Forever Black

By

Sandi Lynn

Cover Design by Meredith Blair

Cover Image by Shutterstock ID: Melissaf84

Acknowledgments

To my husband, thank you for putting up with my endless nights on my laptop writing and editing to make this book possible. Thank you for understanding all the times that I ignored you and told you to be quiet or turn the TV down so I could concentrate. I love you! To my three darling teenage daughters and their never-ending question, "What's for dinner?" To my friend and co-worker, Debbie, who pushed me every day to write this book. Also, to my beta readers, I couldn't have done this without you! Thank you. A special thank you goes out to my friend Lucy D'Andrea, editor and proofreader, who graciously helped me with the editing and proofreading of Forever Black. xo

Table Of Contents

Chapter 1

I stood in the doorway of the bedroom while Kyle packed his bags.

"I just need some space," he said as he threw his clothes haphazardly into his large Nike bag.

"Does this have anything to do with that whore you met at Zoe's the other night?"

"Elle, come on, I told you nothing happened."

I rolled my eyes at him. "You tell me a lot of things, Kyle."

He threw the last of his clothes into his Nike bag and turned around to face me. "We both knew we were heading for this; things have been rocky for a while now, and you know why."

"Rocky for you because you're searching for something that doesn't exist."

He let out a heavy sigh. "I'm sorry, Elle. I just can't do this anymore."

I followed him to the small space we call the living room as he dropped his bag on the floor. He reached into his jean pocket and threw some money on the table. "This is for the next couple of months, so you can pay the rent." He kissed me on my forehead and headed for the door.

I crossed my arms and stared at him. "I don't want your money; I want you to stay. Please, Kyle, don't give up on us."

I was now the most pathetic person in the world, begging my douchebag boyfriend to stay; not because I thought I was in love with him, but because I was afraid of being alone, and being alone was something that was all too familiar to me.

He picked up his bag from the ground and slung it over his shoulder. "Take care, Elle." And just like that, he walked out. I stood in the middle of the living room and looked at the closed door as tears escaped my eyes.

Kyle and I had been together since sophomore year of college. We both attended Michigan State University and met at a frat party when he was a Delta Sigma Phi. Kyle was a good looking guy with his 6ft stature and medium build. He wasn't exactly eye candy, but he was cute. He always kept his jet black hair perfectly combed, and his dark brown eyes reminded me of my one favorite thing in the world—chocolate. Kyle was the person whose presence lit up the room. His charm and romance is what swept me off my feet. He studied Accounting, while I studied Art. It wasn't too long after we graduated that his cousin got him a job at the large accounting firm where he was employed. This is how we ended up moving from Michigan to New York. Kyle worked full-time as an accountant and made pretty decent money, so I was able to take on a part-time job at a record company and finish painting the pictures that I promised the art gallery.

We rented a one bedroom apartment that was small, but it was our home for the past year, and it made us happy—at least I thought it did. I took my teary-eyed self and sat on the couch, curled in a ball, and cried myself to sleep.

I hadn't been sleeping long when I was startled by a knock on the door. I sat up and looked around the room, eyes swollen and red.

"Elle, are you in there?" I heard a familiar voice say as she pounded on the door. I got up from the couch and stumbled to open the door. Peyton always seemed to know when I needed her most. She threw her hands up in the air.

"Elle, it's about time. I thought I was going to have to break down the door." She put her arms around me and hugged me tight. I motioned for her to come in as she pushed her way through and set a large brown bag on the table.

"I come bearing douchebag boyfriend food." She smiled as she rummaged through the bag. She removed the boxes of Chinese food and set them on the table.

"We have Mongolian beef, lettuce wraps, chicken fried rice, wonton soup, and chocolate ice cream for dessert."

Her grin went from ear to ear, but it quickly fell as I dropped my head and curled back up on my couch. Peyton sighed heavily as she walked over and sat next to me.

"Kyle text-messaged me and said he left. He wanted me to come over to check on you and make sure you were ok."

I lifted my head from my arms. Who the fuck did he think he was, sending my best friend over to see if I was ok? I thought as anger burned inside me.

"He said he left because of irreconcilable differences."

"What are we—married?" I growled.

Peyton gave me a sympathetic smile and walked to the kitchen to grab plates and silverware for the food sitting on the table. I couldn't stop thinking about Kyle and how he just left. We were never apart for more than a couple of days, and now we'd be apart forever. Once again, I was alone. I knew why he decided to leave, and for that reason, I hated him. I gave him every opportunity to tell me the truth, but he couldn't even look me in the eye and do that. He was a coward, and I had no room in my life for cowards. Even though I felt sick to my stomach, I got up and made my way to the table as Peyton put some food on my plate.

"Listen, Elle, Kyle's a douchebag, and I'm sorry you wasted the last four years of your life with him. You need to focus on something else. You need to finish your paintings and get them over to the art gallery so that people can find out who Ellery Lane truly is," she said, waving her fork around. I smiled because I knew she was right; if there was one way that I could escape the hurt and loneliness, it was through my paintings. She reached over, put her arm around me, and gave me a squeeze. "Don't worry; I'll be here for you."

I met Peyton at the art gallery the day I stopped by to talk to the owner about displaying my paintings. The minute she asked, "May I help you?" we clicked, and we've been best friends ever since. One thing about Peyton is her personality; it's way bigger than her 5'2", size 0 body. She always sports the perfect look with her long, straight brown hair and perfectly placed makeup that enhances her bright blue eyes. I don't think I've ever seen her dress in a pair of sweatpants. For her, it's all about style with skirts and cute little tops. There isn't a shortage of guys when Peyton's around. They're always flirting with her, but she has yet to find the perfect man to give her heart to.

I didn't feel like eating, but I knew I had to appease Peyton, or she wouldn't leave me alone.

"Do you want me to stay with you tonight?"

I set my fork down. "Nah, I just want to be alone. I think I'll go take a bath."

I got up from the table and headed to the bathroom. I turned the water on and poured a capful of bubble bath in its stream. I twisted my long blonde hair up and clipped it to prevent it from getting wet. I climbed into the bubble-filled bathtub and slid down until my head was resting on the bath pillow behind me. I laid there, closed my eyes, and tried to think of a plan, but I was too grief-stricken, and I needed the proper amount of time to wallow in self-pity before moving on with my life as a single female.

By the time I got out of the bathtub, Peyton had everything cleaned up. She had left me a text message saying, *"Elle, get some rest and call me if you need anything. I'll call you tomorrow. Love you always."*

I smiled as Peyton was about the only family that I had left. My mother passed away from cancer when I was six, and my father died right before my 18th birthday. I had an aunt and uncle back in Michigan, but I haven't seen or heard from them since my dad died. I've always considered Kyle's parents as family, but now that we've broken up, it would be more than awkward to talk to them.

After I made sure the door was locked, I turned off the lights and snuggled in my bed, burying my head under the covers to escape the reality of my life—at least for tonight.

Chapter 2

For the next few days, I did nothing but stay in my pajamas and concentrate on finishing my paintings. I called work and told them I had the flu. They told me to take the rest of the week off which was something that I didn't have a problem with. I was afraid I couldn't afford it, but I needed to get my paintings finished and off to the art gallery. I wouldn't have been good company to anyone anyway.

I made my third pot of coffee of the day and checked my phone to see if I had any messages. Kyle hadn't made any attempt to contact me since he left. How does a person just forget about someone after being with them for four years? A fire stirred in my blood just thinking about it. The way I saw things, I had two choices: I could sit in my tiny apartment and let my life die out, or I could suck up what happened, go out into the world, and live. I opted to go out and live. I wasn't ready to die yet; I had too many things that I wanted to do.

I frantically cleaned my apartment which was long overdue, and I was ashamed that I let it get that way. I took a garbage bag and began tossing everything out that reminded me of Kyle. I was determined to rid this apartment of any sign of him. By the time I was finished, my little home was practically bare. The shelves in the bookcase that housed pictures of me and Kyle now sat empty, reminding me of the emptiness that I felt in my heart.

I finally showered and stood in front of the bathroom mirror. I took my hand and wiped the steam that formed over it. I looked at myself for the first time in days. My ice blue eyes—which Kyle used to tell me they reminded him of the sea—looked tired with bags that formed underneath them. I ran a brush through my long blonde hair and then fingered mousse through it so that it dried wavy. I put on some makeup to try to hide the fact that I've been depressed and locked in my apartment for a week. I stepped into my favorite jeans and was surprised they were loose in places they never were before. My 5'7", size 4 body appeared to have shrunk a bit since the breakup. I tore through my closet for my favorite pink shirt. Once I was ready, I took in a deep breath and called a cab. It was time to step out into the world and start my life again.

Manny pulled his yellow cab up to the curb of my apartment as I walked out the door. Seeing me struggle with the three paintings that I was carrying, he got out of the cab to help me.

"Hey, Elle, let me help you there."

"Hi, Manny, thanks." I smiled at him.

Manny was my favorite cab driver, and I've known him since I moved to New York. When I call a cab, I always ask for Manny; sometimes he's available, and sometimes he's not. He stood about 5'10" with a muscular build. He always wore his black hair in a ponytail, and his brown eyes always sparkled when I'd ask him about his kids. He was a family man and one of the nicest people that I've ever met. His cab was the one that first picked me and Kyle up when we arrived in New York. I sat in front of the cab with him so that my paintings could sit comfortably in the back.

"How's Mr. Kyle doing, Elle?"

"Kyle moved out over a week ago, Manny." I sighed. The expression on his face was sympathetic.

"I'm so sorry, Elle. Are you ok?" I looked over at him, and a light smile came over my lips.

"I'm doing ok. I was a mess last week, but now, I'm adjusting." Was I really? Or was I just a good actress?

14

He pulled up to the art gallery and helped me take the paintings out of the cab. I paid him the fare and thanked him for his help.

"If you need anything, call me, Elle, and I mean that," he said as he pointed at me. Then, he got into the cab and slowly pulled away.

Peyton saw me from the window of the gallery and came outside to help me bring in the paintings. She called the owner, Sal, and told him that I arrived. He came down from his office and kissed me on both cheeks.

"Ah, let me see what you've done here, Ellery," he said as he took the paintings one by one and laid them up against the wall.

I was contracted to submit three paintings to his gallery as a trial. One of the paintings was a romanticism of a man and woman dancing under the moonlight and surrounded by clouds. The second painting was of a garden with a fountain surrounded by beautiful flowers. The last painting was of a child sitting in a field of flowers in a white dress as three angels looked down upon her from the sky. All three paintings spoke something about me.

"Wow, Ellery, these are gorgeous! I'm sure I won't have any problem selling these." Sal smiled.

I felt a little embarrassed because this was the first time that I was going to be showing my work to the world. He led me over to a small wall that was sitting bare.

"This is where your paintings will be displayed. I will call you as soon as one or all of them sell." I thanked him, and as soon as he walked away, Peyton started jumping up and down, clapping her hands.

"Let's go out and celebrate tonight!" she squealed.

Going out was the last thing on my mind. I wasn't ready to do the single girl out at night thing, but Peyton was persistent, and I knew I didn't stand a chance against her. So, I hesitantly agreed.

I left the gallery and started walking down the street. I fumbled through my large purse to find my ringing cell phone. I grabbed it and looked at the familiar number that found its way to my phone a little too much lately. I hit ignore and decided to walk the six blocks home. It wasn't long before the new voicemail alert lit up my phone. By the time I made it home, I was exhausted. I threw my keys and purse on the table next to the door and listened to the message that so annoyingly remained on my screen.

"Hi, Ellery, this is Dr. Taub calling. I noticed that you've cancelled the last two appointments since your last visit. I want to make sure that you're still coming to see me. It is vital that we talk about this. I can help you, Ellery. Please call my office to set up an appointment as soon as possible." I rolled my eyes and shook my head as I hit the delete button.

I walked to the bedroom and decided to lay down for a while as the six block walk home took its toll on me. I had only been sleeping for about an hour when I awoke to the sound of my ringing phone.

Chapter 3

"Hello," I sleepily answered.

"Were you sleeping?" Peyton asked rather loudly.

"I was just taking a little nap." I yawned.

"Get up! I'm on my way over to your place to get ready for the club."

I heavily sighed. "Club? You said we'd go celebrate. I thought maybe that meant dinner, not clubbing." I didn't feel like going to a noisy, crowded club tonight.

"Elle, snap out of it! You've been a humdrum since douchebag Kyle left. Reclaim your life and have fun like you used to; you're the most fun person that I know."

"I don't know, Peyton; I'm not feeling the club scene tonight."

"You'll feel it once you get there, and who knows, maybe you'll meet your Prince Charming tonight."

Did she say Prince Charming? I don't want a Prince Charming. I don't want anything to do with men—period. It was important to Peyton that we celebrate, so I agreed to go.

"Ok, Peyton, I guess I'll go, but I don't want to be out late; I'm tired."

"Yay!" she shrieked. "Oh, my friend Caleb is picking us up at your place. Bye!"

"Wait, who is…"—click—I silently chuckled and hopped into the shower. Peyton's exuberance attracted a lot of different people. I believe that's why we connected with each other so quickly.

As soon as I got out of the shower, Peyton walked through the door and threw a bag from Forever 21 at me.

"What's this?" I asked as I peeked inside the bag.

She looked at me and smiled as she flitted to the bathroom. "It's just a little pick-me-up that I bought for you to wear tonight."

Peyton was generous like that. We always bought each other things that we thought the other would like. I opened the bag and took out the most spectacular silver, glittery knit tank top.

"Peyton, I love it!" I smiled.

"I knew you would. I thought you could wear it with your black leggings and black boots," she mumbled as she brushed her teeth.

I went to the bedroom and put on the top. The length was long enough to cover my ass which made it perfect for leggings. I walked to the bathroom where Peyton was doing her hair. She looked at me through the mirror and whistled. "Look at you, miss thing. Every guy at the club's going to want to tap that hot ass." She smiled as she lightly smacked me.

I rolled my eyes. Peyton's one of those people who doesn't have a filter; she says what's on her mind at that moment and never gives it a second thought. Her mouth spits before her brain thinks.

I smiled as I hugged her. "Thank you; it's perfect."

"Aw, it's nice to see you smile again, Elle." She continued straightening her hair.

I asked Peyton about Caleb, and she said he was a friend of a friend and that they went out a couple of times. I found it odd since this is the first time that I'm hearing his name. She said she started seeing him right when Kyle left me. She didn't think it was appropriate to talk about her dating life so soon. To be honest, I was touched by her thoughtfulness to not mention it, but at the same time, I was pissed she didn't.

I looked at myself in the mirror one last time before going out. I decided to throw some soft curls into my blonde hair that I already straightened, and I rubbed off some of the eye shadow that Peyton painted on me. I was beginning to feel glad that I decided to go tonight; I needed some fun.

Caleb came to the door and whistled at both of us as Peyton opened it. He gently kissed her on the cheek and walked over to me, holding out his hand.

"I'm Caleb. It's nice to meet you."

I shook his hand and told him the same. His grip was firm, and from what I could tell, so was his body. He wore his short brown hair messy but in an attractive way, and his black eyes were piercing. I could see why Peyton was attracted to him. The three of us slid into the cab that was waiting for us outside. Peyton had her arm around Caleb's as they nuzzled each other. Suddenly, I felt like a third wheel.

"So, what club are we going to?" I asked. Caleb broke his gaze from Peyton and looked over at me.

"I thought we'd go to Club S."

I frowned, trying to think of how I knew that club, and then it hit me; my friend from the soup kitchen, Frankie, is a bouncer there. I gasped.

"Isn't that a sex club?"

Peyton looked at me and smiled. "Elle, it's a normal club; it just so happens that some people go there to find others to have sex with," she said it so casually as if it was no big deal. I rolled my eyes and sighed.

"Correct me if I'm wrong, but doesn't the S stand for sex, as in Club Sex?" Peyton and Caleb both smiled at me. "Great, now I'll have to be on the defense all night."

"Live a little, Elle." She laughed.

I crossed my arms and looked out the window as they started making out. I wasn't about to live a little by having a one night stand with some random guy; that wasn't me. I've only had sex with one guy in my life, and that was Kyle.

Chapter 4

The cab dropped us off in front of the club, and I was astounded by the line of people who wrapped around the building for at least two blocks. I smiled because I knew there was no way we were getting in tonight which was ok with me. I preferred to go out for a quiet dinner.

Caleb slumped his shoulders. "Fuck! Look at that line. We should have gotten here earlier."

As the crowds of people in line were patiently waiting to be let in, and I was wishing to get the hell out of there, I heard someone yelling my name. My eyes grew wide as I cautiously turned my head.

"Elle, is that you? Hey, Elle, over here!"

I looked over in the direction where the voice was coming from; it was Frankie waving his hand and motioning for me to come over. The three of us walked to the entrance and stood in front of the large, burly man named Frankie Lasher. His 6'4", wrestler body was enough to intimidate anyone. I could see why the club hired him as a bouncer. He put his arms around me and gave me a squeeze.

"Good to see you, Elle. You guys clubbing here tonight?"

I pulled from his embrace, "We were going to, but wow, look at that line; I don't think tonight's going to be a possibility."

"Nonsense, you three go in."

I gave him a dirty look as he lifted the rope for us. Caleb and Peyton were ecstatic and beaming from ear to ear. Frankie lightly grabbed my arm as I walked past him. "If you don't feel comfortable in there, or if you need me, just come out here, and let me know." I smiled at his generosity and nodded.

We walked through the small hallway that led into the main entrance of the club. I've been to many clubs, and this was by far is the most crowded that I've ever seen. I looked around at the tables that filled the place. A massive bar sat off to the side with fluorescent lights that hung down from the ceiling. The oversized dance floor housed large projection screens that displayed a full color laser show. The walls were suede with soft lights that glowed off them. The music was blaring as the floor was thumping beneath my feet, forcing my body to move with the beat.

Peyton pulled me and Caleb to the dance floor where we danced for what seemed like hours. I needed a drink, so I left them to dance as I made my way to the bar. I took the only bar stool that was available at the end and ordered a Cosmopolitan. I was sipping on my drink when I noticed a man and woman arguing at a table not too far from where I was sitting. She had her shaking finger pointed at him and then proceeded to poke him in the chest several times. I couldn't help but shake my head and laugh. I kept looking over at them to see if they would kiss and makeup, but I noticed he was yelling now. His finger was pointing at her, and his face looked angered. The tall, beautiful woman slapped him across the face, turned on her heels, and scurried off. I stared at him and took notice at the look on his face which showed no emotion whatsoever. He just sat there and stared straight ahead.

I kept looking over in his direction because he was one of the best eye candies that I've ever seen. His light brown, almost blonde hair was shorter on the sides, and his longer top had waves to it. I couldn't help but stare at his prominent square jaw and chiseled cheekbones. I couldn't tell the color of his eyes because he was too far away, and the lighting was inadequate, but I could tell just by looking that anyone could easily get lost in them.

"Yum, Elle, I see that someone has stolen your attention." Peyton smiled as she looked over at him. Oh god, I didn't need her knowing I was checking this guy out because she would be the first one to run over, tell him, and try to set us up.

"He only has my attention because he was just bitch slapped by some woman." She let out a loud laugh, and that was my cue to change the subject. She dragged me out to the dance floor where I danced and endlessly fought off horny guys as I kept getting shuffled in the crowd.

It started to get extremely hot in the club, and I needed some fresh air. I told Peyton that I'd be back as I headed towards the door. As I stepped outside, I saw Frankie escorting Mr. Eye Candy out of the club.

"Ok, Mr. Black, you've had way too much to drink tonight, and it's time for you to go home." He was stumbling from side to side and mumbling something.

"Frankie, what's going on?" I asked casually.

"Hey, Elle, this gentleman has had too much to drink, and he started causing a scene when the bartender refused to serve him."

"What are you going to do with him?"

"I just escort them out. What they do after that is not my concern."

I looked at him and cocked my head. "He can barely stand, so how do you expect him to get home?" My head was telling me to stop immediately because it knew what I was about to do, but my heart was telling me to help him. "I'll make sure he gets home safe," I said to Frankie.

"Elle, that's not a good idea. You don't know who you're dealing with here."

I put my hand up. "I know what I'm doing, and he needs help."

Frankie shook his head. "You have a good heart, Elle, but sometimes, I think you're crazy. Please be careful."

I grabbed my cell phone from my purse and called a cab. Mr. Eye Candy was sitting on the cement against the wall. I took notice of his expensive black tailored suit and the white shirt that was partially unbuttoned, showing off his muscular chest. His 6ft stature was lean but seriously muscular. Like his hair and face, his body appeared to be perfect. I walked over to him and grabbed his arm to help him up.

"Come on, let's get you home."

He looked over at me with his drunken green eyes. "Do I know you?" he slurred.

I patted him on the back and walked him to the curb just as the cab pulled up. Before I pushed him in, I took his wallet out of his back pocket. He stumbled into the seat, and I climbed in next to him. I opened his wallet, took out his driver's license, and handed it to the driver. "Drop him off here." He handed the license back to me, and I took it upon myself to read his name.

I patted him on the arm. "It's nice to meet you, Connor Black."

He looked at me and put his head on my shoulder. I let a small smile escape my lips.

Chapter 5

The cab pulled around to the garage area. "This is where they like to be dropped off. He should have a key that fits that elevator over there, and his name should be on the inside next to the keyhole, telling you which floor he's on. Good luck."

I stared at the cabbie because one: how did he know this, and two: I had no intention of taking him further than the elevator. I opened his wallet and thumbed through his money. I shook my head at the fact he only had several one hundred-dollar bills. I took out a one hundred-dollar bill and handed it to the driver. "Keep the change." I winked.

A large smile swept across his face. "Thanks, ma'am."

"Don't mention it. You can thank him next time."

I opened the door and grabbed his arm, pulling him out of the cab. I put his arm over my shoulder and walked him to the elevator. He kept stumbling and almost taking me down with him. I searched his pocket for his keys. It was that awkward moment when I put my hand in his side pocket and felt something semi hard that wasn't his keys. I pushed the button on the elevator, and he looked at me.

"You're a beautiful woman, and I'm going to fuck you really hard," he said as he grabbed my ass. I sighed and removed his hand from my behind. "Only in your dreams, sweetie, only in your dreams…"

The elevator opened. I escorted him inside and looked at the different keys on his key ring, wondering which one fit the elevator. I turned to him as he was leaning up against the back of the elevator. "Can you please show me which key goes in here."

He flashed me a drunken smile and seductively took the key ring from me, picked a key, and held it up to me. "Thank you." I smiled.

I inserted the key into the lock next to his name as it took us up to the top floor. The elevator doors opened to the biggest and most beautiful penthouse that I've ever seen. Ok, it was the only penthouse that I've ever seen, but it was still beautiful. My full intention was to lean him up against the wall and leave. I had assumed he would pass out on the floor and wake up in the morning, but that was until he looked at me and said he was going to be sick. I rolled my eyes, and I asked him to take me to his bedroom as I figured that would get his attention real quick. He pointed to the stairs, and I held onto him, trying to hold him up as he tripped up each step. We finally made it to the top as I saw a bathroom on the left. He didn't make it; he vomited all over his clothes. I shook my head for this was a sight that was all too familiar to me.

I hurried him to the bathroom where he leaned over and hugged the porcelain of god for a good hour. I stood there, admiring the beauty of his bathroom. The taupe walls and black granite countertops gave it a classic but luxurious look.

I found a washcloth and ran it under lukewarm water. I walked over to him as he sat against the wall with his head down. He smelled like vomit, and I had to get him to change his clothes.

"Come on, buddy, let's see if we can get you changed." I put his arm around me, and with a little help from him, I lifted him off the floor. We made it down the hallway to his bedroom. I opened the double doors that led inside and gasped; his bedroom was bigger than my entire apartment. I took him over to the king size bed and sat him down.

"Are you an angel?" he slurred as he gently rubbed my cheek. His skin felt warm, and his touch felt nice—too nice—as it gave me tiny goose bumps.

I took his hand away. "Yeah, I guess I am."

He drunkenly smiled and fell back on the bed. I knew it was going to take some work trying to get his clothes off, but I couldn't let him sit in his own and vomit all night. I took his shoes and socks off first. I climbed on top, so I was straddling him and unbuttoned his shirt, rolling him from side to side, taking his arms out. It probably would have been easier to take his shirt off in the bathroom, but I hadn't thought about that. I moved down to the button on his pants; oh god, I can't believe I'm doing this. My thought was to let him lie there and sleep it off, but his pants received the worst of his vomit, and he genuinely smelled. I unbuttoned his pants and lifted his hips so that I could pull them off. It was a struggle, but I finally managed.

I couldn't help but look at his sculpted body as he lay there almost perfectly naked and only in his black silk boxers. I'm only human, right? He was lean, muscular, and perfectly defined from head to toe. I felt dirty standing over his passed out body and checking him out, but no one should ever look that perfect; it's just not right. I needed to move him up to his pillow. I put the cool cloth on his head, and he stirred. I grabbed under his arms and pulled him up the best I could. I turned him on his side in case he vomited again, and a slight groan came from his mouth. I found a blanket in the corner of his room and covered him with it. I sighed and looked at the clock on the night stand; it read 1:00 am.

I was exhausted and desperately needed some sleep. It was then I realized I never told Peyton that I was leaving the club. I ran down the stairs and grabbed my purse off the table. I took out my phone and saw a text message from her.

"Frankie told me what you're doing, and I know you like to play Good Samaritan, but I'm worried, so text me."

I quickly replied, *"I'm fine; I managed to get him home, and he's passed out on his bed. I'm heading home now. I'll talk to you tomorrow."*

I stood in the hallway and looked at the stairs. Memories were flooding my mind as I had to walk back to his room to check on him one last time. He had rolled on his back, so I rolled him back on his side. His bed was so comfortable that I decided to sit next to him to make sure he stayed on his side the rest of the night and maybe get a little bit of sleep.

***

I awoke from a dream that I had about my father. I quickly sat up, but my brain hadn't fully registered where I was. I scanned the room and looked over at Connor who was sleeping peacefully. I shook my head in disbelief that I had fallen asleep for so long as I made my way to the bathroom. I splashed some water on my face and downed some mouthwash I found in his cabinet. I ran my fingers through my hair and headed downstairs. I should have just left right then and there, but I needed coffee and so would Connor when he woke up.

I walked to the kitchen and stopped dead in my tracks. The mahogany cabinets topped with dark gray granite counter tops were utterly stunning. A large curved island sat in the middle of the kitchen with a built-in stove on one side as three stainless steel ovens were also built-in opposite the other wall. I found what I needed and made a pot of coffee. I knew a recipe for a hangover cocktail that I used to make my dad every day. I scanned the kitchen, and surprisingly enough, it had everything that I needed to make one. I had my back turned to the doorway, making the hangover cocktail when I heard someone clear their throat. I was startled, and I slowly turned around.

He stood in the middle of the kitchen in a pair of black pajama bottoms that hung low on his hips, outlining his muscular form. I gulped at the sight of him standing there, hung over and still looking as incredible as he did last night. He looked at me and cocked his head to one side.

"Did I not go over the rules with you last night?"

"Huh?" I frowned.

"I don't do sleepovers. You were supposed to leave after I fucked you, so would you mind telling me why you're still here, in my kitchen, making yourself comfortable?"

His tone was arrogant and crude, obviously he didn't remember anything from last night, but I didn't expect he would. His green eyes looked dark and angry, but he'll have to get over it; I didn't have time for this. I set the glass with the hangover drink on the counter and slid it to him. He narrowed his eyes at me.

"I asked you a question, and I expect an answer."

I sighed and rolled my eyes, "Listen, buddy, I don't know what you think happened last night, but you didn't fuck me! I would never give you the pleasure; trust me." Ok, I was lying; I would have given him the pleasure, but he didn't need to know that. He cocked his head and stared at me, narrowing his eyes.

"You drank yourself into oblivion at the club last night, and they kicked you out. I was walking outside when it happened, and being the good person I am, I called a cab to make sure you got home safely. You then proceeded to vomit all over yourself, so I had to get you to the bathroom and out of your clothes, because frankly, you smelled." He raised his eyebrows.

"I was on my way out the door when I decided to check on you one more time. I went back to your room, and you were lying on your back, so I rolled you on your side again in case you vomited; I wouldn't have wanted you to choke to death." He shifted his weight and crossed his arms. "I fell asleep from exhaustion after dealing with you, and when I woke up, I decided to make you a pot of coffee and a hangover cocktail. I was leaving in a few minutes, and I didn't expect you to be up for at least a few more hours."

He took a few steps closer. "So, you're telling me nothing happened between us?" I rolled my eyes. Didn't this man listen to a word I just said?

"No, nothing happened. I just needed to make sure you were going to be ok. You were obnoxiously drunk." I looked down.

"What is this?" he asked as he picked up the glass.

"Just drink it, and you should start to feel better in about 15 minutes. I'll pour you some coffee and be on my way."

I started to feel a little dizzy as I reached for a mug, and it slipped out of my hands, crashing to the floor.

"Fuck," I said as I bent down to pick up the broken pieces.

"Hey, you're going to cut yourself." He walked over to me and bent down.

"I'm sorry," I said, shaking my head and picking up the broken porcelain.

"Stop," his voice commanded.

His voice was startling, but I didn't listen because it was my mess, and I was going to clean it up. He grabbed my hands and turned them over, taking the broken pieces out of them. Our eyes met when he saw the scars on my wrists. I pulled back quickly and stood up. He continued to pick up the pieces. I took my purse from the counter.

"I'm sorry for the mug; I'll replace it for you, and I hope you feel better." I turned and headed out the kitchen.

"Wait," I heard him say.

I turned around and looked at him. "At least let me pay you for your trouble last night."

"I'm not taking your money, and it was no trouble." Ok, it was, but he's alive, and I feel better knowing that I probably saved his life. He rolled his eyes. "Then at least have a cup of coffee before you go." I sighed. I seriously needed it, and one cup wouldn't hurt.

"Fine, one cup and then I'll be out of your hair."

He walked back to the kitchen and put the cup on the island. He drank his cocktail and frowned the entire time. It was fun to watch the disgusted look on his face. He leaned over the counter and looked at me.

"Why on earth would you help me like that? What if I was a rapist or murderer?"

I laughed. "You couldn't rape or murder me even if you wanted to. You were so far gone last night; I could barely get you home." He ran one hand through his hair.

"You shouldn't be doing those kinds of things; it's not safe in this city for a girl to be doing shit like that." He seemed agitated.

I leaned my elbow on the counter, rested my hand on my cheek, and looked at him intently as he lectured me. He stopped what he was saying and narrowed his eyes at me.

"Are you even listening to me?"

I laughed as I got up from the stool. "Thanks for the coffee, but I need to get home." I grabbed my purse and started walking out of the kitchen. "Have a lovely day, Mr. Black, and next time, don't drink so much." I could hear his footsteps following behind.

"Would you mind telling me your name?" The elevator doors opened; I stepped in and turned to face him.

"It's Ellery Lane!" I yelled as the door began to close.

Chapter 6

I stepped out into the bright sunlight and looked up at the sky. I smiled as I waited for the cab to arrive. I kept thinking about Connor, his dumb rule about women staying the night, and the way he looked. There was something about him that made my stomach flutter. I couldn't stop thinking about his tone and how angry it was when he first saw me. I guess I couldn't blame him though; I'd probably be the same way if a strange man was in my apartment when I woke up.

I walked through the door of my apartment, threw my purse down, and took a hot bath. I was exhausted, and I desperately needed some sleep. I craved the comfort of my pajamas and bed. I text-messaged Peyton to let her know I was going to take a nap and that I'd call her when I woke up. If I didn't text her, she'd probably call or come over, and I just wanted to be alone tonight. I looked at the clock, and it was 3:00 pm. I had a plan to sleep till 5:00 pm, make a quick dinner, and do some painting.

I was startled by a knock at the door. I looked at the clock and it was 5:30 pm. Shit, I slept longer than I had wanted to. I got up and headed towards the door.

"Peyton, I said I would call you when…" I flung the door open, and to my surprise, it wasn't Peyton but a young man holding a small white envelope.

"Are you Ellery Lane?" he asked. Suddenly, I got nervous; he sounded serious.

"Yes, I'm Ellery Lane."

He handed me the envelope. "This is for you."

I took the envelope from his hand. He smiled and walked away. My stomach started to tie itself in knots. I didn't know what to expect to find in the envelope, and who was sending me something anyway?

I slid my finger across the top and took out the piece of neatly folded paper that was tucked inside; it read, *"Miss Lane, I'm going to properly thank you for your services last night. I will be waiting for you at Le Sur Restaurant. My driver will pick you up promptly at 7:00 pm. ~ Connor Black."*

First of all, how did he know my address, and second of all, why the hell is he so bossy? I should have had that creepy feeling, but for some reason I didn't. I quickly put it out of my mind when I saw he wants to have dinner at Le Sur.

Since Kyle and I moved here, we've never been able to get into that restaurant. People book months in advance. I called Peyton immediately.

"Hey, girl, what's up?"

"Remember that guy I helped home last night?"

"Yeah…"

"He wants to thank me for helping him, so he's sending his driver over to pick me up to meet him at Le Sur at 7:00 pm."

"What?!" she screamed into the phone. "Elle, who is this guy?"

"His name is Connor Black."

I heard her gasp. "Are you fucking kidding me, Elle?! Do you know who Connor Black is?!" I frowned and twisted my face.

34

"No, but should I?"

"Do you live in a bubble or something? Connor Black is the CEO of Black Enterprises. He's a 30-year-old mega millionaire who took over his father's company when he was 28. Elle, he's hot, he's rich, and he wants to take you to dinner?!" I could hear the excitement in her voice.

"Peyton, first of all, I'm not interested in any guy. I'm in the guy free zone, especially after what Kyle did to me. This man, Connor Black, is rude, bossy, and doesn't have an ounce of respect for women." I didn't want to tell her what he said to me about his rules earlier in the day.

"He can be, Elle; he's rich and hot."

I rolled my eyes at that last comment and told her goodbye. I didn't feel like going out tonight, and I wanted to do some painting, but it was Le Sur, and I've been dying to go there, so I made an exception.

I rummaged through my closet, trying to find something to wear. I pulled out a black dress that I wore to a friend's wedding a couple of years ago. It was simple with spaghetti straps and a v-neck. I put on some light makeup and wore my hair half up, letting the loose curls from the back cascade around my shoulders. I threw some gloss on my lips and looked at the clock; it was 6:58 pm. I checked myself out in the mirror one last time and headed out the door.

Sitting at the curb was a black limousine with a man leaning up against it. "Miss Lane, I presume?"

"Yes, I'm Ellery Lane." I smiled as he opened the door and helped me inside. I took in the comfort and plushness of the limo. I felt like a princess on her way to the ball. I looked to the front where the driver was sitting.

"Excuse me, but what's your name?"

He looked at me in the rearview mirror. "It's Denny, ma'am."

"It's nice to meet you, Denny. Is Mr. Black always so bossy?" I politely asked.

He smiled and nodded his head. "Mr. Black is used to getting whatever he wants." I rolled my eyes and looked out the window. Of course he does.

I walked into the restaurant and up to the desk where a tall redheaded woman asked if she could help me.

"I'm meeting Mr. Black," I answered. Instantly, her eyes looked like daggers as she said, "Follow me." The razor-eyed redhead led me towards the back of the restaurant to the table where Connor was seated. He saw us coming and stood up. He walked over and pulled out my chair. Ok, so far he has some manners.

"Good evening, Miss Lane. I'm glad you decided to join me."

I wanted to tell him that I was only here to experience the restaurant and that if he had chosen anywhere else, I wouldn't have attended. I sat in my chair as he walked over to his.

He wore an extremely expensive dark gray suit. His sun-kissed skin glistened more than I remembered from this morning, and his hair was perfectly styled in the tousled way that was hot.

"Good evening, Mr. Black. Thank you for inviting me, but it really wasn't necessary. Please call me Elle."

He looked at me intently. "Isn't your name, Ellery?"

I took a sip of water. "Yes, but my friends call me Elle."

He took his menu and opened it, and I was astounded by the next words that came out of his mouth.

"But we aren't friends, Ellery."

Ok, I take back the whole—man has manners—thing; he's just downright rude.

I opened up my menu. "Alright then, Mr. Black, why don't we just stick to Miss Lane?" I saw him slightly grin from behind the menu.

"Order anything you like; it looks like you haven't eaten in weeks." I looked sternly at him.

"I eat every day, Mr. Black; not that it's any of your concern." He suddenly looked intrigued as he set his menu down.

"It's just that you're very thin."

What the fuck is this man's problem? First, he says we aren't friends, and then he calls me anorexic.

"This is the way I was born; I've always been thin."

He pressed his lips together as the waiter came to the table with a bottle of Pinot Grigio. He poured the wine in each glass and proceeded to take our order. I looked at Connor as he sat there, staring at me. It was making me intensely uncomfortable, but it was turning me on at the same time. My heart started to beat rapidly, and a familiar ache rose from down below. Two can play this game.

"So, what's your story, Mr. Black?" He brought his wine glass to his lips and took a sip, never taking his eyes off me.

"My story?" he simply asked.

A small smile escaped my lips. "Yes, your story."

"What's to tell? I'm a 30 year old CEO, I have more money than I'll ever need, I don't do relationships, I usually get everything I want, and I do whatever I want." I sat there, staring at him the entire time he boasted about himself.

"Now, that we got that out of the way, what's your story, Miss Lane?"

"I don't have a story, Mr. Black. I'm 23 years old, I moved here with my boyfriend a little over a year ago, I work part-time at a small record company, I paint pictures, and I volunteer at the soup kitchen."

He sat and pondered whether or not he wanted to ask me the next question. "What does your boyfriend think about you having dinner with me?"

"He doesn't; we aren't together anymore. He moved out over three weeks ago." I looked down at the table.

I could sense a tiny bit of sympathy in his voice. "Oh, may I ask how long you were together?" I found it particularly odd that he was trying to get so personal.

"We were together four years; we met at college and moved here from Michigan."

He raised his eyebrows. "Four years is a serious length of time." I decided just to lay it all out there for him since he seemed so interested, but didn't matter anyway; I probably would never see him again after tonight.

"Yep, he came home from work one day and said he needed space. He packed his bags and walked out." I knew the real reason he left, but I wasn't about to tell Connor that.

He struggled with his next words, and it caught me by surprise.

"I'm sorry he did that to you."

I waved my hand in front of my face. "Don't be; nothing lasts forever."

He was taken aback by my choice of words, but it was the truth, and I wasn't afraid to say it.

Chapter 7

Le Sur was just as beautiful as I thought it would be. The ambiance was breathtaking with its low lighting and romantic feel. The marble floors were exquisite as were the paintings that hung on the walls, representing Paris. The tables were lined with satin cloths, and the meals served were on delicate china.

"Do you like it here?" Connor asked as he noticed me looking around.

"Yes, it's a beautiful restaurant." I smiled.

The waiter brought our meals as Connor was about to ask me a question. "You said you volunteer at the soup kitchen; may I ask why?" The look on his face told me that he was a bit intrigued by it.

I took my fork and knife and cut up my chicken as I proceeded to answer his question.

"I like to help people in need; you should know that by now, Mr. Black."

He shook his head. "Yes, but was it a dumb question to ask?"

"I had a rough childhood. Let's just say nobody was there to help me." His eyes never left mine; he listened closely to every word I said.

"What about your parents? Didn't they help you?" I looked down and away from him, trying to find the right words.

"My mother died of cancer when I was six, and my father was an alcoholic who passed away right before my 18th birthday."

The look on his face changed; it went from hard to soft in a matter of seconds.

"Is that why you helped me last night? Because you think that I'm an alcoholic?" he asked. I took the last bite of my dinner and set down my fork.

"No, my father choked to death on his vomit during one of his drunken nights. I found him dead in his bed the next morning. I didn't want that same fate for you. What people don't realize is how easy it is for something like that to happen. I spent my entire life taking care of my father who absurdly drank himself into oblivion almost every night because he couldn't get over my mother's death. So, it's just second nature for me to help people."

He didn't know what to say; I think I shocked him. He held up his glass and motioned me to do the same.

"Well, thank you for your help last night, and as mad as I was this morning to find you standing in my kitchen, I do appreciate it."

"You're welcome." I smiled.

As we were leaving the restaurant, I noticed several women looking at Connor with what appeared to be sex in their eyes. Some were licking their lips as we walked by, and others were eyeing him up and down. It was rather disgusting, but I could see why they did it. He was undoubtedly something to be admired. We walked outside, and I looked at him.

"Want some ice cream?" I asked.

He looked at me with a puzzling look like I was crazy or something.

"No, I don't want ice cream. I'm taking you home and then I have somewhere I have to be." Here comes his rudeness again; I was surprised it took this long.

"Oh come on! It's my treat. I know this cute little ice cream parlor a couple of blocks away that's open 24 hours."

"Miss Lane, I don't want any ice cream, now get in the car so Denny can take you home." His tone was adamant.

I started to walk down the street. I wanted ice cream. If he didn't, that was his problem, but I was getting some with or without him.

I waved my hand as I walked away, "Thanks again for dinner, Mr. Black. I'll see you around sometime."

"Miss Lane, get back here!" he yelled down the street. I rolled my eyes and kept walking. Suddenly, he was beside me mumbling, "Miss Lane, I will not tell you again to get in the car."

I stopped and turned to him, shoving my finger into his chest. "I don't take orders from anybody, Mr. Black, especially people that I've only known less than 24 hours. I'm not your responsibility. You thanked me for my help with a nice dinner, and now it's time for us to part ways. I'm going to get some ice cream, and then I'll call a cab to drive me home."

He stood there stunned and unable to speak. I continued walking, and he followed me. I heard him on the phone, "Denny, it looks like we're getting ice cream. I'll call you when we're leaving." The tone of his voice was angry.

"You don't need to come with me if you don't like ice cream," I said.

"I never said I didn't like it; I just don't want any."

"Then why are you following me, Mr. Black?"

"It's not safe in this city for a beautiful young woman to be walking alone, especially at night. How many times do I need to explain that to you?"

I caught the "beautiful" part and couldn't help but smile. My feet were starting to kill me in my 4 inch heels, so I stopped abruptly in the middle of the sidewalk and took them off.

"What do you think you're doing?" he asked.

"I'm taking off my shoes because my feet are killing me," I said as I used his arm for balance.

"You're going to walk barefoot on this dirty sidewalk?"

I laughed. "Yes, I am, Mr. Black." I could tell he hated the idea; he was so prim and proper. We walked up to the door of the ice cream parlor, and I slipped my shoes back on.

"Hello, how can I help you?" a cheery young girl behind the counter asked. I looked at the different ice creams behind the glass. "I'll have a single scoop of chocolate chip in a waffle cone, please."

"And for you, sir?" the cheery girl asked.

Connor looked at me and sighed. "A single scoop of cherry vanilla in a cup." I smiled at him and bumped my shoulder against his. I went to grab my wallet and pay, but Connor had already handed the girl his money.

"I told you it was my treat."

"Don't worry about it, Miss Lane. I can afford to buy you ice cream." I rolled my eyes and sat down at the wrought iron table.

Connor sat across from me. I watched him eat his ice cream while hiding a small smile. I could tell he was enjoying it.

"How long has it been since you ate ice cream?" I asked.

He looked at me puzzled. "I don't know; since I was a kid, I guess."

"Are you kidding me? You haven't had ice cream since you were a kid?"

"No, is that a problem?"

"No, I'm just surprised."

"I think you'd find a lot of things surprising about me," he said. I twisted my face and glared at him.

"So, where are you going later?" Not that it was any of my business, but he made a point to let me know he needed to be somewhere.

He raised one eyebrow. "Miss Lane, I don't think you really want to know the answer to that."

We finished our ice cream as I saw Denny pull the limousine up at the curb. He got out and opened the door for me.

"Thank you, Denny. You are such a gentleman," I said as I glared at Connor. Thank god I didn't live too far because it was awkwardly silent the whole way home. The limo pulled up to my apartment, and I could see Connor leaning over checking it out.

"You have your own outside entrance?" He frowned.

"I don't live in a fancy apartment building with a doorman and private elevator. This is it, Mr. Black; my little apartment with its own outside entry." He looked at me in irritation.

"I didn't mean anything by it; I just think it is unsafe, and anyone can break in." I looked at him and thanked him for putting that thought in my head. I leaned over and kissed him on the cheek. I found it odd that he flinched at my touch.

"Thank you for dinner and ice cream. I had a nice time."

"You're welcome. Have a nice night, Miss Lane."

I got out of the limo and leaned forward so that I was facing him, and I winked. "Have a pleasant night, Mr. Black."

I shut the door and walked into my apartment. I took off my killer shoes and threw them down; god my feet hurt, but it was worth the pain to eat at Le Sur. My suspicion about Connor and him having to be somewhere was that he was going to pick up some woman for sex. I had the distinct feeling he was that type of guy. He said he didn't *do* relationships, but he's a man; every man has needs, and he was going to make sure his were filled.

I pondered why anyone would want a relationship with him anyway. He's downright rude and arrogant, and not to mention he seems a little controlling. Oh hell, I've never known anyone so controlling, but why does my heart flutter when I'm around him? I laughed to myself, thinking about the night, and how on more than one occasion, I pissed him off as I climbed into my bed and fell fast asleep.

Chapter 8

I spent the next few days going to work and volunteering at the soup kitchen. Saturday came, and it was a beautiful September day. Peyton had called and asked me to go shopping with her, but I told her that I already had plans. Of course, she wasn't happy with my answer, but I was going to Central Park.

Growing up, I would escape my house and find a quiet place to sit and draw. It was the only time that I didn't feel lonely. I liked to draw and paint pictures of places where I could go and hide. My father used to tell me that I got my artistic ability from my mother. I thought about her almost every day and how my life would be different if she hadn't died, but like I say, nothing lasts forever; you can either roll with it or let it kill you. I grabbed my drawing pad and pencils and headed out the door. The walk to Central Park wasn't long, and I enjoyed the fresh air; it made me feel alive.

I've spent more time in Central Park since I've moved to New York than anywhere else. The playgrounds were filled with children playing in the warm New York sun. I made my way to the Conservatory Garden. The magnolia and lilac trees filled the air that provided a soothing and calming effect. It was easy for me to escape the world and take in the beauty of the gardens. It was like a sanctuary for me; a place where I could go and draw just about anything.

I sat down on the bench and noticed a bride and groom over to the right of me, getting their picture taken by the fountain. She was beautiful in her white wedding dress, and he was equally handsome in his black tuxedo. They looked happy. I smiled; this was the perfect place to get married, and that would make the perfect painting.

I was halfway done drawing them when my phone rang. I looked at the unfamiliar number and ignored the call. A second later, the phone rang again, displaying the same number. I'm sure whoever it was had the wrong number, so I answered it to tell them to stop calling. I froze as I heard the voice on the other end.

"Hello, Miss Lane, are you enjoying Central Park?" I started to get creeped out as I looked around from side to side and then behind me; that is when I saw Connor walking towards the bench that I was sitting on.

"I am, Mr. Black, and it looks like you are too." I hung up as he approached me.

I gasped when I saw him. He had a way of making me do that, and I hated it. He was dressed in a pair of khakis and a button down, white cotton shirt with his sleeves rolled to his elbows. His hair, as usual, was perfectly tousled, and his sun-kissed skin glowed in the sunlight. I frowned at him as he sat down next to me.

"What?" he asked.

"How did you get my phone number? I don't remember giving it to you."

"I have my ways of finding out anything about anybody, Miss Lane."

"So, you're a stalker then?"

He threw his head back and laughed. "No, Miss Lane, I'm not a stalker. I just wanted your number in case I needed you to help me home some night." I glared at him but was secretly smiling underneath.

"How did you know I was here?"

"Denny pointed out that he saw you walking down the street, and I asked him to stop."

"Why?" I curiously asked. He pursed his lips together as I could tell he was getting irritated with my questions.

"I don't know. I guess I just thought I'd say hi."

"Then you could have just called since you have my number and all."

He heavily sighed. "Miss Lane, enough with the questions please."

I laughed silently because I was pissing him off again, and I loved it.

"Can I ask you one more thing?" He looked at me and frowned. God, he was sexy when he did that. It's a sin to look that good.

"What is it?"

"Could you please stop calling me Miss Lane, and just call me Ellery?"

He smiled and cocked his head "It would be my pleasure, Ellery." I liked the way my name rolled off his tongue.

Connor glanced over at my pad and saw the scribble of two people on it.

"What are you drawing?"

"The bride and groom over there," I said as I pointed.

"Why?"

"Why not? They're a cute couple, and I think it would make a good painting. I'll call it '*A Wedding in Central Park*'."

"And what makes you think someone would buy that?"

I rolled my eyes at his bluntness; I knew it was only a matter of time.

"People love weddings, and I'm sure any couple that got married here would buy it as a memory of the beginning of their life together."

Connor lifted up his chin. "It's all a bunch of shit if you ask me."

"What is?" I asked as I looked at him in confusion.

"Weddings, starting a life together, relationships; all of it. You even said yourself that nothing lasts forever."

I was surprised by his words and his hatred for relationships. I could see the pain in his beautiful green eyes; he must have been badly hurt. I looked down and continued drawing.

"Well, a lot of people believe in the happily ever after and the fairy tale relationships. Let's not take that away from them."

"Do you believe in any of that?" he asked.

"I don't know. I thought I did once, but I'm not so sure anymore." I continued drawing.

He took his hand and lightly grabbed my wrist, turning it over and softly rubbing my scar with his thumb. I wanted to pull away, but his touch froze me; he was so warm and soft, and what he was doing, sent fire through my body.

"Tell me about these scars," he said in a low voice.

My heart started racing as he let go and let my hand fall back to my pad. I stared at him; why did he care? I haven't known him long enough to share my secrets; hell, I don't know him at all.

"I made a mistake. I was young and stupid, that's all."

"Everyone is young and stupid from time to time, but they don't try to kill themselves," he snapped. It was almost as if he was taking this personally. I sighed and remained calm.

"Connor, you don't know me or anything about me. We aren't friends remember, so what happened to me in my past is none of your business." There, I said it. I put him in his place and politely told him to back off.

"I apologize," he said as he looked straight ahead.

I started to feel a bit of regret for my tone. I got up from the bench. "I'm starving; would you like a hot dog?"

"No, I don't want a hot dog. If you're hungry, then I'll take you to a proper restaurant for lunch."

I laughed as I turned my back to him and started walking away. "Suit yourself, Mr. Black, but I'm going to get myself a hot dog from the hot dog stand." I heard him mumble something under his breath, and before I knew it, he was walking beside me.

"You don't listen to anyone, do you?"

"No, I do what I want."

"I can tell," he mumbled under his breath, thinking I didn't hear him, but I did. I casually smiled and kept walking. We reached the hot dog vendor, and I looked at Connor.

"Are you getting one?"

He frowned at me and growled at the vendor, "Give me two hot dogs."

I grabbed my hot dog and I apologized to the vendor and whispered, "He's mad because I'm forcing him to eat a hot dog when he wanted a fancy lunch."

The vendor and I laughed as Connor walked over to a wooden table. I walked over to the condiment stand and topped my hot dog with relish, onions, ketchup, and mustard. I grabbed a bunch of napkins and sat down next to Connor at the small picnic table. He looked over at my hot dog and then at me with disgust in his eyes.

"That's gross," he said as he took a bite of his plain hot dog.

"Gross? No way man, this is heaven." I took a large bite and watched him stare at me as I chewed.

"You do realize how bad that is for you, right?"

I put my finger up. "You only live once, so we should make the best of it."

He tried to hold back a smile, but I saw it, and it made me smile back. I shoved my hot dog at him.

"Here, take a bite."

"No, get that thing out of my face." He frowned.

"Not until you take a bite, Connor, then you can judge if it's gross."

I kept moving the hot dog closer to his mouth as he rolled his eyes and finally took a bite. He chewed it, and I laughed at the glob of ketchup he had in the corner of his mouth. I took a napkin and wiped it. Instantly, he put his hand on mine like he wanted to jerk it away, but he didn't, and he stared at me with fear in his eyes. I took the napkin away and smiled as if I didn't notice his reaction.

"You had ketchup right there, and I didn't want it to get on your shirt."

He nodded his head. "Thanks."

Chapter 9

The afternoon in Central Park was beautiful. The sun was shining down, keeping a bit of warmth in the air. The tips of the leaves were starting to change, letting everyone know that fall is approaching. The birds were chirping, and the squirrels were running around, gathering up supplies to make their nests for the winter.

"If you don't mind, I want to ask you something," Connor said as he looked at me. I took the last bite of my hot dog and wiped my mouth.

"Go ahead."

"I gave some thought to our recent outing, and I was wondering if you would be interested in being…" He stopped.

"Being…" I motioned for him to proceed.

He cleared his throat and took in a sharp breath. "Would you be interested in being a companion?"

I narrowed my eyes. "What? I don't get it." He heavily sighed at the fact that I didn't get what he was trying to say.

"Would you be interested in being a person who would accompany me to certain functions, no strings attached, and I would pay you of course?" I was in the middle of drinking my water when I spit it out.

"What? You mean like an escort or call girl?!" I yelled.

"NO, NO! That's not what I meant, Ellery," he tried to explain. "I mean like a friend." I smiled at him because that was so hard for him to say.

"You mean go out as friends, like me and Peyton?" He ran his hands through his luxurious hair. I lightly touched his arm.

"Connor, if you want to be friends, then all you had to do was ask. Actually, I already considered us friends, and there will be no money involved either." He pursed his lips, and a small smile escaped them.

"There's a benefit I need to attend tomorrow night. It's a charity function, and I need to attend to represent my company. Would you like to accompany me?"

I bit my lip as I sweetly smiled at him. "I would love to go." He smiled back as we got up from the table and started making our way out of Central Park.

"I'll pick you up at 6:00 pm sharp," he said, looking straight ahead. I smiled silently because I felt different when I was with him. I liked the feeling, but I also hated it because nothing can ever happen between us, and I needed to be extremely careful that nothing did.

Just as we were leaving, I heard someone call my name, "Elle?" I looked to the side and time stopped as I saw Kyle walking towards me. Connor stopped walking when I did and looked at me; he knew something was wrong.

"Elle, how are you?" Kyle asked in a confused tone. I took in a deep breath.

"I'm great, Kyle. How are you?" I managed to smile.

A few feet behind him stood a woman with jet black hair and boobs so fake, I bet they would pop if I poked them with my finger. I looked over at her as she was eye-fucking Connor.

"I'm fine. Who is this?" he asked, pointing to Connor.

"Oh, I'm sorry; this is my friend, Connor Black." Connor extended his hand, and the two of them shook. My stomach was in knots and so desperately wanted to throw up.

"Elle, you look good." He smiled as he looked me up and down.

I faked a smile as Kyle's little plastic bimbo came walking up and introduced herself.

"Hi, I'm Angela; you must be Kyle's ex?"

I rolled my eyes. "Yep that's me; Kyle's ex."

She wouldn't stop looking at Connor and seducing him with her eyes. It was making me uncomfortable. She was practically salivating. I pulled Kyle over to the side.

"Tame your dog, Kyle; she's embarrassing you."

He glared at me. "Let's go, Angela."

I looked over at Connor who was steadily smiling at me.

"What?"

"Nothing, you're just…"

"Just what, Connor?" I asked.

"You're just full of life. Let's put it that way." He laughed. I shook my head as we left Central Park.

Denny had the limo parked and was waiting for Connor. "Are you getting in?" Connor asked as he pointed to the car.

"No, I'm walking," I said as I started down the street.

"Elle, get in the car," he demanded. I smiled because for the first time he called me Elle, which was his way of letting me know we were friends. My back was turned as I walked away and waved.

"Bye, Connor, see you tomorrow."

I heard him sigh, and the car door shut. I walked the majority of the way with Connor's limo following me. I finally turned the corner and stopped. He rolled down the window.

"Are you ready to get in now?" He smiled.

I rolled my eyes and opened the door. I smacked him on the arm and told him to move over. Denny was watching me through the rearview mirror, and he was lightly laughing. We reached my apartment, and as I was getting out of the limo, Connor surprised me by lightly grabbing my hand.

"Thank you for agreeing to come with me tomorrow."

I crinkled my nose and smiled. "That's what friends are for."

I walked through the door and leaned up against it, sliding down until I was on the floor. I cupped my face in my hands and thought about the fire that ignited in my body when he touched me. I was headed for trouble, and I already knew it.

Chapter 10

I awoke the next morning to a text message from Peyton, saying she was on her way over with coffee and bagels. I rolled out of bed just as Peyton was ready to break down the door.

"Some friend you are," she spouted as she flew past me to set the coffee and a bag on the table.

"What did I do?" I yawned.

"I waited all night for you to call me and tell me about your day with Connor, but you never did." She pouted. Peyton loved to pout, and she was such a natural at it. She once told me that she could make a guy do anything just by pouting.

"How did you know about yesterday?"

She looked down and took a sip of her coffee. "Kyle told me," she said as if it was no big deal.

"WHAT?!" I scowled. Peyton pulled a bagel out of the bag and handed it to me.

"He called me and said he saw the two of you in Central Park. He wanted to know how long you have been seeing each other; I could tell he was jealous."

"Who the hell does Kyle think he is? Did he forget he's the one who left me, and he's the one moving on by dating a plastic bitch?"

She leaned over the table. "I told him that Connor was your fuck buddy and to get over it."

I lightly grabbed her arm. "You did not!"

Peyton held up two fingers. "I swear to God I did."

I rolled my eyes as I held my coffee cup in my hands. "Who does he think he is?"

She looked at me as she got up to get a knife from the drawer. "He's a douchebag, Elle, nothing more."

I laughed and was startled by a knock at the door. I strangely looked over at Peyton and got up to see who it was. I looked out the peep-hole and saw a tall, attractive woman standing there. I opened the door. I was still in my pajama pants and tank top.

"Miss Ellery Lane?" the woman asked.

"Yes, I'm Ellery Lane." She pushed her way through the door.

"Very good," she said as she waved her hand, and three other women with garment bags followed behind her.

"Um, what's going on?" I looked over at Peyton as she sat at the table with her mouth open.

"Miss Lane, I'm Camille. We're from Saks Fifth Avenue. Mr. Black sent us to have you pick a dress for tonight's event. He described you, so we chose which dresses we felt would suit you."

"Holy shit, Elle," Peyton said.

I stood there as the women unpacked the garment bags, pulling out the most beautiful and expensive dresses I've ever seen. I tried on each one, feeling like Cinderella. Peyton was giving me thumbs up at the dresses she liked. The tall woman applauded as I tried on each dress. The last dress I put on was a Badgley Mischka black strapless lace gown. I gasped when I looked in the mirror because I had never worn anything more

60

beautiful. Peyton had a tear in her eye as she took my hands in hers and looked me over.

"You look absolutely stunning, Elle."

"It's too much; I can't accept this or let Connor do this for me."

Camille walked over and handed me a pair of Jimmy Choo strappy heels. "Put these on, dear, and let the man buy you a new dress; trust me, if he didn't think you were worth it, he wouldn't have done this." I looked at Peyton and took the shoes from Camille.

"Connor isn't a douchebag. Let him buy you a dress and definitely those shoes." Peyton smiled.

I rolled my eyes as I stood in a designer dress and Jimmy Choos. I felt incredible. I grabbed my phone and sent Connor a quick text.

"Hi, Connor, it's me Ellery. Thank you for the beautiful dress, but it's too much, and I don't feel right accepting it."

Seconds later he replied, *"You're welcome, and it's not too much, see you at 6:00 pm sharp."*

I smiled at Camille. "I like this one," I said as I ran my hands down my body. She snapped her fingers, signaling the other women to pack up the other dresses.

"Mr. Black will be immensely pleased as you chose his favorite." Camille smiled as she walked out the door. I stood in the middle of the room, trying to figure out what Camille meant by his favorite dress. Did he go to the store himself and pick a bunch out for her to bring to me? Then, I wondered if this was a habit of his for all his women.

"You're over thinking, Elle," Peyton said as she unzipped the back of my dress. "Go put your other clothes back on; you don't want to ruin this before tonight. I'm going to call Roger and see if he's available to do your hair and makeup; he owes me a big favor."

I went to the bedroom and put on a pair of jeans and a tank top with a sick feeling in my stomach. My phone rang, and that familiar number was calling again. I ignored it and sent them to voicemail.

***

Peyton and I took a cab to Color Me Beautiful, a hair salon that our friend Roger owns. We walked through the doors of the luxury salon as Roger spotted us instantly. He walked over and embraced me tightly.

"Oh girl, I heard about you and Kyle. I think he's an asshole."

"Thanks, Roger, I think he is too." I smiled. He turned to Peyton and gave her a warm hug.

"Now, tell me where you're going tonight and with whom."

Peyton jumped in, "She's going to a charity event with Connor Black."

"*The* Connor Black? The hot and gorgeous millionaire, Connor Black?!"

I rolled my eyes. "Yes, Roger, that's the one." He looked at me seriously.

"Elle, you do know about his reputation, right?" I looked blank because I didn't know anything about Connor except his one rule about sleepovers and that he didn't like relationships.

"We're friends, nothing more."

Roger waved his hand in front of his face. "Girl, Connor Black doesn't have female friends; he has sex slaves, not friends." I gulped and didn't want to hear anymore. Peyton could tell I was feeling uncomfortable.

"I don't care what he has; I'm going to this benefit tonight as his friend and nothing more."

"Come on, Roger, work your magic and fix up our girl so that every guy at the event will be begging her to take them home." I smacked Peyton's arm as we followed Roger to his station.

I met Roger through Peyton. He used to work at the art gallery part-time while he was trying to launch his salon. He was a handsome man with brown spiked hair and just the right amount of facial hair outlining his oval face. He cut hair and did makeup like nobody's business. He once worked as a hair stylist for Miranda Lambert, but gave that up to stay in one place and build a life with his partner, George. I sat in the chair while Roger worked his magic on my hair and face. I've never felt more beautiful as I did that day.

I stepped into my designer dress and Jimmy Choos and looked in the mirror at my lightly made-up face and elegant curly up-do. For the first time—in a terribly long time—I forgot about all the bad things in my life. I glanced at the clock, and it read 6:00 pm. I rolled my eyes as there was a knock at the door. As promised, he arrived at 6:00 pm sharp. I opened the door as Connor stood there, staring at me and taking in a sharp breath. The butterflies in my stomach started to flutter, and my heart started racing as I looked at him in his black tuxedo.

"Were you afraid that I'd get mugged between my door and your car?" I smirked.

"Very funny, Ellery," he said.

I was surprised that he came to the door himself instead of sending Denny. I bumped my shoulder against his, and he managed a small smile. We got into the back of the limo, and Connor poured us each a glass of champagne.

"You look beautiful, Ellery. What a lovely dress." I looked at him, stomach still fluttering and heart racing.

"Thank you, Connor. I was hoping you'd like this one." I winked as he smirked, and we held our glasses up to one another.

Chapter 11

The charity was for the Autism Speaks Foundation. It was to support the biomedical research for the causes and treatments of autism in both children and adults. Denny opened my door as Connor came around the other side to meet me. He held out his arm and looked at me.

"Do you think that you can behave yourself tonight?" I put my arm in his and smiled.

"I don't know, but I can't make any promises."

We walked to the entrance and stepped inside. The ballroom was breathtaking as were the people who attended. Connor led me over to a reserved table with his company's name on it. I sat down, taking notice of the pilasters around the room as well as the beautifully carved ceilings. The walls were painted in a beige color with mahogany trim as were the chairs that sat at each table. A band and dance floor sat in the middle of the room. Off to the side, was a large wrap-around bar that was complimented by the same mahogany wood and marble tops.

Connor went to the bar to get our drinks. Apparently, he didn't have the patience to wait for the waitresses and waiters walking around the room with drinks on their trays. He came back with a glass of white wine for me and a scotch for him. Even as beautiful as the ballroom was, Connor was the most beautiful person there, and I couldn't help but stare at him. He lightly grabbed my elbow and escorted me over to a couple who were staring our way. Even the slightest touch of his hand sent my body into convulsions.

"Good evening, Connor," the older gentleman said as he shook his hand.

"Hello, Robert, Courtney, I would like you to meet a friend of mine, Ellery Lane."

He took my hand and lightly kissed it. "You have beautiful friends, Connor."

I gently smiled at his comment and looked over at his wife who was eyeing me up and down.

"This is my wife, Courtney." Robert smiled.

"It's nice to meet you." She smiled at me.

Courtney was extremely attractive, and she was about 25 years younger than her husband. Robert put his arm around Connor and walked him over to the side, whispering so we couldn't hear. Connor shook his head, and the two of them came back to where we were standing.

"What was that about?" I asked.

He looked at me at strangely for even asking. "It's just business."

He lightly put his hand on the small of my back and escorted me back to the table while he excused himself to the restroom. I was taking in the beautiful sound of the band playing soft melodies as Courtney came over and sat next to me.

"So, you're Connor's new toy," she remarked. I looked at her, trying to absorb what she meant.

"Connor and I are nothing more than friends."

She shook her head. "Right, well I'm only saying this for your own sake, woman to woman, because you seem like an innocent and nice person. Stay away from Connor Black."

66

I narrowed my eyes at her then looked around to see if Connor was on his way back. "Why would you say something like that?" I asked.

"Because Connor will use you till he emotionally breaks you down and physically wears you out, then he'll toss you to the side like a piece of trash." She got up from her seat and put her hand on my arm. "It's just some friendly advice."

She walked away and left me sitting there, pondering her words. The way she spoke led me to believe that she was a victim of Connor's. I didn't want to think about it as I got up and headed to the bar for another glass of wine. I glanced over to the side where there was a small hallway and raised my eyebrow when I saw Connor talking to the same woman who slapped him at the club. His eyes looked angered as he grabbed her arm and led her out of sight. My stomach tied itself in knots. What the hell was I doing here? I don't even know anything about this man I was with.

I was standing at the bar when a gentleman approached me. "Hello, I'm Andrew. I was wondering if a beautiful woman such as you would like to share a dance with me?" I looked around, and Connor was nowhere to be found; the nerve of him just to leave me alone like this.

"It would be my pleasure." I smiled.

I didn't mind dancing with Andrew; he was handsome with brown hair and hazel eyes. He was tall, and as he put his arm around my waist, I could feel his strength. Before we had a chance to finish our conversation, Connor came up from behind.

"Excuse me, Andrew, but she's here with me."

Andrew looked at Connor. "Mr. Black, I apologize. I didn't know she was yours."

He stepped away as Connor took his place. His? I'm not his or anybody else's. Connor stared at me as he put his arm around my waist and took my hand in his. "I leave you alone for a minute, and you go off and dance with strange men? Is that what you call behaving?"

I narrowed my eyes at him. "You leave me alone to go disappear with the woman who slapped you at Club S."

His look turned to fire. "You saw that?"

I nodded my head. "I think a lot of people saw that."

"So, let me get this straight, you saw me before you found me drunk outside?"

"Yes, I was sitting at the bar. Why do you ask?"

The corners of his sexy mouth curved up. "Interesting."

I cocked my head at him. "What's interesting?" Then it hit me. "Oh, I get it now. You think I had my eyes set on you from the start."

He wickedly smiled at me. "Your words, Miss Lane, not mine."

I rolled my eyes and leaned into him, taking in his alluring scent as I whispered in his ear, "You are a delusional man, Mr. Black."

"May I ask why this specific charity?" I asked.

He looked at me and took in a breath. "Why not this charity?" I dropped the subject about the woman in the hallway and where he disappeared to, but I wouldn't let this one go.

"Why did you though?"

He stopped looking at me and looked straight into the crowd. "It's just a charity that my company is involved with. Why is it so important that you know a specific reason?" His words came across as cold, almost as if he didn't trust me enough to tell me.

"Just forget I asked." I kept my eyes straight ahead refusing to look at him.

"You're mad," he spoke.

"You'll know when I'm mad, Mr. Black," I responded.

The song ended, and we walked back to the table that was now filled with some associates from Black Enterprises. Connor went around and introduced me to some of his staff. I glanced over at the next table, and there she sat, the beautiful tall woman from the club. Her straight, jet black hair sat just above her shoulders, and her tanned skin glowed beneath the ballroom lights. She sparkled in her silver long dress and silver high stilettos. Diamonds took their place in her ears and on her neckline, and she didn't miss a beat when it came to applying makeup. She was a stunning woman, and she kept staring at me—or should I say glaring at me.

Dinner consisted of Filet Mignon or Fish. Connor took the liberty to order me the Filet since he felt I needed to put some meat on my bones as he so kindly put it. During dinner, a man stepped up to thank everyone for coming and thanked Black Enterprises for donating five hundred thousand dollars to the charity; everyone applauded.

I excused myself to the restroom as I heard someone call my name. I turned around and froze when I saw Dr. Taub coming out of the men's bathroom.

"Ellery, fancy meeting you here," he said.

"Dr. Taub, I'm here as someone's guest and would appreciate it if he didn't see us talking." My stomach felt sick, and my heart was beating faster.

"You haven't returned my calls or rescheduled your appointments. You need to finish our sessions, Miss Lane; it's important, and you know it."

"Dr. Taub," I whispered as I looked around to make sure no one, especially Connor, saw us talking. "I will; just give me some time, please."

"Time is not on your side, Ellery. It's important you schedule your appointment."

"I can't talk about this here, please, Dr. Taub." He walked away, shaking his head.

I walked into the restroom and checked my hair and makeup. I glossed up my lips, and as I opened the door to step out, I was startled to see Connor standing against the wall with his arms folded. He glared at me as I spoke, "Uh, hi? Why are you standing there like that?"

"Because you've been gone for quite a while, and I was checking to make sure you're ok. I was giving you five more seconds before I was opening the door and coming in after you."

I walked away from him. "Wow, stalker much?"

I heard him sigh. "For the last time, I'm not a stalker; I was concerned for your safety." I rolled my eyes; he had safety issues, and it was starting to annoy me.

We walked back to the table, and as we passed the *one* next to us, Connor looked over at the tall beautiful woman. She smiled at him.

"Are you ready to leave?" he asked.

"I am if you are."

He smiled, and we walked outside where Denny was waiting for us. He stopped and turned to me. "I'm going to have Denny take you home; I have something that I need to wrap up here." He took my hand and lightly kissed it. "Thank you for coming with me tonight. I hope you had a good time." His lips were warm on my skin, but I was focused on the fact that he wasn't coming to drive me home.

I looked into his eyes. "I had a wonderful time, Connor. Thank you for inviting me."

He nodded and opened the door. I slid into the back seat and waved goodbye, trying to hide the disappointment in my eyes.

"Good evening, Miss Lane," Denny said as he looked in the rearview mirror. "Hi, Denny," I replied as I looked out the window.

Chapter 12

The night air was exceptionally warm for September, and I wanted to do something other than go home to an empty apartment. "Denny, could you please drive me to the beach?"

He looked up in the rearview mirror. "Sorry, Miss Lane, but my orders were to take you straight home."

I politely smiled. "Denny, either you can drive me to the beach, or I will call a cab the minute you drop me off at home. Mr. Black doesn't own me nor does he have the right to tell me what to do. I don't care if he told you to take me home; I'm telling you otherwise. Now, please, drop me off at the beach."

"Fine, Miss Lane, if you say so." he sighed.

"I do say so, and if Mr. Black has a problem with it, then I will deal with him."

***

I took off my shoes and carried them as my feet hit the soft, warm sand. The ocean looked beautiful at night with the moonlight shining down, illuminating each wave that pushed its way to the shore. I threw my shoes down and ran to the edge of the water. I laughed as the cold water stung my feet, making me feel alive and exhilarated. The peaceful sound of the waves lapping against the shore and the sweet smell of the salt water was enough to let me escape into a world of my own; a world I created. I was enjoying the serenity of my world when I heard, "What the hell do you think you're doing?" I sighed, for I knew that angered voice all too well. I turned my head to see Connor standing a few feet away from me.

"What are you doing here, Connor? Don't you have things to

wrap up?" I considered the possibility that his wrapping something up involved sex and the tall beautiful woman.

"I'm here because you didn't make it home and forced my driver to disobey my orders," his voice sounded angry.

"Well, it was such a beautiful night, and I wanted to be here; it's my favorite place to visit."

"There's a time and place for that, Ellery, and now is not the time."

"I'm sorry you feel that way, but I'm not done here yet, and I'm not leaving."

He raised his voice, "Let's go now, Ellery."

Who the fuck does this man think he is? "Don't be so grouchy, and if you want me to go, then you'll have to catch me." I laughed as I started running down the beach.

"For fuck sake, Elle, you're pissing me off!" he yelled as he started chasing after me.

I turned my head and looked behind me as he was catching up; I swear I saw a small smile escape his lips. He was a good runner, but he had an advantage; he wasn't wearing a long dress. I started to run out of breath and slowed down as he came up from behind me, picked me up, and put me over his shoulder. I kicked and screamed, "Put me down, Connor Black!"

"Not a chance! You'll just run again, and I'm done playing games."

Out of breath I said, "I won't, I promise. I'm out of breath anyway if you couldn't tell."

He gently put me down, and I sat on the sand. He looked down at me, shaking his head as I held out my hand for him to sit next to me.

"I'm not sitting in the sand in this tuxedo."

"Live a little, Connor, life is too short," I said as I stared out into the moonlit water. He sighed and sat down next to me.

We sat in silence for a moment, and I was feeling somewhat emotional—I'm blaming the wine—when I started to speak.

"It was my 16th birthday when I was diagnosed with cancer." I felt him look at me as I just stared ahead, listening to the whispers of the ocean. "Hey, happy sweet 16! Guess what, you have cancer." I felt the tears starting to sting my eyes.

Connor took my hand and whispered, "You don't have to do this." I wouldn't look at him because if I stared into his beautiful green eyes, I would have lost it. I proceeded with my story.

"I couldn't bear the thought of my father having to go through that torture and pain again like he did with my mother, so I decided I was going to spare him from having to."

"Ellery," he whispered as he leaned closer to me.

"He was going out on one of his drinking binges, and I knew he wouldn't be home until the middle of the night, if at all, so that was my opportunity to put my plan into action. I filled the bathtub with hot water, laid back, and took a razor blade to both my wrists." I heard him take in a sharp breath as he was gently rubbing my scar with his thumb.

"Can you believe it was the one night he forgot his wallet and came back to the house? Talk about fate, right? He found me and called 911. I almost didn't make it; I had lost so much blood."

Connor didn't say a word, but he didn't have to; I could tell he was choked up.

"I guess God had other plans for me. I went through a year of chemo and went into remission. I was given a second chance at life, and for that, I'm grateful. Like I said yesterday, I was young and stupid, and I made a terrible mistake."

Connor let go of my hand, put his arm around me, and pulled me into him. I rested my head on his shoulder. He was firm, and it felt good to be held.

"That's why you have this overwhelming need to help others, isn't it?" he asked as he lightly kissed the top of my head. "You're a good person, Ellery Lane," he whispered in my ear.

I smiled and closed my eyes. I felt his strong arms pick me up as he carried me across the sand and to his car, which wasn't his limo; it was a Range Rover. He carefully laid me down on the front seat, and as I stirred he whispered, "Sleep, angel."

He pulled up to my apartment, opened my purse to find my keys, and then carried me to the door. My arms were tightly wrapped around his neck. He inserted the key into the lock and lightly kicked the door open with his foot. He carried me to the bedroom and laid me gently on the bed. I was somewhat aware of what he was doing, but I was too exhausted to move.

He covered me with a blanket and brought the back of his hand to my cheek as he softly rubbed it. "Sleep well, angel, and sweet dreams."

Chapter 13

The next morning was a work day, but I didn't have to be there until noon. I dragged my ass out of bed and got out of my evening gown. I was thankful he didn't undress me, ok maybe I wanted him to because the moments we shared on the beach were something that I never wanted to forget. I felt something change in him last night.

I stood under the hot water and let it overtake me. I couldn't stop thinking about Connor and how sweet and gentle he was with me last night. I exposed my deepest secret to him, and now regret was settling in. I shouldn't have shown him that side of me; it was too dangerous. I dressed in my leggings and long tunic top, put my hair up in a ponytail, and headed to the kitchen to make some coffee. I couldn't shake the feeling of stupidity for telling him; sometimes I just don't know when to keep my mouth shut.

As I waited for the coffee to brew, I went into my purse and grabbed my phone; there was a text message from Connor.

"Hi, I hope you slept well. I just wanted to see if you were up and how you were feeling."

A small smile escaped me as I replied, *"Good morning, Connor. I slept well, and I'm feeling fine; thank you for your concern. I hope you have a terrific day, and don't work too hard!"*

"I'm glad you're feeling fine, and I always work hard; it's why I'm as successful as I am."

"I believe that, and thank you for taking care of me last night. I owe you one!"

"Consider it repayment for when you got me home safe. I have

a meeting that I need to get to. TTYL!"

"Bye, Connor."

I poured some coffee into a mug that read: "I'm not gay, but my ex-boyfriend is," compliments of Peyton. I walked over at the desk that housed my laptop, opened the drawer, and took out the piece of paper that sits neatly on top of a magazine. I looked over the paper, and with a pen, I scribbled on it and put it back in its place until I needed it again.

I stepped outside and walked down the street. I had an hour before I had to be at work, so I decided to walk the few blocks it took to get there. The air was cooler today as the sun hid behind a stream of clouds. Today was a different sight than it had been in months. People had broken into their fall wardrobe and pulled out their *chilly* day clothes. Pants, long sleeves, cardigans, and light jackets graced the streets of New York City as people prepared for the arrival of fall.

I passed Starbucks on my way to work, and of course, I had to stop as I needed more caffeine. I walked in and stood in a line that took up half the café. I reached in my bag and grabbed my phone; I promised Peyton I would call and tell her about last night. I dialed her number and waited for her to answer; after a few rings, it went to voicemail.

"Hey Peyton, it's me. I had a fabulous time last night with Connor. I'm on my way to work. Call me later for girl talk. Love you."

It was finally my turn as I ordered a Grande Cinnamon Dolce Latte. I paid the barista, walked outside with my coffee in hand, and made my way to work. As I walked down the crowded street, I noticed a black limo parked across from a tall building. The limo door opened as a familiar woman got out, and then came Connor, following her and adjusting his tie. My stomach felt sick, and my heart started racing, not out of passion, but out of nerves. He looked over and saw me standing there a few feet away. I couldn't let him know the rage and jealousy I was feeling at that moment, seeing them together, so I smiled and waved just like any friend would do. His face looked pained when he saw me. He didn't smile back; he could only manage a small wave. They walked up to the tall building and went inside. As I walked past, I noticed the name of the business on the large double doors, Black Enterprises. I never realized that's what this building was as I passed it all the time.

I continued walking as a wave of betrayal coursed through my veins. There was no reason for me to feel this way. Connor and I are friends, and nothing more; there could never be more. I struggled with my emotions all the way to work and tried to reason with myself that he did nothing wrong. If he and I were going to remain friends, then I would have to get used to seeing him with other women. He wasn't mine, and I wasn't his. I kept saying that as I finally arrived at work.

It was a slow day at work, which sucked because it gave me more time to think about Connor and the tall beautiful woman that got out of the limo. I had no right to even think about them, but after the moment we shared last night, I couldn't help but wonder that maybe he had feelings for me. Who was I kidding? Connor Black is a player, and I've already been warned about him. I needed to do some serious soul-searching, and the best place to do that was at my favorite pizza place.

The workday finally ended. I grabbed my phone and purse and headed out the door. I came to a standstill when I saw Denny leaning up against the limo parked at the curb. I narrowed my eyes at him.

"Hi, Denny, what are you doing here?" I curiously asked.

"Hello, Miss Lane, Mr. Black sent me to pick you up and take you to the restaurant where he will meet you in 15 minutes for dinner."

"Is that so?" I asked as I put my hands on my hips. He looked at me with a smirk on his face because he knew what was coming next.

"You can tell Mr. Black that I'm not available this evening. I have other plans."

I started walking away as I turned my head back. "Also, tell him that if he wants to have dinner with me, then he can pick up the phone and ask me himself." I put my hand up and waved. "Bye, Denny, have a great night."

Pizzapopolous was a couple of blocks away, and the chilly evening air was settling in. I sat down at a table close to the window and opened the menu. The restaurant was small with about 20 tables that took up the space. The white walls were decorated with photographs of all the celebrities that dined there. The tables were decorated with red and white gingham tablecloths and white napkins. The atmosphere was casual and quaint, and they had the best pizza.

I was digging through my purse for my phone when I saw the shadow of someone sit down across from me. I looked up and there was Connor glaring at me; I rolled my eyes.

"So, this is where you want to have dinner?" he asked.

I tilted my head to the side and looked at his smoldering face. "Yes, Connor, this is where I'm having dinner tonight, and I don't believe you were invited."

He put his hand over his heart. "Ouch that stings, Ellery. I invited you to dinner, and you turned me down, so I took it upon myself to join you."

"How do you know I want company?"

He put his hands on the table and folded them. "I don't, but since I'm here, we might as well dine together," he said as he looked around the restaurant.

The whole point of this dinner was for me to do some soul-searching, and that was going to be extremely hard with him sitting across from me.

The waitress came over and started drooling when she asked Connor what he would like to order. He looked the menu up and down and decided on a salad. I looked at him and grabbed the menu out of his hand.

"You can't sit in a pizza place and only get a salad."

I looked at the waitress and cleared my throat to divert her attention away from Connor. "We'll have a large deep dish with pepperoni, mushrooms, and black olives, and a large antipasto salad with an order of bread sticks."

Connor brought his finger up and rested it on his lips. "Do you actually think I'm going to eat that pizza?"

"I don't think you are; I know you are." I smiled.

I set my phone on the table and looked at him. If he so rudely wanted to interrupt my dinner plans, then he'll have to answer some questions. "Who's that woman that you're always with?" The words just came out before I could think about them. He shifted in his seat.

"She's a friend, Ellery," he answered my question softly. I knew he was lying. Perhaps she was a friend, but what kind of friend is what I wanted to know.

"What kind of friend, Connor?"

His green eyes turned dark as he glared at me. "She doesn't matter, Ellery; she's a friend, and that's all you need to know."

I raised my eyebrows. "I think after what I told you last night you would be willing to tell me a few things."

"I'm not in the habit of discussing my personal life. It's called personal for a reason, Ellery."

He didn't realize it, but at that moment, he made a decision for me. The waitress brought our pizza and put it in the middle of the table along with the salad and bread sticks. I picked up a slice of pizza with the spatula and put it on his plate. He sighed and grabbed his fork and knife.

"What, are you kidding me?! Put that down right now, Connor Black!"

He looked startled. "What? What the hell is wrong?"

I leaned over the table and grabbed the fork and knife out of his hand. "You are not eating pizza with a fork and knife."

"Then how the hell am I supposed to eat it?"

He was so damn sexy at that moment. I picked up my pizza and took a bite. With a mouthful, I said, "Like this; pick it up and bite into it."

"That's disgusting, and don't talk with your mouth full."

"If you won't do it, then I will." I picked up the pizza from his plate and held it up to his mouth.

"Bite," I demanded.

He raised his eyebrows at me. "Do you have any idea how sexy that sounds?" He winked.

I couldn't help but let out a light laugh as I hit him on his arm. He rolled his eyes—which was sexy as hell—opened his mouth, and took a bite of the pizza. I smiled as I put the pizza back on his plate.

"My turn." He smiled.

"Your turn for what?"

He took the pizza from my plate and held it up.

"Bite," he demanded.

I took a bite, and a wide grin graced his perfect face. I think that may have been the first time since I've known him that I've seen him smile like that. It was the most beautiful and warm smile that I've ever seen, and it made my heart flutter.

We ate more pizza, talked, and ate some salad. The waitress kept walking by our table, giving Connor flirtatious smiles.

"Don't you ever get sick and tired of all the ogling you get from women?"

He laughed. "Don't you get sick of all the ogling you get from men?"

I twisted my face in confusion. "I don't get that."

"Yes you do, Ellery; I see it every time I'm with you. The only difference is men are more discreet about it than women are."

I never noticed men ogling me before; I'll have to start paying more attention. As we were laughing and enjoying our conversation, my phone rang; it was my Aunt Patti's number. I looked at Connor. "I have to get this." He nodded his head and took out his phone.

"Hello," I answered. The voice on the other end was my cousin Debbie.

"Ellery, it's Debbie. I wanted to let you know that mom and dad were..." She started sobbing. "They were in a car accident, and they were both killed."

Her sobs grew harder as a tear fell down my cheek. Connor looked at me and reached for my hand resting on the table. "Debbie, I'm so sorry; I will be there as soon as I can."

"Thank you, Elle. I'll call you with the details."

I hung up and looked at Connor who was staring at me with a worried look in his eyes. "Ellery, what happened?"

"My aunt and uncle were killed in a car accident. I need to get out of here, Connor."

I grabbed my purse and took out some money. Connor grabbed it from my hands and shoved it back in my purse. "I got this."

I couldn't fall apart in front of him; I had to hold it together— at least till I got home where I'd be alone.

He threw some money on the table and followed me out of the restaurant. My head was in a daze, and I was confused. I looked in both directions, forgetting which way I needed to go. He put his arm around me and pulled me into him, leading me to where Denny had parked the limo. I stumbled a few times, but the strength of his arms held me up. He opened the door and helped me in. I slid to the other side as he got in and sat beside me. He didn't say a word; he only wrapped his arms around me and pulled me into his chest. Feeling the warmth and security of him, I clenched his shirt in my hands and started crying. He rubbed his hand up and down my back as his chin rested on my head. At that moment, I didn't care that he saw me like this. I just needed to be with someone right now, and he was more than willing to be that someone.

Chapter 14

We walked into my apartment. Connor shut the door behind him. I threw my purse on the table and walked to the kitchen to grab a bottle of wine.

"Are you ok?" Connor asked as he followed closely behind. I scratched my head. "Yeah, I'm fine. Do you want some wine?"

"Ah no; I really have to go. I have a meeting with someone."

I rolled my eyes with my back turned to him because I'm sure his meeting had to do with getting laid. I opened the bottle, poured some into a glass, and turned around, putting one hand on his chest.

"Thank you, Connor. I want you to know that I truly appreciate you being here for me."

He put his hand to my face and gently wiped away a couple of tears that were left with his thumb. "I know you do, and you are welcome."

Fire swept through my body, heating every part that ached for him at this moment. This was a side of him that was tender and gentle; a side I wanted to know better. My heart started racing, and the butterflies fluttered around every time he touched me. I was vulnerable at this moment, and all I could think about was kissing him passionately. I restrained myself because I wasn't about to ruin our friendship.

I patted him on the chest. "You better go to your meeting Mr. Black; it's rude to keep someone waiting."

He managed a small smile. "If you need anything, anything at all, please don't hesitate to call me," he said as he pressed his lips against my forehead.

"I will. Now, go have a good night."

I shut the door behind him and sat down with my wine. For someone my age, I have experienced death more times than I should have. I needed to call Peyton and let her know what was going on. As I got up and reached for my phone, there was a knock at the door. I looked out the peep-hole and saw Connor standing there.

"Hey, what are you doing here?"

He walked inside. "Pack a bag because you're staying with me tonight."

I looked at him with a stunned look. "No, I'm not; I'm staying right here."

He sighed. "Elle, for once, just once, please do as I say."

"I'm not a child, Connor, and frankly, you can't order me around. I thought we had this discussion already?"

He walked over to the corner of the room where my easel was and looked at the unfinished painting sitting on it. His tone changed, "I don't think you should be alone tonight after the news you received, and my place has a guest room. I would feel better knowing you weren't alone."

He struggled with every word he just spoke; I now realized that he had a hard time with emotions.

"Ok, Connor, give me a minute." He nodded his head, never taking his eyes off the painting.

I threw a few things in a bag and walked over to him standing by the easel. "This is what you were drawing in Central Park, isn't it? The bride and groom in front of the fountain?"

"Yeah, I started painting it that night."

"From what I can see, you're a very talented artist."

"Thanks, Mr. Black. Now, let's go." He smiled and took my bag from me; he was full of surprises today.

His penthouse was breathtaking, from the marble floors in the hallway to the white walls and two story windows. The living room housed a beautiful dark gray sofa, a large square wooden table in the center, and two leather wingback chairs in a soft gray shade. Long curtains hung from the floor to ceiling windows, and the marble fireplace was the focal point of the room. Black and white pictures hung vertically on the walls in groups of three with various city scenes from around the world. He came up behind me as I was staring at the pictures.

"Do you like these?"

I smiled. "Yes, they're beautiful. Where did you get them?"

"I took them."

I whipped my head around, and the look on my face must have amused him because he started laughing.

"You took these?" I emphasized each word.

"You look so surprised, Ellery. Photography is a hobby of mine."

"Well, how would I know that, Connor, especially since you refuse to tell me anything about you?"

I stood there and studied the photographs. I smiled, because at that moment, I realized we had something in common; we were both artists. I painted pictures, and he took them.

"Your home is beautiful; did you decorate it?"

"No, my sister did."

I looked at him confused. "You have a sister?"

"Yes, and she's an interior designer. She did this place and my office building."

I nodded my head up and down. "I get the impression that talent runs in the family."

He laughed as he walked over to his bar. "Drink?" he asked.

"Shot of Jack, please."

"Are you sure?" His eyes widened.

"Does that surprise you?"

He reached for a shot glass. "It doesn't, well, maybe it does; I just don't know any women who do shots of Jack Daniels straight."

He handed me the shot glass as I held it up. "You do now." I threw it back as it burned all the way down, but it felt good.

"I thought you didn't do sleepovers, Mr. Black?"

He looked at me and grinned. "I don't, Miss Lane. I never have, but tonight I made an exception for a friend," he emphasized the word friend, "Because I felt she shouldn't be alone." He poured another shot and held up the glass.

90

"Another shot?" he asked.

"Are you trying to get me drunk?"

He looked at me in that sexy way that made my body ache. "Should I be?"

I threw back the shot and sat down on the couch. Connor walked over with his glass of scotch and sat next to me. "Are you ok?" he asked.

I looked up at him and sighed. "I was just thinking about how I can visit my mom and dad's grave when I'm back in Michigan."

I looked at him, blue eyes staring into green, and seriously spoke, "When I die, I don't want a funeral. I don't want people staring at my dead body and crying over me. I want to be cremated and have my ashes scattered around Paris."

Connor stared at me and gave me an irritated look. "Stop talking like that. You have many years to decide what you want."

"Connor, I'm serious; I want people to drink and celebrate me. I want them to remember the good times, not mourn in the death of me."

"Ok, you need to stop because you're talking as if you're going to die tomorrow."

"You never know what each day will bring, and that's why I believe that nothing lasts forever."

"Ok, I think Mr. Daniels has gotten to you. Let's get some sleep; I have to work in the morning."

We walked upstairs, and he showed me to my room. "Good night, Elle, sleep well," he said as he walked out and towards his bedroom.

"Good night, Connor."

I changed into my nightshirt and climbed into the comfy king size bed that occupied the room. I took in the luxurious feel of the satin sheets as I looked around at the classically decorated room. The taupe walls with carved moldings were astounding. There was a beige dresser with a large round mirror that sat above it and matching night stands on each side of the bed. The large window had built-in bookcases on each side with a window seat that was covered with the same material as the bed comforter. I could curl up here and stay forever, residing in its beauty and comfort.

It was too late to call Peyton, so I decided to text her and let her know what was going on.

"I got some terrible news today. My cousin called me earlier; my aunt and uncle died in a car accident. I'll be going back to Michigan in a couple of days for the funeral. I wanted you to know so that you didn't worry."

"OMG, I'm so sorry, Elle. Do you want me to come over? You shouldn't be alone."

I'm fine, I'm staying at Connor's tonight; he was with me when I got the call."

"Seriously, Elle? What the hell is going on between the two of you? Did you sleep with him?"

"NO! We're just friends, and I'm staying in the guest room."

"Shut the fuck up. Go get into that man's bed, and let him make you forget about everything bad—at least for tonight."

"LOL! Good night, Peyton. I'll keep in touch."

"Live, Elle! Have you ever heard of friends with benefits? Nighty night..."

She was right; when I'm with Connor, he does make me forget about everything bad, but the ironic thing is he's the one who's bad for me. One of us will have our heart broken by the other, and I can't have that in my life right now.

Chapter 15

I rolled over and opened my eyes as the sunlight peeked through the sheer curtains that hung perfectly from the windows. I threw on some yoga pants and a T-shirt and followed the aroma that led me straight to the kitchen. Connor was sitting at the table, typing away on his laptop.

"Good morning, Ellery, I hope you slept well."

I smiled and headed to the cabinet for a coffee mug. "Good morning. I slept very well in that monstrous bed."

He lightly laughed. I poured some coffee and sat at the table across from him. "There are bagels over there; please have one."

"Thanks, but I'm not hungry."

He looked at me with his morning green eyes. "You have to eat, Ellery."

I sighed. "I never eat when I first get up, but don't worry, dad, I'll have one in a little bit."

A slight irritated smile graced his face. "You're even a smart ass first thing in the morning." I held up my cup and smiled.

"What are you doing?" I asked as I pointed to his laptop.

"Just sending some emails and rearranging some meetings."

"Did you over-schedule or something?"

He looked at me and cocked his head. "You question everything, don't you?"

I looked up at the ceiling. "I guess I do." I smiled.

I sat and stared at him as he was looking at his computer screen. He was freshly showered, and his hair was still damp and perfectly sexy.

"What are your plans today?" he curiously asked. I set my cup down and wrapped my hands around the mug.

"I have to call work and tell my boss that I won't be in because of the funeral; then I think I'll stop over at the soup kitchen and volunteer this afternoon."

Connor looked up from his laptop. "You really enjoy volunteering there, don't you?"

"Yes, I love it. Even though they are homeless and whatever problems they may have, they're human beings, and they need help."

He looked at me for a second and then continued on his laptop. I took a sip of my coffee and looked out the enormous window at the view of New York City.

"I rearranged my meetings because I'm taking you to Michigan."

"What?" I asked.

He got up from the table and put his cup on the counter. "It's not up for discussion, Elle; we're leaving tomorrow morning, and we're driving."

"Driving? That's a 10 hour drive, Connor!"

He turned around and faced me. "I know how long of a drive it is; consider it a road trip."

I sighed. "A road trip? Flying will get us there in an hour and a half."

"Do you have a problem being in a car with me for 10 hours?" he casually asked.

"No, but…"

He walked over to where I was sitting and stood over me as if he wanted to touch or kiss me, but he didn't. He just said, "No buts; we'll go by car."

"I don't think Denny wants to drive us to Michigan."

He laughed and walked away. "Denny isn't driving; I am."

I rolled my eyes and heavily sighed; why was he going anyway? I'm more than capable of going back home by myself, and that's the way I prefer it. Ok maybe not; the thought of being in a car with him for 10 hours was exciting. I smiled and got up from the table.

**

I grabbed my bag and stepped into the elevator; Denny was waiting for me outside by the limo.

"Morning, Denny, where's Connor?" I asked as I looked, and he wasn't in the limo.

"Good morning, Miss Lane. Mr. Black took the Range Rover to work today."

"Can I ask you a question, Denny?"

"Sure, Miss Lane," he said as he looked at me through the rearview mirror.

"Did Mr. Black tell you why he's driving me to Michigan?"

"No, Miss Lane, he did not. He just told me to take the next few days off because he was going on a road trip. Miss Lane, can I tell you something?"

I looked curiously at him. "What is it?"

"I've worked for the Black family for the past 10 years. I was his father's driver as well. I've never seen Mr. Black behave in such a way as he has since he's met you. Maybe I shouldn't be telling you this."

I smiled. "Nah, it's ok, Denny; we're friends, and maybe all Connor needs is a really good friend." It saddened me that it's the only way things can be.

I stepped into my apartment and headed to the bathroom to take a hot bath. I needed to think about everything before I headed back to Michigan. I climbed into the hot, bubbly water and closed my eyes, taking in the lavender scented bubbles. My phone rang just as I was starting to relax.

"Hey Peyton," I answered. There was a screech from the other end.

"OMG, Elle; I have the best news!" Even though I couldn't see her, I knew she was jumping up and down.

"Elle, all three of your paintings sold!"

I sat up. "What? Are you kidding?"

"No, I wouldn't kid about a thing like that. The best part is the same person bought all three paintings and paid triple the amount for them. They said your paintings are the most beautiful they've ever seen. Elle, Sal wants to talk to you about becoming a regular artist for the gallery; he wants to contract you for more paintings.

Listen, the money you made off those three alone, you can quit your job to paint full-time."

"Who was the buyer?" I asked.

"I don't know. Sal said it was some woman. I have your check; can you meet for lunch later?"

"Lunch sounds great. I'm going to volunteer at the soup kitchen for a couple of hours then we can meet after that; I'll text you."

I hung up the phone and laid back against the tub, reveling in my good news. I never dreamed any of my paintings would sell, especially all three of them. I couldn't wait to tell Connor. I wanted to text him, but he was at work, and I'm sure he was busy, so I figured I shouldn't bother him. I got out of the tub, pruned skin and all, and threw on a pair of skinny jeans and a long sweater. I walked across the hallway as a wave of dizziness came over me. Suddenly, everything turned black.

I awoke lying on the floor and my head hurting. I laid there dazed and confused, trying to focus and remember what happened. I was pretty sure I fainted. I sat up as I felt something dripping down my face. I took my fingers and swiped them across the drips and looked in horror at the blood all over them. I took a deep breath and got up to look in the mirror. I had a deep cut above my eye, and it was bleeding pretty badly. I opened the medicine cabinet, took out some gauze, and applied pressure to the wound. I kept begging God to make it stop and not have to go get stitches. I reached back inside the medicine cabinet. I took out the box of butterfly bandages that I had left over from when Kyle cut his finger with a knife. I applied the bandage and hoped for the best. Why now? Why did this have to happen now? Just an hour ago, I was basking in the glory of the sale of my paintings, and now I was standing in front of the mirror with a gash above my eye that may or may not require stitches.

I went to the cupboard and pulled out the bottle of Motrin. I took two caplets and headed over to the record company to give my notice. Peyton was right; if Sal wanted to contract me, then painting would become my full-time job. I just hope I would make enough money to live on.

Chapter 16

I was walking down the street as I felt the wetness through the bandage. Shit, I knew I was going to need stitches. I reached in my bag for my cell phone and dialed Peyton.

"Peyton, I fell and cut my head. It won't stop bleeding, so I'm heading over to the hospital to have it looked at."

"Elle, are you ok? I'll meet you there, don't worry."

Before I could tell her not to go, she hung up. I was nowhere near the hospital, so I tried to catch a cab. Of course, when I desperately needed one, they wouldn't stop. As I was standing on the curb with my hand on my head, a limo driving by pulled up and rolled down the passenger side window. "Miss Lane, are you ok?" Denny asked with concern. I couldn't believe he was here at this moment.

"Denny, thank god, can you drive me to the hospital? I had a little accident, and I need to get it checked out."

"Of course; get in the front seat, and let me take a look."

I opened the door and climbed in the front seat. Denny removed my hand, and his eyes widened. He opened the glove box and took out a small white towel and folded it. "Here, keep this over that cut and apply pressure," he said as he pulled into traffic and drove me to the hospital.

We arrived at the hospital, and he helped me out of the car. I thanked him as I saw Peyton waiting in the lobby for me. He walked me into the ER as I introduced him to her.

"Thank you for all your help, Denny."

He smiled. "Not a problem, Miss Lane. Take care of that and feel better." I gently hugged him as he left through the automatic doors.

A nurse named Carla sat me in a wheel chair and pushed me through the corridor to a room. She helped me out of the chair and onto the bed where she made me lay down to prevent any more injuries. Peyton sat down in the chair next to my bed and cursed at me for not coming to the hospital sooner. I hated hospitals; I saw and been in enough of them to last me a lifetime.

Carla was a larger woman, and by the looks of her, she wasn't one who played around. She was funny. She had me and Peyton laughing our asses off with the way she talked about the nursing staff and some of the doctors.

Not too long after she took my vitals, Dr. Beckett came in. Peyton was in the middle of a sentence, and when she saw him, she fell silent. He was a hot young resident with short black hair, baby blue eyes, and suntanned skin.

"Hi, I'm Dr. Beckett." He smiled as he held out his hand.

Peyton jumped up and held out her hand. "Hi, I'm Peyton Bennett." She flirtatiously smiled.

I rolled my eyes, which hurt because of the cut. "So, Ellery, tell me how this happened," he spoke as he examined the wound.

"I'm not sure; I took a bath and got dressed. I started to feel a little dizzy as I was walking down the hallway, and I think I passed out. I must have hit my head on the corner of the wall or molding."

"Is it normal for you to get dizzy suddenly?"

I looked straight into his baby blues and said, "No."

"Ok, well I'm going to get my suture kit, put in a few stitches, and get you out of here." I smiled and nodded my head as Peyton drooled over him.

"OMG, he's gorgeous! I'm obviously getting his number. Did you see a ring on his finger? Elle, did you?"

Just as I was about to answer, the curtain opened, and there stood Connor looking as sexy as when I left him this morning. Peyton's eyes widened. "Oh god, another one; I think I've died and gone to heaven." I frowned at her and lightly smacked her on the arm. Connor stood there, holding the curtain in his hand.

"Elle, my god what happened?" He walked over to me and put his hand on my head. "Are you ok?" I looked at his face; he genuinely seemed worried. It's a look that I haven't seen before.

"Connor," I put my hand on his arm, "I'm fine."

"So, you're Connor Black?" Peyton tilted her head and asked.

"I'm sorry, Connor, this is Peyton; Peyton, this is Connor."

"Nice to finally meet you, Peyton; I've heard a lot about you."

Peyton smiled. "I've heard a lot about you too."

Twenty shades of red covered my face as he responded, "Is that so?"

Just before Peyton could embarrass me any further, Dr. Beckett walked in with a small silver tray. "Let's get that nasty cut sewn up; I promise to stitch it well so the scar will barely be noticeable, if at all."

Connor took my hand and started lightly rubbing it with his thumb. Dr. Beckett worked his magic and put four perfect stitches above my eye. The only feeling I felt was the warmth from

Connor's touch and the rapid beating of my heart as he softly stroked my hand.

"Ok, all fixed, Miss Lane. Do you live with someone?"

"No, I live alone. Why?"

He cleared his throat. "You'll have to get someone to stay with you tonight. You'll need to be monitored for a concussion. Sometimes, with head injuries, even minor cuts, a concussion can settle in after the brain and the trauma settle down. I'm going to write you a prescription for some pain medication; take it only if you need to." He glanced over at Peyton and smiled as he spoke to me, "Take care, Miss Lane, and call if you have any questions." I thought Peyton was going to die as he walked out of the room.

"I'm staying with you tonight," Peyton said as she got up.

Connor looked over at her. "Ellery will be staying with me tonight, Peyton."

She started to pout. "Elle, is that true? We can have a girl's night?" I looked over at Connor then back at Peyton and couldn't believe these two were fighting over who I was staying with.

I took Peyton's hand. "Listen, you're my best friend, and I love you, but I think it's best if I stay at Connor's tonight anyway; we're leaving in the morning for Michigan."

Her mouth dropped. "What? The two of you are going to Michigan together? Why?"

"Connor and I are taking a road trip." I looked at him and winked.

"Fine, but as soon as you get back, we're having a girl's

night."

I smiled and hugged her. "We will. Now, go find Dr. Beckett; I didn't see a ring on his finger, and I could tell he liked you."

A gigantic smile grew across her face. "Do you think?"

"I know so, now go."

Peyton started to walk out of the room, but she turned around and looked at Connor. "You better take care of her and make sure she's alright. She's like a sister to me." He smiled at her.

I looked at Connor who was helping me from the bed. "Why would you pass out like that? Is there something wrong?" he asked.

I grabbed my purse. "I just took too hot of a bath."

"You need to be more careful." He lightly took a hold of my arm as we walked down the corridor. My eyes widened as I saw Dr. Taub walking in the opposite direction towards us. My heart started racing as I didn't want to talk to him, especially in front of Connor.

"Miss Lane?" he said as he looked at the bandage above my eye.

"Dr. Taub, it's lovely to see you again." I faked a grin.

"Miss Lane, what happened to you?"

"Oh, I fell and hit my head; I tripped in the hallway."

He looked at me curiously. "How have you been feeling?"

"I've been feeling great, Dr. Taub. Now, if you will excuse me, I have to get this prescription filled."

"Yes of course," he said as he looked directly at Connor.

"Have a good day, Dr. Taub." I smiled as I couldn't get away from him fast enough.

"How do you know him, Ellery?"

I knew that brief encounter would trigger questions. I looked straight ahead at the sliding doors.

"He's my family doctor; I've seen him a couple of times since I've moved here."

"A couple of times and he knows you like that? Why would he ask you how you're feeling?"

Shit, why does he have to ask so many questions? He doesn't explain anything to me when I ask him questions.

"I saw him a couple of months ago for a bad cold I had. He's a good doctor and truly concerned for all of his patients." We walked out the door as the cold air hit me and cooled my burning body.

We slid into the back of the limo as Denny turned and looked at me. "I'm glad to see you're doing better, Miss Lane."

I gave him a heartfelt smile. "Thank you, Denny, I appreciate it."

Connor looked over at me and smiled. "Denny almost got fired today."

I looked at him; shocked expression on my face. "What! Why?"

"He didn't pick me up for my meeting. It wasn't until he called and told me that he drove you to the hospital because you cut your head."

I looked at him with a confused look. "Didn't you drive yourself to work this morning?"

"Yes—yes I did," he answered.

I ran my tongue across my lips to moisten them, "Then why didn't you just drive yourself to the meeting, especially if he was running late?" I heard Denny lightly laugh from the front seat, and I think Connor did too by the irritated look on his face.

"I suppose I could have but…"

I tilted my head. "There's no but. You were going to fire him for not picking you up when you had a vehicle the whole time? I'm sorry he couldn't call you, but he was concerned about me, Connor Black, and for that you should be grateful. I could have bled to death on the streets of New York." I was silently grinning.

He looked at me and rolled his eyes. "Now you're being a drama queen."

I let out my silent smile. "I know, and I'm good at it too."

Connor laughed as he took my hand and gently squeezed it. I laid my head his shoulder as my body warmed from his touch, and my heart started beating faster.

Chapter 17

I walked into my cold apartment and headed straight to my room to pack my bags. "Help yourself in the kitchen; there's not much, but if you can find something, it's yours!" I yelled. I grabbed what clothes I needed from my closet and drawers and folded them neatly into my suitcase. I looked up and saw Connor standing in the doorway with his arm up on the frame of the door.

"Why did you lie to that doctor and told him you tripped over something in the hallway?"

Oh shit, he wasn't going to let this go. I looked down and continued packing. "I don't know. I wasn't going to tell him I fainted. He would make a big deal about it and want me to get a bunch of tests done. That's what doctors do."

"You said you took too hot of a bath."

I stopped and looked at him, now seriously irritated. "I did, Connor, now let it go for fuck's sake. You talk about me asking a billion questions, but it's different when it's you, right?" my voice grew louder.

He walked over to me and put his hands on my shoulders. "I'm sorry. I didn't mean to upset you."

My first mistake was looking into his beautiful green eyes, because before I knew it, I cupped his face in my hands as I so desperately wanted to kiss him, taste him, and feel him. I was vulnerable at that moment, and for one second, I didn't care; all I knew was I needed him in ways every woman needs a man. Then reality hit me. "I'm sorry that I raised my voice; I'm just tired."

I let go of his face and turned to zip up my suitcase. He

grabbed my arm, turned me to face him, and wrapped his arms around me, pulling me into a warm embrace. This was the first real hug we ever shared. His arms were strong, and he made me feel safe. I closed my eyes as I took in his scent that made me weak but excited. He didn't say a word, and it felt like we stayed in each other's arms for eternity. He broke the embrace and turned away like he did something wrong. "We should get going."

Suddenly, it hit me; I never made it to my work to give my notice. I shook my head and sighed.

"What's wrong?" Connor asked.

"I was on my way to the recording studio to give my notice, and I just realized I never made it there."

"Give your notice? Why are you quitting?" Connor grabbed my suitcase, and we walked out into the living room. My face lit up as I was about to tell him the good news.

"I completely forgot to tell you; my paintings sold, all three of them," I excitedly said. "Now the owner wants to contract me and my paintings, and that's a full-time job."

He smiled at me. "That's brilliant news, Ellery, congratulations."

As I grabbed the last of my things, my phone rang; it was my cousin Debbie. I asked Connor to go in my desk drawer and grab a piece of paper and pen so that I could write down the name and address of the funeral home. I took down the information and hung up. I turned around as Connor was staring at my list that I keep in the drawer.

"What's this?" he casually asked.

I walked over and took it from him. "Just a list of things I would like to do in my lifetime. I wrote it after Kyle moved out, kind of a new start on life list."

He looked at me only the way Connor could and said, "Ok, ready to go?"

I locked up the apartment and headed to the limo. I called my boss at the record company and explained to him what happened and how I was on my way to give my notice. I explained to him how much I liked working there but my painting was now going to become a full-time job. He congratulated me and told me if I ever needed a job he would take me back.

***

We arrived back at Connor's penthouse, and he took my suitcase upstairs. I followed him and fell back onto the large comfy bed.

He looked down at me. "Do you like this bed?"

I smiled. "Yes, it's the most comfortable bed that I've ever slept in."

He held out his hand to help me up. "Are you up for some Chinese food?"

I smiled as my stomach growled. "That sounds delicious."

We walked down to the kitchen where Connor opened the drawer, pulled out a menu, and sat on the bar stool next to me. "What do you like?"

I leaned closer as his scent filled me with excitement. I wanted to respond, I like you, but that wouldn't be a cool move. "I like just about anything; surprise me."

He looked at me. "Sweet and sour pork, chicken fried rice, Mongolian beef, and egg rolls?"

"That's a lot of food, Mr. Black. Is anyone joining us?"

"No, I'm going to make sure you eat."

I rolled my eyes and then held my hand over my cut. "Ouch."

He smiled as he looked at me. "Stop rolling your eyes at me, and it won't hurt."

"Then stop making me roll my eyes at you, and I will."

He chuckled and grabbed his phone to call in the order. He poured us some wine and led me to the living room where we sat on the couch. The fireplace was on and had warmed the room nicely. I sat with my leg under the other and faced him.

"I want to know more about you, Connor Black."

He looked surprised as he responded, "What's to tell?"

I took in a deep breath. "We're friends, right?"

He nodded his head. "Of course we are."

"Friends know things about each other. It doesn't have to be intimate or deeply personal things, but I want to know about where you come from and about your family or even your business. Of all the time we've spent together hanging out, you've never told me anything about your family, other than I know you have a sister who's an interior designer. You know a lot about me, and I know nothing about you. I feel like this friendship is one-sided, Connor."

He stared at me as he drank his wine, being cautious as to what he was going to say to me. He ran one hand through his hair.

"You're right, and I'm sorry; I just don't like to talk about my life with anyone. It's not that it's a bad life; I'm just a very personal person, and I like it that way." I looked down disappointed as he leaned over and cupped my chin in his hand. He lifted it so that I was looking into his eyes. "Give me some time; this friendship thing is new to me. You need to understand that I've never been just friends with a woman before."

The thought of the tall, beautiful woman entered my mind as he said that, and with me and my big mouth I said, "But you said you and that woman you're always with are just friends, so you have other women that are friends, right?"

He looked at me intently. "It's different with Ashlyn, and I'd rather not discuss it now."

The doorbell rang, and he got up to answer it. I sat there, wondering what the hell I was doing. Was I playing a game? Was I his game? Was he using me to prove something? He came back with the cartons of Chinese food, plates, and silverware.

"Can I have the chopsticks please?" I asked. He looked in the bag, pulled out a pair, and handed them to me.

"What are you doing?" I asked him as he started to put food on our plates.

"Um… serving dinner?" He looked at me with a—are you stupid—look. I shook my finger from side to side.

"Let me," I said as I grabbed the cartons. "Grab your chopsticks," I told him.

"I don't know how to use chopsticks; I could never get those things right."

"I will teach you then."

"Ellery, let's just eat."

"We're going to eat, but my way." I smiled.

He sighed and took his set of chopsticks out of the bag. I took the sweet and sour pork container, inserted my chopsticks, and grabbed a piece of pork. "See, it's easy." If looks could kill, I'd be just about dead now.

I took his chopsticks and placed them properly between his fingers. The feel of his soft skin sent shivers down my spine. I guided his chopsticks inside the carton and helped him pull out a piece of pork. He looked at me and smirked.

"See, it's not hard with the proper training."

I took a piece of beef and held it to his mouth as he took it and smiled. He was enjoying this new found way of eating Chinese food even though he would never admit it. He still had some trouble, but managed to get a piece of pork and brought it to my mouth. He laughed when I grabbed the chopsticks between my teeth and refused to let go. This moment we were sharing felt so right and comfortable, and it scared the hell out of me.

When we finished eating, he took his thumb and gently stroked the area above my cut. "Does it hurt?" he asked sympathetically.

"Not anymore," I answered as I looked down. His touching me like that was killing me. It stirred up heat in me that I never knew existed. Kyle never made me feel the way Connor does, and I was bothered by that. I shouldn't have these feelings for him; we're friends, and that is all we can ever be. I believe we met for a reason, but I have yet to find out why.

"What are you thinking?" he softly asked. I took his hand and removed it from my head, holding it up to my face as I gently kissed it. I could feel him tighten as his breathing grew heavier, but I didn't and wouldn't let go.

"I was just thinking about how lucky I am to have a friend like you." I smiled.

He smiled and pulled his hand away. "We need to leave early in the morning; we should get some rest."

I got up and started walking upstairs. "Do you want a pain pill?!" he yelled from the kitchen.

"No, I'm fine," I responded. I slipped into my nightshirt and got under the absurdly warm covers.

I was looking through my phone when Connor knocked on the door. "Come in." He walked into the room, wearing dark gray silk pajama bottoms that hung off his hips. His muscular frame stared at me as my butterflies awoke, and the fire ignited in my blood. He sat down in the chair and reclined it back. "What are you doing?" I asked.

"Getting some rest."

"Here?"

"Yes, do you have a problem with that?" The only problem I had was trying to keep my hands off him and having my way with him.

"As a matter of fact, I do mind, Mr. Black."

He sat up and looked at me. "Why? The doctor said you need to be watched for a concussion. How am I supposed to do that if I'm in the room down the hall?"

"I'm fine, and besides you can't sleep all night in that chair.

You'll be hurting in the morning, and we have a 10 hour drive to Michigan."

"I'm following the doctors' orders, Miss Lane, so deal with it. You're not getting your way with this one."

"Now, you're making me feel bad." I took in a sharp breath and wanted to crucify myself for what I was about to say. "At least come sleep in the bed."

His eyes widened. "I don't think that is a good idea, Ellery."

"Why not? We're friends. Peyton and I sleep in the same bed when we have sleepovers, and my bed is tiny compared to this one. You have your own side way over there," I pointed. "If you don't, then I'm leaving, and you know I will."

"You're not going anywhere, and I'm not sleeping in that bed."

I threw the covers back, got out of bed, and started to put on my yoga pants. Connor jumped up from the chair and grabbed my arm. "Stop it Ellery, you need your rest." His voice was angry, and his face was irritated.

He took in a long sharp breath. "Fine, I'll sleep in the bed, just please get back in it and leave those pants on." I smiled at him and climbed back into bed. He walked to the other side, climbed in, and turned the other way. "You are the most stubborn and defiant person that I've ever known, Ellery Lane."

I smiled as I closed my eyes. "So I've been told, Mr. Black, Good night."

Even though I couldn't see him, I could feel him smile. "Good night, Ellery."

Chapter 18

I awoke the next morning, and I was alone. I got up and headed to the bathroom when I heard yelling coming from downstairs. I stepped a little closer to the top of the step when I heard Connor's raised voice. "That's too bad Ashlyn; I have to go out-of-town for a few days on business. No, you can't; I don't have time. Don't you dare come over here; I'm leaving. I'll call you as soon as I get back. I know it's been a while, but I can't help that; I've been busy. No, she has nothing to do with it. I've been working. Ashlyn, I promise we'll get together as soon as I get back. I'm going to send an envelope over with Denny; I'll talk to you soon."

My stomach felt sick, and my heart ached after I heard that conversation. I leaned my head against the wall and felt the sting of tears fill my eyes. My inner voice started to yell, "Stop it Elle—just stop it; he's your friend. You knew from the beginning it could never be more than friendship. You knew what you were getting into, and I warned you." I looked up at the ceiling to stop the tears from falling.

I heard footsteps coming up the stairs, so I ran into the bathroom and started the shower. There was a knock at the door.

"Elle, make sure the water isn't too hot," Connor said.

"No worries; it's not."

I stood in the shower and let the warm water fall on me. I was going to have to put an end or distance to this friendship when I got back from Michigan. I silently cried as I buried my face in the water, drowning my sorrows. I turned the shower off and stepped out; I wrapped a towel around me and noticed I didn't bring any clothes except my nightshirt that was lying wet on the floor. I opened the door and jumped when I saw Connor leaning against the wall across from where I was standing.

"Shit, Connor; you scared me." Not to mention the fact that I was half-naked, standing in front of him, and the towel was barely covering my ass.

He looked at me with a hunger in his eyes as he blushed. "I'm sorry; I just wanted to make sure you didn't take too hot of a shower. I didn't want you getting dizzy and pass out again. You do have a habit of not listening to anybody."

I rolled my eyes and headed to the bedroom. "Ouch."

"See, I told you not to roll your eyes at me, and you didn't listen!"

I smiled as I shut the door and got dressed. When I came out, he was downstairs in the kitchen. He set a cup of coffee on the counter and a plate with scrambled eggs, bacon, toast, and potatoes. "Did you make all this?"

"I sure did, but you sound surprised."

I took a bite of the eggs. "To be honest, I am. I didn't think you knew how to cook."

He sat down next to me at the island and started eating. "How hard is it to cook eggs? Plus, I can cook a little." He smiled.

I wanted to bring up the conversation that I heard earlier, but we were heading out in a little while, and I didn't want to upset him.

"So, did I harm you in any way last night?" I asked.

He looked at me and frowned. "No, in fact, you put your arms around me, started rubbing my chest, and calling me Peyton. I was quite turned on."

My mouth dropped until he smiled and then I knew he was joking. I went to smack him as he laughed and grabbed my wrists, holding them, rubbing my scars, and looking straight into my eyes. The atmosphere was no longer playful as it turned serious.

"My scars really bug you, don't they?"

He let go of my hands and stood up, taking his plate to the dishwasher. "They sadden me, that's all."

"Why, Connor? I didn't even know you when this happened. Why would my scars sadden you so much?"

He kept his back turned to me. "It saddens me that someone could think so little of their life to want to do such a thing."

That comment hurt me deep down to my core, and I wanted to break down and cry. He stood, staring out the window with his hands on the counter.

"I told you why I did it, and it wasn't because I thought so little of my life. I did it to lessen the pain for my father, and how dare you, Connor Black."

It was too late; the tears started falling, so I left the kitchen. He came after me and grabbed me, pulling me into him as he held me.

"I'm sorry, I didn't mean it; I swear I didn't. I just get sad when I see them because it reminds me of what you went through." His voice was sincere, and I could tell he regretted saying what he did.

I looked up at him. "It's ok; let's just forget about it and head out."

He gently wiped away my tears and put his forehead on mine. "I'm an insensitive bastard." He sounded wounded and broken. Those words were from pain, and I wanted to know what happened in his life to make him this way.

I put my hand on his firm chest. "You're in luck as I'm quite fond of insensitive bastards."

He smiled and kissed me on the head. "Let's go."

We took the elevator to the garage and set out on our road trip to Michigan.

The Range Rover was comfortable, and I had an easy time settling into my seat with my iPod in hand. I looked over at Connor; his seat was slightly leaning back. He had one hand on the steering wheel, and his other arm was resting on the console in the middle. The way he drove was sexy, and I couldn't help staring at him. Everything this man did was sexy, even when he tried to control me.

He looked over at me. "Why are you staring at me?"

"I was just wondering about Connor Black, that's all."

He sighed and looked back at the road. I looked out the window and put my headphones on. I pressed play and started singing as we merged onto the U.S. Route 1-9. Connor tapped me on the arm. I took out my headphones and looked at him.

"Are you going to ignore me the whole way there?" he asked.

"Are you going to tell me a little bit about Connor Black?" I smiled in a cocky way.

He sighed and shook his head. I could tell I was pissing him off, so I put my headphones back on. He yanked the headphone out of my ear. "Hey, what the hell, Connor?"

He laughed. "Take those things out you stubborn girl, and I'll talk."

I knew I'd win; I always do, but if it got to be too much for him, I would tell him to stop.

"My sister's name is Cassidy, and I had a twin brother, Collin."

I gasped as my eyes widened. "How the hell could you not tell me you were a twin?"

He sighed and took a hold of my hand. "Are you going to ask a million questions, or are you going to let me finish?"

I twisted my face, contemplating what to say. "Ok, I promise not to ask any questions at all; go ahead."

"Are you sure?" he seriously asked.

I nodded my head and made the zip-my-lip motion across my mouth. He smiled and continued. "Collin died when he was seven years old from a virus that attacked his heart." I swallowed hard. I wanted to throw my arms around him and comfort him because I knew how hard this was for him to tell me.

"My mom and dad had a hard time with his death, and their way of dealing with it was to get pregnant with my sister. When Cassidy was 18, she got pregnant from some guy who tossed her to the side when he found out. You asked me why my company is involved with the autism charity; it's because my sister's five-year-old son. My nephew is autistic."

I put my hand on his leg. "I'm sorry, Connor, you don't have to say anymore."

My sympathy ran deep for him, and my stomach was in knots for behaving the way I did and forcing him to tell me about his family.

He put his hand on top of mine and glanced at me. "It's ok; I want to tell you."

"My father built Black Enterprises from the ground up and started grooming me when I was around 13. I worked hard, learned fast, went to Harvard, and two years ago, he retired. He handed over his company to me, and in those two years, I doubled the company's profits. So, now you know about my family."

"What about past relationships?"

I knew that was crossing the line with him, but I was hoping he would feel comfortable enough to tell me since he was telling me about his family.

He pressed his lips together and took in a deep breath. "I don't talk about my past relationships; there's no point, and why revisit it revisit the past? I don't have a girlfriend, nor do I want one."

His comment hurt deep down; just hearing him say he didn't want a girlfriend was heartbreaking. It's for the best though, because I could never be his girlfriend, and he could never be my boyfriend. I figure if I keep telling myself that, I'd actually convince myself.

"Why don't you? Even if you've been hurt before, you just have to pick yourself up and move on. Everyone's been hurt at least once in their life, some more than others, but you have to make a choice what to do with that pain." I sounded way too casual

about that, and who was I to tal

"It's not that simple, Ellery

"So, you don't ever want t do the whole perfect family thin

He looked at me with such never want any of that, and to qu

I could just kick myself for s I didn't mean to live a life of lonel

"You really need to stop qu took it the wrong way."

"Regardless of which way I t don't do relationships, and I mean t

I looked out the window. "I kno

I was starting to regret asking l think it was better if I didn't know, hurting so much.

Chapter 19

We'd been driving about four hours as Connor pulled off the expressway and stopped for gas. "I'm going to fill her up and then we'll stop for something to eat," he said as he got out of the car. I got out and walked around, stretching out my back and legs. I walked over to the gas pump where Connor was pumping gas and kissed him on the cheek.

"What was that for?" he asked.

"It's just a thank you for telling me about your family." He gave me that heart melting smile of his.

"I'm going in the shop to get a couple of things."

I entered the store and headed right to the candy isle. I scanned the rows, trying to decide what I wanted when Connor came up behind me. "You're going to fill your body with this junk?" he asked.

I turned quickly to face him, and a wave of dizziness fell over me as I stumbled into him, and he caught me. "Ellery, are you alright?"

I held my head. "I'm fine; I just got a little light-headed." He held me until it passed.

"I knew we should have waited an extra day to leave. You're not ready to travel yet. You need more time to recover from your fall."

I was feeling better and could have lifted my head up from his chest, but I liked where it was. "Connor, stop being so protective. I'm fine; it's probably the pain meds I took," I lied; I never took any, but I didn't want him worrying about me.

"Well, I'm finding us a hotel, and we're stopping for the rest of the day. We'll continue first thing tomorrow. We'll be in Michigan in plenty of time for the funeral."

"Ok, but let's get something to eat and drive for a couple of more hours before stopping for the night. Go grab one of those little baskets over there," I said to Connor as I pointed by the door.

"You aren't seriously buying that much, are you?"

"Ok, Mr. Black, if you must know the truth, it's my PMS time."

He took a step back and put his hands up. "Whoa, enough said."

I grinned as I picked up a bag of Fritos, Cheetos, a Hershey bar (king size), a Twix bar, a small pack of chocolate donuts, three cans of coke, a bag of tiny twist pretzels, and a jar of Nutella. Connor looked in the basket and then at me with a horrified look on his face.

"Hey, you're the one who wanted to take me on this road trip. I'm just trying to keep the peace because without these foods for a woman at that time of the month," I waved my hand, "Well, you don't really want to know."

I put the basket on the counter. The cashier overheard our conversation; she looked at Connor and said, "Trust her; we girls are two sheets short of psycho when it comes to our special little time."

He just stood there and looked at both of us, speechless, as she rang up the food. She gave me the total, and I looked at Connor.

He looked at me in confusion. "Really? You want me to pay for this crap?"

The cashier leaned over the counter and looked at him straight in the eyes. "Remember, two sheets short of psycho."

He pulled out his wallet and paid as he was mumbling under his breath. He took the bag and headed out. I looked at the cashier and high-fived her. "Thank you."

"We girls need to stick together," she said. I walked out of the store, smiling as he sat in the car waiting for me.

We headed back to the interstate as he looked at me.

"What?" I smiled.

"You're crazy; I just wanted you to know that."

I laughed. "Aw sweetie, I know, but I promise it's only for a few days."

He shook his head, and I saw how hard he was trying to fight a smile. We saw some signs on the interstate for some restaurants. I was going to be polite and let him pick where he wanted to eat. He got off at the next exit, and we entered restaurant heaven.

"Take your pick, Mr. Black, the call's yours," I said as I moved my hand around.

"You really don't care where we eat?"

I looked at him and tilted my head. "No, pick wherever you want. I like just about anything."

"Ok then," he smiled. "There's a seafood restaurant over there."

I pressed my lips together and didn't say anything. I didn't like seafood, but I said it was his pick, and if that's what he wanted, then that's what we'll have. They should have something non-seafood. We got out of the car as he held his arm out for me. I hooked my arm around his as we walked into the restaurant.

"Wow," I said as I looked around at the sharks and swordfish mounted to the walls. A cute little blonde girl walked over to us and said there was about a 30 minute wait; this was my chance to get the hell out of here. I didn't like staring at those things on the wall; they're creepy.

"30 minutes is a long time to wait, Connor; maybe we should go somewhere else."

He looked at me with a smile. "30 minutes is nothing, and time will fly by. Go look at those lobsters over there."

I flinched because I hated to see them in those glass tanks, moving around not knowing they were next to be thrown into a pot of boiling water. He grabbed my hand and led me to the bar. "We'll sit here and have a drink until they call us."

I sat on the stool as the bartender, a very attractive woman with long, brown curly hair and large perky boobs, walked over to us but only made eye contact with Connor. She leaned over the bar, not taking notice that I'm sitting right next to him, and with her low-cut top and cleavage hanging out she says, "What will it be, handsome?"

He gave her a flirtatious smile and leaned in closer. "I'll have a sex with the bartender." I gasped, and with a horrified look on my face, I looked at him.

"One sex with a bartender coming right up, stud." She winked.

He looked over at me as I clenched my jaw and took in a deep breath. I couldn't believe he just did that right in front of me. I bit the inside of my cheek and contemplated.

"Um, sweetheart, when you get his drink, don't forget to bring those luscious boobies over here." I smiled. The look on Connor's face was priceless after that statement.

"Ellery, what the hell are you doing?" he whispered.

"What? Am I embarrassing you Mr. 'I'll have sex with a bartender'?"

She came over and handed him his drink, looked at me, and in an irritated way, asked me what I wanted. I looked at her and pouted. "Don't you think it's only fair that you give me the same kind of service that you're giving him? Why should he be the only one to get to see your boobies?"

Connor threw some money on the bar and stood up. "Come on, honey, I think our table is ready."

I smiled and winked at her as she gave me a dirty look and turned away. Connor leaned over to me and whispered in my ear, "Point taken, you *bad* girl."

"You love it, Mr. Black, and you know it." He smiled as the waitress showed us to our table.

I opened the menu, and guess what, no non-seafood items existed. Shit, I thought to myself. What was I going to order? Well, I do have a car full of junk food if it comes down to it.

"What are you going to order, Ellery?"

I looked up from my menu and glared at him. "I'm not sure; I'm torn at the moment."

The waitress came by and asked to take our drink orders. Connor spoke up before I could tell her that I wanted a Cosmopolitan.

"I'm set, and she'll have a coke."

I frowned. "I wanted a Cosmo, Connor."

"Not after that little stunt, and who knows what that bartender would do to that drink."

I laughed and continued looking at the menu. As soon as the waitress brought my coke, she asked us if we were ready to order. Connor closed his menu and looked at me. I glanced up at the waitress and bit my lip. Connor looked at her. "Give us a minute, please." I looked at him; I think he realized I didn't like seafood.

"You don't like seafood, do you?" I stared at him while biting my lower lip.

"Why didn't you say something?" he asked as he ran his hands through his hair.

"Well, I wanted you to have what you wanted."

He looked at me with those beautiful green eyes, and suddenly, they turned evil. He didn't say a word, but he was scaring me as he waved for the waitress to come back.

"I'm going to order for us," he said. Uh oh, now I'm in trouble.

"We will start with an order of calamari, crab legs, and a lobster tail for each of us. Also, please throw in an order of broiled scallops.

The waitress looked at me, and I managed a slight smile.

Connor crossed his hands and placed his elbows on the table.

"Remember the times when you made me eat things; the pizza, hot dog, and let's not forget the use of the chopsticks?"

I just stared at him. Two can play this game.

"Yes, I do, and I'm fine with everything you ordered."

"We'll see about that." He smirked.

I leaned over the table. "You're a vicious man, Connor Black."

He leaned in closer until we were face to face. "Not as vicious as you, darling." I sat back, smiled, and reveled in the moment when he called me darling.

The waitress came and set the calamari in the center of the table. I looked at it and then at Connor. I got out my phone and Googled calamari; my eyes widened as "squid" appeared. I looked up at Connor; he was laughing at me.

"You Googled 'calamari', didn't you?"

I nodded my head and took a sip of my coke. His laughing subsided, and he looked at me with a serious face.

"You don't have to eat it, I'm sorry."

I took in a deep breath. "No it's ok, and I'm going to try it. It's the least I can do for everything you've done for me." He smiled as I took a piece from the plate and inspected it.

"Seriously, Elle, don't; I know you don't want to."

I took a small bite and started chewing; his eyes intently watched me as I was eating the calamari and making faces. He took out his phone and started taking pictures of me. "This is classic." He laughed. The calamari wasn't as awful as I thought it would be.

"Ok, bad boy, bring on the next one."

Connor threw his head back and laughed as the waitress brought the scallops and lobster tails. I stabbed a scallop with my fork and held it up to my mouth as he smiled and took a picture. I ate it, and to my surprise, I enjoyed it. I held up the lobster tail and pouted at it as he took another picture. We both laughed and talked throughout dinner. I'll admit I liked it all; this new seafood experience agreed with me. We finished up and left the restaurant. Connor put his arm around me and pulled me close. I put my hand on his chest and my head on his shoulder as we walked to the Range Rover.

We drove until we found a hotel. We only passed a billion of them, but Mr. Fancy pants had to have the best, so we drove out-of-the-way to the Ritz Carlton.

Chapter 20

We pulled up as he let the valet park his Range Rover. He walked up to the desk and gave them his last name. I watched the girls behind the counter giggle and eye him. He must have seen it too because he flashed them his flirty smile. I rolled my eyes.

The bellhop took our suitcases and led us in the elevator. "Good evening, Mr. and Mrs. Black, and welcome to the Ritz Carlton."

I looked over at Connor as he began to speak, "Oh, we're not—" I cut him off.

"Thank you so much. What my husband is trying to say is that we won't be staying long." Connor gave me a perplexed look.

The elevator took us to the Presidential Suite. The door opened, and I glanced over at Connor. "The presidential suite, really, just for one night?"

"I will have nothing but the best room for my beautiful wife. Isn't my wife beautiful?" Connor asked the bellhop with a wide grin.

"Yes, sir, she's very beautiful." I glared at Connor and then smiled at the bellhop.

"Darling, husband, make sure you tip this nice young man well."

He pulled out a wad of money from his pocket and started thumbing through the bills. I walked over to him and grabbed a one hundred-dollar bill and handed it to the bellhop. "Do you have a wife or girlfriend?" I asked.

"Yes, I do, thank you, ma'am, and thank you for your generosity."

"Go buy her something beautiful, perhaps a nice necklace." Connor looked at me and clenched his jaw.

"Thank you, ma'am, sir, thank you," he said excitedly as he walked out, shutting the door behind him.

"Really, a one hundred-dollar tip?"

"Well, it's what you tipped the cab driver."

"Cab driver, what are you talking about?"

"The night I brought you home, I had to pay the driver, and I didn't have enough money, so I went in your wallet and gave him a hundred; that was before you told me you were going to fuck me really hard."

His jaw dropped. "I said that to you?"

I smiled. "Yeah, but you were drunk, so I forgave you."

He started walking towards me. "A one hundred-dollar tip, Ellery?" he kept saying as he was smiling with a playful look in his eyes.

"Connor, relax, it's only money, and you said yourself that you have plenty of it."

He was heading straight for me. I screamed and ran behind a chair; he started to chase me around the suite saying over and over, "A hundred dollars?"

He caught me as I ran into the bedroom, and he threw me on the bed. He straddled me and pinned my arms over my head. We were both out of breath as he looked down at me, staring into my eyes. I stopped fighting him and held his gaze; my heart was racing and my skin was on fire. My body ached for him, and my lips begged him to kiss me. He held my wrists and lowered his head until his lips lightly brushed against mine. He looked at me again and let go of my wrists. He softly stroked my cheek with the back of his hand and stared into my eyes as I moved my hands through his hair. He swallowed hard as I could hear the rapid beating of his heart; he felt the same way as I did. He stared at me as if he was searching my soul; then his lips touched mine as we kissed, and he fell onto me as our tongues met for the first time. This was our first kiss, and it was filled with such passion and emotion. He was gentle and not forceful. He took his time exploring my mouth in such a way that made me feel loved. He abruptly broke our kiss and pulled back, getting off me and sitting on the edge of the bed.

"I'm sorry, Elle, but I can't."

He can't? He basically rapes my mouth, and now, he sits there and says he can't? A wave of hurt and rejection overtook my body.

"Why not, Connor? Is it because I'm not one of your whores?" The words flew out of my mouth before I could stop them.

He got up and wouldn't look at me. "You're not a whore, Ellery, and I just can't."

I sat up and pleaded with him. "Please just tell me what's wrong and why you don't want me."

"I do want you, Ellery, that's the problem; I want you too fucking much."

"How is that a problem?!" I yelled.

He turned and looked at me with rage in his eyes. "You don't want to know the real me. I'm not a good person; I use women for sex. I can't have real relationships; I don't want to."

"We don't have to have a relationship; we can just be friends with benefits."

Yep, there it was, the thing I hated the most; I just yelled to the man I was falling in love with. He stood there and ran his hands through his hair. I stepped closer to him. "Connor, please; I need you." A single tear fell from my eye.

"Don't, Elle, don't do this to me, to us; I can't sleep with you."

Anger and rage grew inside me. He wouldn't give me a straight answer or explanation, so I did what I do best.

"Fuck you, Connor Black!" I turned and walked out of the room, grabbed my purse, and headed towards the door. Connor followed after me.

"Don't you dare walk out that door, Ellery!" he yelled.

I put my hand on the knob and held it there for a second as I took in a deep breath. I started to open the door when Connor came up from behind me and slammed it shut. He turned me around and pushed me against the door.

"I fuck women for the pleasure, that's it. There's no emotion for me when I fuck them; there never has been!" More tears fell from my cheeks.

"I seduce them, use them, fuck them, and leave them. Is that what you want? Is that how you want me to treat you?!" he screamed at me. "You're different, Ellery, and you scare me. You make me feel things that I've never felt before. You're all I think about, both day and night. I feel empty inside when you're not around. Don't you understand? It isn't supposed to be this way, and if I sleep with you, this will all be ruined."

"What happened to you to make you this way?" I whispered.

He looked away from me as he still had my body pinned against the door.

"I had a girlfriend when I was 18. She started to become obsessive and wanted to spend every waking minute with me. It became too much to try to keep her happy, and it let me to feel I was suffocating, so I broke up with her." He paused and looked up at me as his eyes started to fill with tears.

"She committed suicide two days later. She left a note, explaining that if she couldn't have me, then she didn't want to live and told everyone to blame me for her suicide." He took my wrists and turned them up.

"You see, this is why I feel sad when I see these on you. It's a reminder of what I did, and how I killed her." I gasped at his words as I broke his grip and cupped his face in my hands.

"You did nothing wrong, Connor. It wasn't your fault that she killed herself. It was her weakness and inability to cope; you cannot blame yourself."

"I swore then I would never fall in love or get emotionally involved with another woman, but with you, it's too late. I'm already emotionally attached, and I'm doing everything I can to stop myself, but I can't." He turned away; his breathing was rapid.

I went to him and wrapped my arms around his waist. "I'm emotionally attached, and everything inside me said to stay away, but I see a side of you I don't think you let other people see; a sweet, tender, and caring man who would give his world for someone he cares about."

He turned around and looked at me. Before I knew it, his lips were on mine, kissing me passionately and warmly. Our tongues danced with each other as he picked me up and carried me to the bedroom. My heart was racing with his, and my body was aching for his touch. He sat me gently on the bed as he lifted up my shirt and gently took it off. He tore the shirt off his back and unbuttoned his pants, never taking his eyes off me. I stood up, took off my jeans, and threw them on the floor. I laid myself down on the bed in just my bra and panties as he examined my half-naked body.

"You are so fucking beautiful," he whispered as he ran his hand up and down my stomach. He climbed on top of me as I wrapped my arms around his neck. His lips met mine for a brief second until his tongue started to explore my neck. I moaned and tilted my head back to give him full access. I arched my back as he took down my bra straps and exposed my breasts. He groaned as he lightly sucked each nipple and ran his tongue in circles down my stomach. I pressed my hips against him and felt his erection, which made me ache for him even more.

I took my hand and pushed it down the front of his pants as he moaned. He lightly traced the edge of my panties as his fingers made their way to the spot that needed him the most. He circled his fingers around before gently inserting them inside me. "You're so wet, Ellery; god, I want you," he moaned as he brought his lips to mine. He moved his fingers inside me and then in a delicate in and out motion.

"I promise I'll be gentle with you. If I get too rough, please promise me that you'll stop me."

I nodded my head as I helped him take off his jeans and boxers. He took himself and gently inserted himself in me, looking into my eyes with each small thrust, slow and steady. Once he

about that, and who was I to talk anyway.

"It's not that simple, Ellery; trust me."

"So, you don't ever want to get married or have children and do the whole perfect family thing?"

He looked at me with such seriousness it startled me, "No, I never want any of that, and to quote you, nothing lasts forever."

I could just kick myself for saying that to him. It was true, but I didn't mean to live a life of loneliness and misery.

"You really need to stop quoting that, Connor. I think you took it the wrong way."

"Regardless of which way I took it, I already told you that I don't do relationships, and I mean that."

I looked out the window. "I know."

I was starting to regret asking him to tell me about himself. I think it was better if I didn't know, and maybe then, I wouldn't be hurting so much.

I put my hand on his leg. "I'm sorry, Connor, you don't have to say anymore."

My sympathy ran deep for him, and my stomach was in knots for behaving the way I did and forcing him to tell me about his family.

He put his hand on top of mine and glanced at me. "It's ok; I want to tell you."

"My father built Black Enterprises from the ground up and started grooming me when I was around 13. I worked hard, learned fast, went to Harvard, and two years ago, he retired. He handed over his company to me, and in those two years, I doubled the company's profits. So, now you know about my family."

"What about past relationships?"

I knew that was crossing the line with him, but I was hoping he would feel comfortable enough to tell me since he was telling me about his family.

He pressed his lips together and took in a deep breath. "I don't talk about my past relationships; there's no point, and why revisit it revisit the past? I don't have a girlfriend, nor do I want one."

His comment hurt deep down; just hearing him say he didn't want a girlfriend was heartbreaking. It's for the best though, because I could never be his girlfriend, and he could never be my boyfriend. I figure if I keep telling myself that, I'd actually convince myself.

"Why don't you? Even if you've been hurt before, you just have to pick yourself up and move on. Everyone's been hurt at least once in their life, some more than others, but you have to make a choice what to do with that pain." I sounded way too casual

122

He sighed and shook his head. I could tell I was pissing him off, so I put my headphones back on. He yanked the headphone out of my ear. "Hey, what the hell, Connor?"

He laughed. "Take those things out you stubborn girl, and I'll talk."

I knew I'd win; I always do, but if it got to be too much for him, I would tell him to stop.

"My sister's name is Cassidy, and I had a twin brother, Collin."

I gasped as my eyes widened. "How the hell could you not tell me you were a twin?"

He sighed and took a hold of my hand. "Are you going to ask a million questions, or are you going to let me finish?"

I twisted my face, contemplating what to say. "Ok, I promise not to ask any questions at all; go ahead."

"Are you sure?" he seriously asked.

I nodded my head and made the zip-my-lip motion across my mouth. He smiled and continued. "Collin died when he was seven years old from a virus that attacked his heart." I swallowed hard. I wanted to throw my arms around him and comfort him because I knew how hard this was for him to tell me.

"My mom and dad had a hard time with his death, and their way of dealing with it was to get pregnant with my sister. When Cassidy was 18, she got pregnant from some guy who tossed her to the side when he found out. You asked me why my company is involved with the autism charity; it's because my sister's five-year-old son. My nephew is autistic."

Chapter 21

I awoke the next morning, snuggled in Connor's arms. He was holding me tight as my head rested on his chest. I opened my eyes, and for the first time in my life, I felt peace and serenity. He made me feel whole and safe like I've never felt before. We made love three times last night, and it was the most beautiful experience that I've ever had; nothing like when I was with Kyle. I felt passion and love with Connor; it was like we couldn't get enough of each other.

We finally had our moment, and now, I faced a new problem. I have a secret that could destroy this man who finally gave himself to me.

"Good morning, baby," Connor said as he kissed me on the head.

I looked up at him and smiled. "Good morning; did you sleep well?"

"I slept great; how about you?" he asked.

I lightly ran my finger around his muscular chest. "Yes, I did, but someone wore me out." He smiled as I moved up closer to his face, covering my mouth with my hand. "I have morning breath."

He laughed, and before I knew it, I was lying flat on my back with him on top of me.

"I don't care; it doesn't bother me one bit."

I looked over at the clock. "Look at the time; we need to get out of here, or we'll never make it to the funeral on time."

Connor slid off me, got out of bed, and held his hand out. "It looks like we'll have to shower together to save time." I bit my bottom lip as I took his hand, and we walked to the bathroom.

I would have preferred the water a little hotter, but with what we were doing, I was getting hot enough. He pinned my arms against the shower wall and took me from behind, kissing my neck as he moved in and out of me. He let go of my arms as he cupped each breast in his hands, rubbing and feeling them as deep groans came from the back of his throat. He moved flawlessly and had me ready to come the minute he touched me.

"Are you ready, Elle?" he panted.

I moaned with each deep thrust. "Yes, come with me, Connor," I begged. The words were enough for him as his sexy moans grew louder. He pushed himself harder into me, and I felt his warmth fill my insides. He held me tight as we both sank to the shower floor and sat there in pure bliss.

Once we were able to get ourselves out of the shower, we dressed, and I sat on the bed for a moment as I was starting to feel a little weak and tired.

"What's wrong, baby?" Connor asked as he stood over me.

I smiled to mask what I was actually feeling.

"Nothing's wrong; I'm just sitting here, wishing we could spend another night in this beautiful hotel room."

He took my hand and helped me up. "Don't you worry; there will be plenty beautiful hotel rooms in our future." I smiled as he used the word future, which to me meant a relationship.

What have I done? I need to tell him something, but I can't, not now. Once we get back to New York, I'll tell him everything and watch his perfect heart break. Tears started to fill my eyes as he looked at me.

"Ellery, what's wrong? Why do you look like you're going to cry?" He wrapped his arms around me.

"I'm just so happy, that's all; you've made me so happy."

"You've made me happy too, baby; I can't even tell you how much."

He kissed me and grabbed our suitcases as we headed back on the road to Michigan. I followed behind him, trying to fight back the tears.

We were driving and deciding whose music to listen to. He liked mostly classic rock, and I was more of a pop, contemporary kind of girl, so we compromised and took turns listening to each other's music. I would eventually get him over to my side of music, but that was going to take some work.

His phone was sitting between us on the console, and it rang. I glanced over and saw Ashlyn's name appear. Suddenly, my stomach tied itself in knots; I felt sick, and I started to sweat. There was no way in fucking hell he was going to continue to talk to her or see her. He pressed ignore and kept looking straight ahead at the road. She was someone that I needed to know about, and it wasn't going to be painless, but Connor's mine now, and he's going to have to tell me the truth.

I took in a deep breath. "Who is she, Connor?" I reached over and turned off the radio.

He heavily sighed. "I knew you were going to ask me."

"Ok, then you must tell me about her if we're going to move forward."

He took my hand and held it up to his lips. "I don't want to talk about her now, Ellery. This isn't the right time or place to do that."

"Fine, I'll wait, and we'll discuss her later. But whatever you tell me will be ok because things with us are different now, and we're putting all our baggage in the past, right?"

He looked over at me and smiled, "You bet we are."

"I have a question for you," I said as I took the wrapper off my Twix bar. "Denny told me that you've been different since you met me."

He rolled his eyes. "Denny shouldn't be saying things like that, but it's true. I was intrigued by you the minute I saw you in my kitchen. When I woke up and heard someone making a lot of noise, I walked downstairs to yell at whoever it was for being so loud. Imagine my surprise when I saw this beautiful stranger, standing there making coffee."

"Yes, but you yelled at me about your rules."

He shrugged. "Well, I thought that I'd brought you home from the club; I'm sorry about that." I smacked his arm. He smiled as he looked at the road ahead.

"When you told me what you did for me and gave me quite the attitude, it was that moment I knew I couldn't let you walk out of my life. Denny knew it too because I kept talking about you without realize it." I laughed and reached over to kiss his cheek, but instead I shoved the Twix bar in his mouth.

We arrived in Michigan, and I grew nervous to be back to a place that harbored such bad memories. Connor must have sensed it by my reaction. When I saw the 'Welcome to Michigan' sign, he grabbed my hand and held it tight. My phone rang, and it was Peyton calling.

"Hi, Peyton," I answered.

"Oh my god, Elle, I just had to tell you about my fantastical date with Dr. Hottie last night."

I started to laugh. "So, did you manage to get him to ask you out?" I put her on speaker so Connor could hear.

"No, I asked him out, and we went to dinner, then to a club and back to his place. Elle, he was phenomenal. He fucks like no one ever has before." Connor looked at me and started laughing.

"Wow, Peyton, that's great." I rolled my eyes.

"Seriously, Elle, he made me do things that I never thought of doing before and shit is he big. I was worried when I saw it that it wouldn't fit inside me. Elle, I got nervous that I wasn't going to be able to experience this hot man."

Connor's mouth dropped as he was in shock by Peyton's openness. I was used to it so it didn't faze me.

"Peyton, sweetie, I have you on speaker, and Connor heard every word you just said."

"So, I have nothing to hide. Maybe you two should try it. Live a little, Connor; take that girl to bed and show her your sexiness." I wanted to die right there in the leather seat of Connor's Range Rover.

He unexpectedly shouted, "I already did, and she was amazing; she made me do things to her that even shocked me." I hit him on the arm and shot him a look.

"Woot, you go girl! We'll swap notes when you get back. I

have to go; Dr. Hottie is summoning me back to bed." She giggled.

I hung up and shook my head at him. "How could you tell her that?"

"Oh please, love, like you haven't embarrassed me before."

I couldn't argue with that, especially with the bartender at the restaurant and then the bellhop. I laughed and looked out the window at the all too familiar place I was heading to.

We pulled into the funeral home, and instantly, my stomach felt sick. I got out of the car and took a deep breath.

"This is the same funeral home where we held the services for my mother and father," I said as I stood in front of it.

Connor put his arm around me. "You don't have to do this; you can call your cousin and tell her you got sick or something."

"No, that's the coward's way out. I can't escape reality. Besides, I have you with me."

As we walked through the doors, my cousin, Debbie, saw me and swiftly walked towards me, and we hugged each other tight.

"I'm so sorry for your loss, Debbie."

She started to cry on my shoulder. "I know, and I'm sorry for you too; I know they were like your surrogate parents growing up.

"What happened?" she asked as she pointed to my stitches.

"It's no big deal; I just fell and hit my head."

I looked over at Connor. "Debbie, this is my friend Connor."

She shook his hand and then whispered to me, "I heard you

and Kyle broke up; I'm sorry."

I smiled. "I'm not, but thank you anyway."

She led us to the room where my aunt and uncle laid in their beautiful wooden caskets. I walked over and kneeled down in front of them, praying to God to keep them safe. Connor stood behind me with his hands clutching my shoulders. I stood up and made my way through the crowd, saying hi to old friends and making small conversation with distant family. I could hear the whispers of people talking about my attempted suicide seven years ago. I could hear the pity in their voices. The whispers went on about my dad; how he was an alcoholic and couldn't stop drinking enough to raise his only daughter. They went on to say that if my mother was alive, I wouldn't have tried to take my life. I had become the center of attention at someone's funeral, and I was starting to get pissed. Connor overheard the soft talks as he put his arm around me.

"Don't listen to them; they don't know what they're talking about."

I took in a deep breath, but I couldn't control myself any longer when I heard a woman say, "She's the one who tried to commit suicide to save herself from her alcoholic father. He was too wrapped up in the death of her mother to even realize she existed. She should have been taken away from him and then she wouldn't have tried to—"

Before she could finish her sentence, I rudely interrupted her, "Who the fuck do you think you are, talking about my father and family like that?!"

I pushed my wrists in her face. "Here, see the scars? That's right, take a good look at them; it wouldn't have mattered if they took me away or not, they would still be there."

The whole room was standing in silence, staring at me. Connor grabbed my hand. "Come on, baby, let's go. It's not worth it." I turned as he led me out of the funeral home. The cold air cooled my burning skin.

"I must say, you can put on quite a show." Connor smiled to lighten my mood.

"I'm sorry, I just couldn't take anymore; I knew this was going to happen if I came back here."

He held me and whispered, "It's ok, you've said your goodbyes to your aunt and uncle, you told off a few people, and now we can go; unless you want to stay?"

I shook my head. "No, let's get out of here."

Chapter 22

We hopped back into the Range Rover as Connor searched for hotels on his GPS. "If you're looking for luxury, then I suggest the Athenuem Suite Hotel."

He looked over at me and smiled. "Funny; that's what my GPS is telling me. I can reserve the Presidential Suite right here online." He did just that and then took my hand. "Where do you want to go?"

I brought his hand to my lips and gently kissed it. "I need to go visit my mom and dad's graves; it's not too far."

He punched the address in his GPS as we headed toward the cemetery. I asked if we could make a quick stop at the flower shop so that I could pick up some flowers.

We arrived at the cemetery. I directed Connor where to park to make it easier to get to their graves. We got out of the car. I took his hand and led him to where my parents were buried. The air was brisk for the end of September. I remembered warmer days this time of year. We walked to the graves of my mother and father that sat side by side.

"My father made sure to buy the plot next to where my mother was buried because that way they could be together forever. He loved my mother very much, and he considered her his soul mate; that's why when she died, a part of him died with her."

Connor knelt beside me and kissed me on the head. "That's beautiful." I put the flowers on my mother's grave first and then my fathers. Connor got up. "I'm going to give you some privacy," he said as he walked a few feet away.

I sat down on the grass and placed my hands on each of their graves. "Hi mom, hi dad, I can't believe it's been over a year since I've visited you last. A lot has changed in the past year. I moved to New York and started selling my paintings in a small art gallery. I met an incredible guy there; in fact, he's here with me now. I know you'd like him, daddy. He's sweet, charming, kind, really sexy, and I believe he would do anything for me."

I leaned in closer to their graves and whispered; I love him, mom and dad; for the first time in my life, I'm truly in love. We're leaving Michigan tomorrow, so I wanted to stop by to say hi and let you know I'm doing well." Tears swelled in my eyes. Connor walked over and put his hands on my shoulders. "I love both of you very much, and I miss you." He helped me up as I took in a deep breath and composed myself.

Connor took me in his arms and held me. "You're far too young to have experienced so much death, Ellery; it hurts me to know what you've been through."

My chest started to tighten, and panic began to settle in. I needed to tell him my secret, but I was too scared about how he was going to react. I couldn't lose him; not now, I loved him too much.

He stood with me and stared at my parent's grave. "I can't even imagine losing my parents, especially at such a young age. You amaze me with your strength, Ellery, because I don't know if I could have made it through if I was in your place."

I let go of him and bent down to pull some weeds that were surrounding the grave area. "That's something you decide whether or not you're going to do. You can move on and try to live your life as normal as possible, or you can make the decision to let go of life and let sorrow consume you. I'm a big believer of fate, and I believe God took my dad so his pain and suffering could stop, and he could be with my mother again." He stroked my hair and ran his finger along my cheek.

"You're amazing; I don't know what I did to deserve to have you in my life." I kissed his cool lips and smiled as we walked back to the Range Rover and headed for the hotel.

We arrived at the hotel and took the elevator up to the Grand Room. I was getting use to this Presidential Suite thing. Connor went to the fireplace and turned it on. I walked over to him and wrapped my arms around his waist. "You feel so good," I said as I took in his scent.

"Not as good as you feel, baby," he whispered as he buried his nose in my head.

"Dance with me," I said.

A beautiful smile graced his face. "I would love to dance with you, but let me put on some music first.

He walked over to the small stereo that sat on a table by the window. He walked back to me and wrapped his arms around my waist. We held each other and slowly moved to the soft melody coming from the radio. He stared into my eyes as he leaned in and brushed my lips with his. My hands moved up and down his back as our soft kiss turned passionate, and we gently made love by the fire. We laid there, staring into each other; our naked bodies wrapped in a blanket.

"Are you hungry?" He asked as he kissed my shoulder.

"Yes, I'm hungry for you." I smirked.

He smiled as he stroked my cheek with his soft fingers. "I'm always hungry for you, but we'll eventually have to eat real food. I hate to break it to you, baby, but we can't survive on sex alone."

He started to tickle me as I laughed and tried to grab his hands. He finally stopped when I said ouch because my eye started to hurt. He softly kissed my stitches before getting up and ordering room service.

It wasn't too long before room service was delivered as we got up and got dressed. "Are you feeling ok, Elle? You look a little pale."

"I'm fine, sweetie; I'm just tired, and I think I have you to blame for that."

He flashed me his sexy smile. "If I recall, you were the one who did all the work."

I blushed as I got up from my seat and held out my hand. "Would you care to join me for a hot bath, Mr. Black?"

"I would love to, Miss Lane, just not too hot; I don't want you passing out." I snickered as we walked to the large marbled bathroom.

The bathtub was large enough for four people. Connor started the water and got in as I removed my robe and twisted my hair up so it didn't get wet.

"Damn you're so sexy." He smiled as I walked towards the tub.

"Not as sexy as you are." I smiled as I slid into the tub and leaned my back against his firm chest. He put his arms around me, and we laid there, taking in the warmth of the water and the softness of our wet skin. He softly kissed my neck. "I love it when

152

you wear your hair up."

"Is that so?" I smiled as he continued to plant small delicate kisses down my neck.

"You have no idea how bad I wanted you that night of the charity event. I did everything I could to restrain myself and not take you in the bathroom to have my way with you."

I lightly rubbed his arm with my finger. "I wish you would have."

"No, you don't. I would have been too rough, and I might have scared you off."

"You can never scare me off."

I turned my head so that I was facing him. "Infinity is forever, and that's what you are to me. You are my forever, Mr. Black."

He kissed my lips. "There's no limit to what I wouldn't do for you. Just ask, and it will be done, no matter the sacrifice."

I traced his lips with my fingers. "Those are the most beautiful words that anyone has ever said to me."

"They're true, every last word," he whispered as our lips met one last time before we headed off to bed.

***

The next morning, Connor and I were drinking coffee in the room when a text message from Kyle came through.

"Elle, I heard you were in town. Where are you staying? I need to see you; it's important." I sighed as I read it.

"Who's it from?" Connor asked.

"Kyle says he needs to see me. He says it's important, and he wants to know where we're staying."

"Tell him then; obviously he needs to see you about something." Connor seemed calm about it, but I had a terrible feeling.

I text-messaged Kyle back and told him which hotel I was at, wondering what the hell was he doing in Michigan. Connor and I got dressed and finished packing our things to head back to New York. Before long, there was a knock at the door. I walked over and opened it.

"Hi, Kyle, come in." I glared at him.

"Hey, Elle." He walked in and froze when he saw Connor come from the bedroom. Kyle looked at me. "I didn't know he was here with you."

"Hey, Kyle." Connor waved to him.

Kyle gave a small hello and looked at me. "Ellery, I need to speak with you in private."

"If you have something to say, you can say it in front of Connor." Kyle looked sternly at me.

"I don't think you'd want him to hear this."

My stomach tied itself in knots, and I started to get extremely nervous.

"Kyle, what is it? Spit it out for fuck's sake; we are heading back to New York in a little while, and I don't have time for games."

He looked at Connor who started to walk towards the

154

bedroom. "I'll give you two some privacy."

Kyle nodded and turned to look at me. "I made a terrible mistake, Elle; I never should have left you."

I gasped because that was totally unexpected. "It's a little too late; you did what you did, and I moved on, and so did you."

"No, that's what I'm trying to tell you; I didn't move on. Hell, I dated a few girls, but none of them are you; I love you, baby. We had four fucking years together; you can't just throw that away."

Rage started to take over my body. How dare he tell me that I threw our relationship away when he's the one who packed up and left? My voice became uncontrollably loud.

"*I* can't throw that away? You're the one who fucking walked out on me, leaving me alone because you needed space, and now you come back here to our hometown and expect me to take you back?!" Connor heard me yelling and emerged from the bedroom.

"I was scared, Elle. I ran because I was scared, but I now realize what a screw up I am, and I want you. I want us back for as long as we can be."

I pointed my finger at him. "Get the hell out of here, Kyle!"

His eyes turned cold as he looked over at Connor. "Does he know, Elle? Did you tell him?"

Connor walked over and looked at me. "Tell me what?"

I stared at Kyle with pleading eyes. "Kyle, please leave; please, for both our sake."

His eyes grew wider. "You didn't tell him?"

"Kyle, stop, please," I begged.

Connor turned to Kyle. "What hasn't she told me?"

Tears filled my eyes as Kyle began to speak.

"I'm sorry, Elle."

He looked at Connor and proceeded to talk. "She has cancer, and she refuses to go and get treatments; she's just going to let herself die. That's why I left her. I couldn't sit there and watch her die."

The tears were flowing freely down my face as Connor looked at me with a horrified look on his face. "Ellery, is that true?"

Kyle turned around. "I'm sorry, Elle," he said as he shook his head and walked out the door.

"Ellery, is that true?!" Connor screamed.

I flinched and nodded my head. "Yes, it's true."

He clenched his fists and tightened his jaw. "You've known your cancer was back even before I met you, but you still hid it from me after everything we've been through? What kind of person are you?!"

I've never seen or experienced such rage and anger in a person like the one standing in front of me. His eyes turned dark as he looked at me with shame and disgust.

"Please, Connor, let me explain."

"Explain what? What's left to explain? Were you just going to tell me one day you were dying? And why the fuck aren't you getting any treatment?"

"Please, calm down, Connor," I pleaded.

"Calm down? You expect me to be calm when I just found out that the woman I love and want to spend the rest of my life with is dying? I don't want to hear anything from you. You make me sick, Ellery. I can't do this; I can't even look at you." He turned towards the bedroom. I ran after him and grabbed his arm.

"Please, Connor, don't do this; let me explain."

He jerked his arm away, and I fell back onto the floor. He turned and looked at me, his voice now calm but pained, "Your dizzy spells and your tiredness, it's all part of the cancer. You're getting worse, and you knew it, but you still didn't tell me. I bared my soul to you. I told you things nobody in this world knows. I shared myself with you. How could you do that to me, Ellery?" His eyes filled with tears as he turned to the bedroom and slammed the door.

My heart shattered, and I started to shake. I sat on the ground in shock at how quickly my life had just changed. An hour later, he threw open the door and came out with his suitcase, walking past me.

"Connor wait, please," I said as I jumped up.

He turned around and pointed at me. "Stay away from me. I booked a flight for you back to New York; it leaves in two hours, so compose yourself and be ready. I'm driving back by myself. I can't stand to look at you right now, let alone ride in a car with you for 10 hours."

I covered my mouth with my hand as he opened the door and stormed out. I fell to my knees. It felt like the wind had just been knocked out of me. I couldn't breathe, and I begged God to take me right then and there. He was gone. He left me just like everyone else in my life.

I got up from the floor and somehow managed to call the desk, telling them I needed a car to take me to the airport. I stumbled to the bathroom and looked in the mirror at the black streaks of mascara that stained my face. I took a washcloth and wiped them away. I didn't need water; my tears were enough to soak the washcloth. I put on my sunglasses to hide my red swollen eyes and headed to the lobby with my suitcase. I was unsteady and still shaking.

The car was waiting for me as the driver took my suitcase and opened the door. All I kept thinking was had I told him the truth from the start, maybe things would have been different. I was to blame for his pain, and I hated myself for that. He didn't deserve this. I knew he could forgive me, if he would let me explain why I didn't tell him.

As I sat in the airport, I dialed his number. It went straight to voicemail. My flight was called, and I boarded the plane. I couldn't think about anything but Connor and how I felt like I had just killed him. Who am I? I searched deep in my soul for that answer. The only thing that came to mind was a cold-hearted bitch that was selfish and only thought of herself.

I never should have let the relationship with Connor get that far. I knew it was wrong, but he made me feel things that I've never felt before, and he loved me. I never felt love from anyone in my life; not my dad, and certainly not Kyle. Our relationship was out of convenience. There were times I knew Kyle cheated on me, but I chose not to say anything because I was afraid to be alone. I spent my whole life alone. Don't get me wrong, I did love Kyle, but I was never in love with him.

**

I arrived back in New York and was walking out of the airport when I saw Denny standing next to the limo. I stopped as he walked over to me, hugged me, and then took my suitcase. I tried so hard not to cry, but my eyes didn't listen. I sobbed and sobbed in the back of the limo while Denny drove me home.

"I'm so sorry, Miss Lane."

"What did he tell you?" I sniffed.

"He told me that he won't be seeing you anymore and that I needed to pick you up from the airport and drive you home."

"He didn't tell you why?"

"No, Miss Lane, he didn't."

I guess I was going to be the one to tell him. He deserved to know the truth.

"I'm sick, Denny. I have cancer. Connor left me because I didn't tell him." I started sobbing again.

He pulled up to my apartment and followed me inside with my suitcase. I turned to him as he hugged me.

"Miss Lane, he'll come around."

I shook my head. "Not this time, Denny; it's too late."

He took my hand and handed me a piece of paper. "This is my phone number. I want you to call me if you need anything, and don't worry, I won't tell Mr. Black."

I looked at the paper and hugged him as we said goodbye. I shut the door behind him and looked around my apartment; it was a representation of how I felt, dark, lonely, and small.

Chapter 23

I walked to the bedroom and fell on my bed. The rage was growing inside me as I gripped my comforter with both hands and screamed. I sat up and looked around my small bedroom. The pain inside me was far worse than I ever imagined it could be. My chest felt heavy, and my shattered heart pierced me from within. I clenched my jaw as my hands gripped the bed. I tore my comforter off the bed and threw it across the room. I ripped off my sheets and balled them up so that they masked the sounds of my screams. I walked to the kitchen for a glass of water to try to calm down, but I threw the glass at the wall and watched as it shattered into tiny pieces like my heart. I looked around. I took my desk and tipped it over as the drawer fell out, and my list was lying on the floor. I picked it up and looked at it. I held my bucket list in my hand. A list of all the things that I needed and wanted to do before I died. I crumpled the paper and threw it on the ground.

I went into the bathroom. I was so angry at my life and for what I did to Connor that I couldn't see straight. I reached into the bathtub and grabbed my razor that was sitting on the edge. I took the blade out and held it to my wrist; I was going to end this pain now. I looked at the blade that perfectly matched up with my scar as the memories of that night came flooding back in my mind. I threw the blade down. What the hell was I doing? I fell to the ground, sobbing as I felt someone's arms wrap around me.

"It's ok, sweetie; I'm here," Peyton whispered. She looked down and picked up the blade and then she looked at my wrists. "Jesus, Elle."

We sat on the bathroom floor for what seemed like an eternity. She helped me up and walked me to the bedroom.

"I see you went on a destruction spree."

I sat on the floor with my knees to my chest as she remade my bed. I felt like I just had a nervous breakdown; like everything that happened in my life just hit me. Peyton took me by the shoulders and helped me up. She went to my drawer and pulled a nightshirt out and helped me into it. I felt like a rag doll as my arms and legs felt limp. I climbed into my bed as Peyton covered me with the blankets. She scooted next to me and put her arms around me.

"Connor called and told me everything. Elle, I'm sorry, and I wish you would have told me about the cancer, but now is not the time to talk about this," she said as she pushed my hair out of my face. "Get some sleep, I'm not going anywhere, and if you're up to it, we'll talk when you wake up."

I didn't say a word; I couldn't. I just nodded my head and drifted off into a deep sleep.

***

I woke up and looked around the room. I sat on the edge of the bed as Peyton walked in. "Finally, you're awake."

I yawned and ran my hand through my hair. "How long have I been sleeping?"

She put her hands on her hips and twisted her face as if she didn't want to tell me. "Two days."

My eyes widened. "What? Two days? Peyton, why didn't you wake me?"

She came over and sat on the edge of the bed. "Sweetie, you obviously needed it. When I found you on that bathroom floor, god, Elle, I thought you..." She turned her head and looked at the wall.

I lightly took her hand. "I know, Peyton, and I'm sorry."

She laid her head on my shoulder. "The only thing that matters is that you didn't do it. You're awake now, and you need to eat. Henry made the most delicious chicken noodle soup."

I looked at her with a frown. "Who's Henry?"

She tilted her head and smiled. "Dr. Hottie, he's been here helping me out while you've been sleeping."

I rolled my eyes. "Seriously, Peyton, you told him everything?"

"Yeah, Elle, I did; we're seeing each other now, and I needed someone to talk to. Besides, he's been the biggest help."

I got up and felt light-headed. Peyton grabbed my arm. "You need to eat, Elle; it's been two days."

She helped me to the kitchen. All I could smell was the aroma of the chicken noodle soup, and it was amazing. I didn't feel like eating, but my body told me that I had to. I sat at the table as Peyton set the bowl of soup in front of me. "Eat up."

"Where's my phone?" I asked her.

"It's over there on your desk; I charged it for you."

I walked over, pulled it out of the charger, and turned it on. I patiently waited for it to turn on so that I could see if Connor text-messaged me or called. There was nothing, not even a voicemail. I should have started crying, but there were no tears left in my eyes.

Peyton sat across from me as I slowly ate the soup Henry had made. "Ellery, why didn't you tell me about your cancer coming back? I thought we were best friends?"

I couldn't look at her, because I was ashamed. I knew my secret would hurt the people close to me. I've already lived it, and I couldn't go through it again.

"Peyton, I'm so sorry that I didn't tell you. I wanted to tell you, please believe me, but I couldn't bear to stand in front of you and see the look on your face after I told you. It was bad enough that I had to tell Kyle."

She reached over and touched my hand that was resting on the table. "Elle, I would have stood by you and supported you. I seriously can't understand why you wouldn't tell me. I get that you were scared, and you didn't want me to worry, but what were you going to do? Just go off and die alone?"

I got up from the table and sat on the couch, hugging my knees to my chest and burying my head in my hands. "My life has been made up of hurting people, Peyton. I need you to understand that. After my mother died, I was left as a reminder of her to my dad, and that hurt him so much, he had to drink himself to death just to cope. Then there was my suicide attempt and cancer." I could feel the tears starting to spring back to life.

Peyton sat down beside me and put her arm around me, pulling me closer. "I do understand where you're coming from, Elle, but do you want to know what I think? I think you made the wrong decision not to tell anyone, especially Connor, and now you have to deal with the consequences. I'm sorry; I don't mean to kick you while you're down, but by you not telling anyone has caused more pain than if you would have been honest from the beginning."

I leaned my head on her shoulder, "I'm sorry Peyton; I hope

164

you can find it in your heart to forgive me."

"I can and have forgiven you, Elle, but you have to promise me that you'll call the doctor and start treatments right away because…" Peyton started to cry. "I can't imagine my life without you in it."

I turned towards her and hugged her tight. "I'm sorry; I promise to get help."

Peyton got up to clean up the kitchen as I went to take a shower. I got dressed and put on my coat.

"Excuse me, where do you think you're going?" she asked.

"I have a couple of things that I need to do."

"I don't think it's a good idea that you go anywhere."

I lightly laughed. "Are you my mother now?"

"No, I'm not, but I worry about you, and I want you to be safe. Oh god, I sound like a mother." She smiled.

"I won't be gone long; I promise."

I walked out the door and headed down the crowded streets. You would think that the coldness of the air would chill my bones, but every part of my existence was already numb.

I walked over to the next block to a church that I've admired since I moved to New York. I needed to seek solace in the house of God. I had unanswered questions and unfinished business. I reached the steps of the church and pulled open the heavy door that led inside. I've wanted to visit this church since I moved here, but Kyle wasn't a church fan and wouldn't go with me.

I looked around at the beauty of the stained glass that overtook the windows and many rows of wooden pews that stood before me. I knelt at one of the pews and said hello to God before I sat down. I stared at the altar as memories of my childhood flashed before my eyes; memories of me sitting in a pew just like this one in the front row, staring at the large wooden casket that held my mother. My father was holding his face crying as strangers all around gave me their sympathetic looks.

A single tear fell from my eye. As I wiped it away, a man in a white robe sat down next to me.

"Good day, my child. Is there anything that I can do for you?"

"Hello, Father, I'm just here because I have some unfinished business with God."

He gave me a surprised look and said, "Unfinished business, huh?"

I looked down and laced my fingers together. "Yeah, I need some questions answered about my life, and I was hoping to get them here."

The priest sat and listened to me as I told him about my life. I confided in him about my mother and father's death, my past and recurrent battle with cancer, and how I hid the truth from Connor. I didn't tell him about my suicide attempt, but it wasn't too hard to hide when I lifted my hand and pushed my hair behind my ear. The priest looked at me and lightly touched my wrist.

"You're a survivor, and God gave you a second chance at life."

I shook my head. "I know that Father, but what good is that second chance if I'm not going to live a long, full life?"

He patted my hand softly. "You don't know whether you won't live a long, full life, and it doesn't matter what you went through before; what matters is that you survived it. God won't give you more than you can handle. He knows you're strong enough to handle this again."

I looked down and bit my lip. My emotions were all over the place. "The chemo was awful," I whispered.

"Chemo isn't supposed to be fun, but you survived, and it made you stronger. What you need to understand is that by you refusing to get treatment is just another form of suicide."

I looked up at his face; my eyes stinging with tears. He was right. I never thought that what I was doing was a form of suicide. He took my hand and patted it once more as he smiled and walked away.

Chapter 24

I was walking down the street, not knowing exactly where I was going, thinking about my conversation with the priest when I stopped in front of Pizzapopolous. My stomach tied itself in knots as I stared through the window, remembering how I made Connor eat pizza with his hands. I smiled as I stepped into the Starbucks that was next door. The aroma of coffee was making me salivate as I ordered a mocha latte. I took my latte and sat at a table towards the back. I looked at the time on my phone; it was already 2:00 pm. I dialed the phone number that kept consistently calling me for the past four months.

"Good afternoon. Dr. Taub's office, how may I help you?" the perky voice on the other end spoke.

"Hi, this is Ellery Lane; I need to make an appointment to see Dr. Taub"

"Oh ok, well, the first appointment I have is on November 5th at 3:00 pm."

I sighed. "Do you realize that it's September 30th, and November 5th is very far away?"

"Sorry, but that's his first available appointment."

I was now starting to get agitated. "May I please talk to Dr. Taub?"

"I'm sorry, but he's with a patient right now; may I take a message for him?"

Once again I sighed. "Yes, tell him Ellery Lane called, and that I'm ready. He'll know what I mean." I hung up before she could say anything else.

I put my phone on the table as I looked up and had a near heart attack when I saw Connor walk through the door. He looked rough—like he hadn't slept in days. He wore dark jeans and my favorite gray T-shirt that defined his muscular chest. A few days' worth of stubble sat upon his face. His hair was tousled in a different way, but he still looked perfect and hot as hell. I panicked. I didn't want him to see me, so I did the only thing I could; I hid under the table.

The place was packed with people conversing and studying, so the chances of anyone seeing me under the table were slim; with the exception of Dr. Hottie who knelt down and peered his head under the table.

"You ok down there, Ellery?"

I waved my hand to shoo him out of the way so that I could see when Connor left.

"I'm hiding from him," I mumbled, pointing to the line.

"I've got this." He winked.

Henry stood up, walked over to Connor and shook his hand. He kept him talking until Connor got his coffee and then patted him on the shoulder as he walked out the door. I got up off the floor and sat back in my chair. Henry walked over and sat across from me.

"Thank you; I owe you one."

He smiled and took a sip of his coffee. "Nah, now we're even."

I cocked my head to the side and raised one eyebrow. "What do you mean?"

He lightly laughed. "If you wouldn't have needed stitches that day you came to the hospital, I never would have met Peyton."

I pursed my lips together. "You really like her, don't you?"

The grin on his face was priceless. "I do, and I know it's soon, but I'm going to ask her to move in with me."

"I know she's crazy about you; I'm glad my injury brought you two together." I smiled.

He leaned over the table and brought his hand above my eye. "I must say, I did an exceptional job with those stitches." He smiled. "I have to go; I have rounds at the hospital. I'll talk you soon, Ellery." I waved goodbye as he walked out the door.

My phone, face down on the table, started to ring. My imagination went wild with the hopes that maybe it was Connor. I picked it up and looked at it. It was Dr. Taub's number.

"Hello?" I answered.

"Ellery, it's Dr. Taub. I'm glad you called. I want you to come in for some blood work tomorrow morning. After I get the results, we'll go ahead and schedule the Chemotherapy. I'm happy you changed your mind."

I wanted to throw the phone at the wall because I wasn't looking forward to going through that again.

"Me too, Dr. Taub. I'll see you tomorrow." I sighed and took a sip of my latte.

When I got home later that day, Peyton had told me that Henry was taking her somewhere special for dinner. I was truly happy for her and that someone was worthy of her heart, even if my own was shattered beyond repair.

"Guess what else?" She jumped up and down. Henry asked me to fly to Colorado tomorrow to meet his parents."

I looked at her, put on my happy face, and jumped up and down with her. I didn't want to ruin her trip by telling her I was going to be starting chemo soon, so I didn't tell her about the phone call from Dr. Taub.

"Are you going to be alright, sweetie?" She pouted.

I waved my hand in front of my face and walked over to the sink. "I'll be fine. I'm going to lose myself in my paintings, so don't worry about me."

She hugged me tight. "Ok, I have to go home and pack. We'll be gone for two weeks, so if you need anything or you just want to talk, you better call me, Ellery Rose Lane. Do you understand me?" She grabbed her coat and opened the door.

"Peyton," I called.

"Yeah?" She turned and looked at me.

"I'm really happy for you; go have fun and keep in touch," I spoke with a fake happiness.

"Thanks, Elle, I will. I love you!" she yelled as she shut the door.

It wasn't that I wasn't happy for her; I was. I was just feeling sorry for myself because I screwed things up with Connor. How could I be so stupid? What the hell was I thinking? I knew what I had to do and the first step was to apologize to him.

172

***

I called a cab and stepped out into the brisk night air. I had the cab driver drop me off at the soup kitchen; I wanted to volunteer one last time before I started chemo. Once I start, I can't be around groups of people, especially the homeless with their colds and illnesses. I volunteered for a couple of hours and told Julius what was going on.

"Oh, Elle, I'm sorry."

"Don't be, Julius. I've been through it before and beat it, and I can do it again."

He high-fived me. "That's my girl! I know you will, and if you need anything, anything at all, you call me or anyone here, and we'll be by your side in a flash."

"Thanks, Julius, I will, and tell your wife that I said hi." He flashed me a smile and nodded his head.

I walked to the next block to a tattoo parlor where my friend Jack works. "Why, if it isn't Ellery Lane; it's good to see you, sweetheart," Jack said as he walked over and bear-hugged me. "I haven't seen you in a while. How's Pey?"

"Hey, Jack, she's good."

He stared at me and twisted his face. "What's going on in that pretty little head of yours? Are you thinking about a tat Elle?"

I bit down on my bottom lip. "Yep, I sure am."

"Come sit over here. Let me finish her up, and then you're next." He winked.

The girl sitting in the chair was getting a tattoo of angel wings on her left shoulder with the inscription, "Forever Yours." I looked at her. "Nice tattoo."

She smiled over at me. "Thanks; it's for my boyfriend. Tomorrow's his birthday, and this is my way of letting him know that I'm forever his and no one else can have me."

I looked into her 18-year-old eyes. "Wow, forever, huh?"

She giggled. "Yeah, he said that we'll be together forever."

Jack looked at me and rolled his eyes. I had to keep myself from laughing. He finished her tattoo and gestured for me to sit in the chair. "What do you want and where do you want it, Elle?"

I held out both my wrists. I pointed to my left scar; "I want 'CONNOR' on this one and the infinity symbol on this one." I pointed to my right. "Make sure the scars are totally covered."

Jack looked at me and frowned. "Who's Connor?"

"It's a long story." I shook my head.

"It's going to hurt, Elle; you do realize that, right?"

"I know it will Jack; let's just get it over with." Nothing could hurt me as bad as I was already hurting.

Chapter 25

Jack was a great guy. He was one of those guys that had tattoos covering on every inch of both arms, down his chest, and his back. He was an artist like me, and he proudly displayed his work. His black eyes matched his long, dark hair, which he frequently wore back in a ponytail. He started with Connor's name on my left wrist. The sting was bearable. Don't get me wrong, it felt like a thousand tiny pins were being poked in me, but I've been through much worse. After a couple of hours, Jack was finally finished. I looked at my wrists and smiled.

"The redness will go away in a few days. Just make sure you keep moisturizer on them so that it won't itch as bad.

"Thank you, Jack. They're beautiful."

"Do you have a ride home?" he asked.

"I'm going to call a cab."

He looked at the clock. "It's midnight; I'll have Donny close up, and I'll take you home."

I smiled. "It's ok, Jack, really; I'll just call a cab."

He grabbed his coat, yelled for Donny to close up, and told me to get in his car.

"If I'm not mistaken, you live by my girlfriend, and I'm heading that way anyway; it's no problem."

I walked into my apartment, and the first thing I did was grab my laptop, change into my pajamas, climbed in bed, and opened my email. The first step in getting on with my life was apologizing to Connor, and I owed him a big one. I hit the compose button as a blank page came up.

Dear Connor,

I hope you're reading this and didn't delete it before you opened it when you saw my name. If you are, then you'll see this is my heartfelt apology to you. Words cannot explain how sorry I am for not telling you about my illness from the start. I never meant for us to get as close as we did for that very reason. The night I took you home, I had every intention of leaving and never looking back; if I had, we wouldn't have met, and you wouldn't be hurting right now. I will never forgive myself for not telling you the truth. I believe in fate, and it was fate that brought us together. I told you I was saved for a reason, and I think it was to save you. You have a beautiful heart and soul, and you don't deserve to never love someone. You will never know what you've done for me, and how you've changed my life. I never would have experienced love the way I have with you, because what you showed me, and how you made me feel, was a first for me in my lifetime. I never loved Kyle. I was with him because he was there, and I was afraid of being alone. Loneliness is what my whole life was made of. My decision to not receive treatment at the time was out of pure selfishness on my part, and I've come to understand that now. I want to thank you for your love and kindness. If I had one last breath left, I would use it to tell you how much I love you, because I do, and I always will.

Love forever,

Ellery.

Tears filled my eyes as I hit send. I took in a deep breath, closed my laptop, and fell asleep.

I threw on a pair of leggings, my pale pink long sweater, and my black boots. I put some curls in my long hair and applied some makeup for the first time since Michigan. I opened my laptop and checked my email—nothing. I didn't expect there to be any reply from him, but one could only hope.

I called a cab and headed to Dr. Taub's office for blood work. I examined my wrists and smiled at the beauty of both Connor's name and the infinity symbol. I entered the office building and took the elevator up to the fourth floor.

"Hi, I'm Ellery Lane, and I'm here for some blood work," I said to the young girl behind the desk.

"Yes, I have your file right here. I just need to copy of your ID, please." I dug through my purse, retrieved my driver's license, and handed it to her. She took notice of my wrist with Connor's name.

"Oh my god, that's awesome," she said.

I smiled and thanked her as I showed her my other wrist. The scars were barely noticeable, and for people who didn't know, they wouldn't see them. The nurse called my name and took me back to the drawing station. She asked me if I was nervous about needles, and I laughed.

"I've been through chemo before, so giving blood is nothing."

She managed to force a smile; I don't think she thought that was too funny. She drew three vials of blood and told me to have a good day.

I left the medical building and decided to walk around for a while before calling a cab and heading home. I walked a few blocks, doing some window shopping when a text came from Peyton.

"Hey, girl! I'm on the plane, headed to Colorado. Please tell

me you're doing ok?"

I smiled and replied as I walked down the street. Unaware of my surroundings, because I was too engrossed in text-messaging my best friend, I collided into someone.

"Oh shit, I'm so sor…" I started to say as I looked up at the man that I just ran into head on. I took in a sharp breath and looked down. "Connor, I'm sorry; I didn't mean…" I couldn't even look him in the eyes; I was so ashamed. My heart started pounding so hard it felt like it was going to jump out of my chest.

He stood there, staring at me. "No, it's my fault. I should have been paying more attention."

We stood there in front of each other awkwardly, with his hand lightly touching my arm. I pulled away; the pain was too strong, and I felt my throat closing up.

"I have to go," I mumbled as I turned the corner and didn't look back. I reached an alleyway between buildings, and I stood with my back against the brick, trying to catch my breath. All the emotions that I tried to force away came flooding back and bruising what was left of my soul.

I ended up walking home which was about 10 blocks from where I was. I didn't care; I needed to try to clear my head. I walked through the door, panting and completely exhausted. I made a pot of coffee, and as it brewed, I sat down in front of my easel and continued my painting of the wedding in Central Park. I wanted to get at least two more paintings finished before I started chemo. I was up till 2:00 am, and it was finally finished. I painted it with the vision of how I would want my wedding to be; just a delusional thought from my head. I took my brushes over to the sink and let them soak as I went to bed. Tomorrow, I would paint a new picture.

Morning had come and gone. I was woken up by my cell phone ringing. "Hello?" I sleepily answered.

"Ellery, it's Dr. Taub. Your blood results came back, and I'm a little concerned about your hemoglobin level. It's a little low, but I'm going to go ahead and start chemotherapy anyway. I'm going to schedule your first treatment one week from today, but first, I'm going to prescribe you some iron pills that I want you to start taking immediately."

I rolled my eyes. "Ok, Dr. Taub. One week from today at 9:00 am."

I looked at the clock as it read 12:00 pm; I couldn't believe I slept in that late. I put on a pot of coffee and rinsed my brushes. I took a quick shower and got dressed. I noticed the pile of clothes lying in the laundry basket that needed to be washed; I hadn't done laundry in a while. I sighed as I picked up the basket and set it by the door. I filled a mug with coffee and headed off to the laundry mat; thank god it was only around the corner. After a couple of hours, I finished my laundry and walked back to my apartment where I saw Kyle leaning up against the door.

"What do you want, Kyle?!" I yelled before I approached the walkway. He was standing there with his hands in his pockets, staring at me.

"I wanted to see how you were doing."

"You could have text-messaged me and not just shown up here."

This is just what I needed; this asshole to ruin my day. I wasn't in the mood, and I needed to start painting.

"Here, let me help you," he said as he took my key and opened the door. I walked in and set the basket in my room. When I came out, I noticed him staring at my painting.

"Elle, this is beautiful."

"Yeah, isn't it? Now, what do you want Kyle?"

I was being mean, but I didn't care; I loathed this boy standing in front of me and for what he did.

"Like I said, I wanted to see how you were doing."

"Bullshit Kyle; I'm fine, and now you know; now you can leave."

"Elle, stop acting like this, baby," he said as he swiftly moved closer to me. Before I knew it, his mouth was on mine. I pushed him away with force.

"What the fuck are you doing?"

"Elle, don't fight it; I know you still love me, and I want you so bad." I stood there in shock by his words and by his actions; I didn't know what to say.

"Really, Kyle, you think I love you? Let me tell you something you scum-sucking, loathing little worm; you leaving me was the best thing that ever happened in my life. I never loved you. You were a convenience for me; someone to fill the lonely spot in my world."

His face turned red and angry. "You're a fucking bitch, Elle!" he screamed.

"It takes one to know one, Kyle. Now, get the fuck out of my house before I seriously hurt you."

"I'd like to see you try," he said.

I picked up a vase that sat on the corner of my desk and threw it at him. He ducked as it shattered against the wall.

"You are one crazy bitch; I'm out of here."

I ran and locked the door, avoiding the tiny pieces of glass that were scattered across my floor. I heavily sighed as I cleaned up the mess I made, remembering the first time I met Connor in his kitchen, and I dropped the mug on his floor.

The whole week I never left the apartment except when I went to the hospital to have a port put in for chemo. I concentrated on finishing my paintings, and successfully, I did. Sitting in front of my easel was the only time when I felt somewhat normal. My heart was still shattered, and my soul was empty. I felt lost and broken, and no matter what I did, I couldn't shake the feeling, so I just existed.

My first treatment was tomorrow morning, and I was scared. I had no one to be there with me. The first time I went through chemo, my dad managed to stay sober long enough to be there for me during my sessions, but as soon as we left the hospital, he hit the local bar. Now, I was all alone facing cancer and chemo once again—by myself.

Tears came to my eyes as I threw myself a little pity party. I had some friends, but I was in no way going to have them stop their lives to help me. I took the paintings to the art gallery and terribly missed seeing Peyton's smiling face greeting me at the door. She had one more week left in Colorado. Sal shook his head when he saw my paintings.

"Ellery, these are beautiful! You're so incredibly talented; I know these will sell quickly," he said as he moved them over to the empty wall. I gave him a hug and thanked him.

Chapter 26

Chemo day arrived. I put on my yoga pants, a baggy sweatshirt, and threw my hair up in a ponytail; there was no going to chemo looking fashionable. I grabbed my blanket and my kindle and stepped inside the cab that was waiting for me outside. I arrived at the hospital and headed to the cancer center where I would be a frequent visitor once a week for the next six months. Because I waited longer than most to have chemo after I was told my cancer came back, the doctor and I agreed to do a little more aggressive treatment that would shorten the duration of my therapy, hopefully.

Nurse Bailey called me back into the room where a total of 16 oversized blue chairs lined the walls of the sterile white room. There were eight chairs on one side and eight on the other; each chair having its own IV pole and curtain. I never felt comfortable with my chemo treatments. People always looked at me like I was way too young to have cancer. I was the youngest one there for the first eight months until a nine-year-old girl named Molly showed up.

"Is anyone here with you, sweetie?" Nurse Bailey asked with a smile.

"No, it's just me."

She patted my hand and gave me a sympathetic look. "Well, don't you worry, I'm here with you."

She was an older woman, probably in her fifties, with short salt and pepper hair. Her voice was soft but perky. She told me about her ex-husband and her three grown children as she sat me in the chair and did some prep work. She excused herself and said she'd be right back. I looked around the room at the six chairs that were filled by people who were here for the same reason I was. It was weird because being complete strangers, we all shared a common bond.

"Someone is here to see you," Nurse Bailey said in her perky voice. I looked up from my phone and practically went into cardiac arrest when I saw Connor standing there. I felt like I was going to suffocate.

"What are you doing here, Connor?!" I managed to ask.

He sighed and sat in the chair next to me.

"Hello, Ellery."

I continued to look down at my phone, and I refused to look at him. "I asked you a question," I demanded.

"Nobody should have to go through this alone."

"I'm not alone, I have Nurse Bailey." I pointed, still looking at my phone.

Before I knew it, he grabbed my phone from my hands and put it in his pocket.

"What the hell, Connor?!" I snarled.

Nurse Bailey came walking over. "Ok, sweetie, here's your cocktail, bottoms up." She smiled as she inserted the needle into my port and hung the bag on the pole. I gently smiled at her. "Cheers."

Connor looked at me. "I'm here as your friend, Ellery."

"Can I have my phone back please?" I asked nicely as I held

out my hand.

He took in a sharp breath, reached in his pocket, pulled out my phone, and handed it to me. Our fingers touched as he put it in the palm of my hand. My heart started racing like it always did when he touched me.

"This is how this is going to work," he spoke. "I'm going to bring you here every week and then take you home. I've hired a private nurse to come to your apartment daily to tend to you and make you comfortable."

All kinds of thoughts were running through my head; why was he doing this for me? Is this his revenge; to kick a girl during her chemo sessions?

"Why, Connor? Why are you doing this?" He looked at me with cold eyes.

"I owe you."

"What the fuck are you talking about?"

"You took care of me once, so now, I'm returning the favor. I know you don't have anyone else."

So, now I've become his charity case—great. "The night you brought me home from the beach and put me to bed, you said we were even. You don't need to stay. I'm fine; you can go."

He looked down and laced his fingers together. "I'm staying Ellery, and you're in no position to say otherwise." I rolled my eyes and tried to think of a million ways to run.

"By the way, how did you know I started chemo today? And how did you know I was here?" I glared at him.

"I know a lot of things, Ellery; I've told you before that I can find out anything."

I shot him a look. "Stalker."

I sat there reading while he sent emails and did business from his iPad.

"You don't need to be here; I'm sure you have better things to do than sit in a room, watching people get chemo for five hours," I randomly said.

"Whether I have better things to do or not, this is how it's going to be, so let's be quiet, and don't worry about it," his voice was flat and cold.

Didn't he realize I was pissed off at the world at that moment, and he was making it worse? I didn't want him here because it was bringing back all the emotions that I tried to bury, but I did want him here because I had a bit of hope in the back of my mind that he still wanted to be with me and that he possibly forgave me. I looked down at my kindle and tried to read, but as I looked at the words, the only thing registering in my mind was Connor.

"How are you doing, sweetie?" Nurse Bailey cheerfully asked as she checked my chemo drip.

"I'm doing fucking fantastic, Nurse Bailey, because I know that probably by tonight, I'll have my head down the toilet for a good hour or two."

Connor looked at me and then at Nurse Bailey. "Ellery, that's enough."

The nurse looked at him sympathetically. "It's alright, she's angry right now and needs to let it out. I'm used to it. I just try to make my patients as comfortable as possible."

Connor leaned closer to me and whispered, "Could you please stop being a smart ass? She's only trying to help you."

I couldn't look at him because if I did, I was going to slap him right across the face. I didn't say a word. I was more than ready to rip that chemo line right out of me and run as fast and as far away as I could. This is what I wanted to prevent; the hostility, the anger, and the resentment. I just wanted to live my life—with the time I had left—happy.

That was the longest five hours of my life. Nurse Bailey removed the chemo drip from my port and gave me a hug goodbye. Connor grabbed my blanket, and I tore it out of his hands. "I got it." He heavily sighed and followed behind me as I exited the hospital. Connor opened the limo door for me as I slid into the seat.

Denny turned and looked at me. "Hello, Miss Lane." He was the only person of the day that got a smile from me.

"Hi, Denny."

Connor climbed in next to me. "How are you feeling?"

I looked out the window. "I'm fine right now; it takes a few hours or even a few days for the chemo to hit you." The ride to my apartment was silent.

Connor got out of the limo and followed me inside. "I want you to start packing."

I turned and looked at him. "For what?"

He took in a sharp breath. "You will be staying in the guest room at my penthouse." I felt the blood drain from my face, and my heart started to beat faster.

"I'm not going anywhere; this is my home. This is where I'm staying!" But the idea of sleeping in the enormous, comfy bed was appealing.

"Listen to me," his voice was raised, "I don't want you staying here alone."

I walked over to him and put my finger to his chest. "I'm not your fucking charity case Connor Black, and I don't need your help. Besides, you hate me anyway, why would you want to help me after what I did?" I slowly turned around and walked to the sink for a glass of water. I stood there with my hands on the edge.

He slowly walked up behind me. "Ellery, I don't hate you; please don't ever say that again. Yes, I will admit that I'm still angry, and that I probably will be for a very while, but I need to put all that aside because you are my friend, and you need help. Please put your stubbornness aside, and let me help you."

His voice was soft and his words sincere. I wanted to throw my arms around him and cry into his shoulder, but I couldn't, he admitted he was still angry and that he was only my friend.

"You said you hired a nurse to come here."

He sighed again. "Well, I'm making other arrangements."

"Fine, let me get my things." I gave in because I didn't have the strength to fight him, and I was scared of being alone.

He turned around and looked over at the wall that was missing a chunk of drywall. "What happened over there?"

I came from the bedroom as he walked over and grabbed my bags. "I threw a vase at Kyle."

He let out a laugh. "Are you serious?"

"Yeah, he wouldn't leave, so I threw a vase at him; needless to say, he left after that." Connor shook his head and continued to laugh.

Chapter 27

I threw myself on the bed I've grown to love as Connor set my bags down in the corner.

"I'm going out tonight; if you need anything, you're welcome to help yourself."

I looked at him and gave half a smile. "Thanks."

He walked out and shut the door. Did he just make it a point to tell me he was going out? I could feel the burning and the rage rev up in my body; jealousy was setting in. This wasn't a good idea, but if it got too unbearable staying with him, I would pack up and leave.

I didn't have much of an appetite, and I was tired, so I decided to turn in early. I was woken up by the sudden feeling of nausea that overtook my body. I looked at the clock. It was 2:00 am. I flew out of bed and into the bathroom that was directly across the hall. Thank god I made it as I started to vomit uncontrollably. Here we go. I knew it wouldn't take long; it didn't the last time. As I leaned over with my head in the toilet, I heard the door slowly open.

"Ellery," I heard Connor say as he grabbed my hair and held it back.

I didn't want him to see me like this. Moving here wasn't a good thing to do, and now I regretted it.

"Get out of here, Connor. Please, just go."

He knelt down beside me as he held my hair. "I'm not going anywhere until you're back in bed."

I threw up a few more times; mostly dry heaving as he walked to the sink and wet a cloth with tepid water. He folded it up and put it on my head. I quickly grabbed it out of his hand. I managed to get up and take small steps towards the door. I was so weak that I wanted to collapse right on the marble floor. Connor lightly took a hold of my arm and helped me into bed. He pulled the covers over me, and as he turned to walk away, I grabbed his hand. He turned around and looked at me.

"This is nothing. You have no idea what you've gotten yourself into, Mr. Black."

He stared at me without saying a word then walked out the door, leaving it open a crack. I was too exhausted to think of anything. I just wanted to sleep peacefully.

***

I opened one eye at the sunlight peeking through the curtains that hung on the windows. I stretched and rolled over on my side, taking in the view of the city that stood outside my window. So much for the anti-nausea meds Nurse Bailey fed me. I heard the door slightly open.

"Ellery, are you awake?" I heard his voice whisper.

I rolled over and looked at him standing there in his dark jeans and a black cotton button down shirt that he left un-tucked. His hair was messy and damp, but in that sexy way that made me ache for him.

"How are you feeling?" he asked from the doorway.

I sat up on the edge of the bed. "I'm feeling ok at the moment. I think I'll take a shower."

His eyes stared into me as if he wanted to reach out and touch me.

"When you're done, come downstairs and Claire will make you some breakfast."

I got out of bed and opened my bag to dig out my clothes for the day. "Who's Claire?" I asked.

"She's my housekeeper."

"Oh, I didn't know you had a housekeeper; you never mentioned her."

He ran his hand through his hair. "The opportunity never came up, I guess."

I walked past without even looking at him. I walked into the bathroom as he followed me and stood in the doorway.

"I'm going to the office to do some work; I'll be home later."

I kept my back to him as I turned on the shower. "Ok, see you later."

My words were flat with no emotion. I climbed in the shower and sat on the floor. I curled myself into a ball and cried.

After my shower, I walked down to the kitchen. "You must be our new house guest Ellery, right?" she asked as she walked over and hugged me.

I greeted her warmly. "Yes, and you must be Claire?"

"I sure am, honey. Now, sit down and tell me what you'd like me to make you."

Claire was a breath of fresh air in this house. She was an older woman with brown hair that sat just above her shoulders. Her smile was as warm as her deep brown eyes that lit up when she saw me. Maybe she was happy to have another female in the house. I sat at the island as she put a cup of peppermint tea in front of me.

"Drink up; it will soothe your stomach." I took a small sip and set the cup down.

"Mr. Black told me that you were sick last night, so how about you start with some toast and scrambled eggs?"

I nodded my head. I was curious as to how much she knew about me and our situation, so I asked an obvious question.

"What else did Mr. Black tell you?"

She smiled as she put the bread in the toaster. "He only tells me what I need to know. Mr. Black is a very private person. He says you're a friend, and he wanted to help you. He's a very generous man."

I rolled my eyes. If the chemo doesn't kill me, then staying here with the man whose life I pretty much ruined will.

"Ah I see you two have met," Connor said as he lightly stepped into the kitchen.

"I thought you left," I said with a—I don't like you very much right now—attitude.

"I had to finish up some computer work here first, but don't worry, I'll be leaving soon."

Claire eyed me and then looked at Connor as he sat over at the table.

"Here, honey, try to eat something. You'll feel better if you do."

I saw Connor look over at me out of the corner of my eye. I picked up the fork and started to eat some eggs. The food was starting to help a bit, or maybe it was the tea; who knows.

Connor finished his coffee and walked over to me. "I'm leaving now, so if you need anything, Claire will be here all day." I didn't look at him as I waved my hand.

"This is going to be more difficult than I thought," he mumbled as he left the kitchen.

I didn't know if he meant for me to hear it or not, but I did, and it pissed me off.

Claire studied me for a moment. "Calm down, honey; it's not worth getting upset over."

I decided that if I was going to stay here, Claire had a right to know what happened between me and Connor. I told her everything.

She sat down next to me, holding her coffee cup. "I figured something was going on between the two of you. You must have been the reason why Mr. Black was always in a good mood and smiling all the time not that long ago."

She saw the look on my face and took my hand; she pushed back my sleeve and looked at my wrist, and then took my other hand and did the same. "Does he know about this?"

I shook my head. "No, but he will soon enough; it's not something that I can keep hidden for long." Claire smiled and patted my hand.

I grabbed my coat and stepped outside. The air was a little warmer than it had been. The sun was shining bright, and there wasn't a cloud in the sky; it was a perfect October day. I needed to get lost in myself, so I decided to take a walk to Central Park. I needed to be alone, and what better place to think about how much my life sucked at the moment than in the park. I made my way to the Conservatory Garden and found a spot in the middle of the grass. I laid the blanket on the soft grass and sat down with my knees to my chest. My phone started to ring; it was Connor. Someone must have tipped him off that I escaped. I hit ignore. I figured he would go to my apartment first, then probably to the art gallery or soup kitchen. He'll eventually figure out where I am, so I wasn't worried, and I honestly didn't care. I inhaled through my nose, taking in the mild October air. I studied the flowers that were around me for soon they would be gone.

I laid myself down on my back and stared up at the sky. I had a little talk with God and asked him to give me the strength to endure this process all over again. Connor kept calling me, so I turned my phone off. As I asked God for a sign to let me know he would help me through this, I felt a tiny drop of rain fall on my cheek. That was good enough for me until a few clouds rolled in, and it started to pour—so much for my perfect October day. I laid there staring up at the sky that was falling down upon me. I wanted so badly for the rain to wash away my illness and my fears. I continued to lay there in my delusional state until I heard a familiar voice call my name.

"Ellery, what the hell do you think you're doing? Are you crazy?!" I looked at him as he was walking towards me holding an umbrella.

"Aren't you the crazy one for coming out here after me?!"

I saw his jaw tighten as he approached me. "Look at you, you're soaked; get up now before you get sick."

I laughed. "I'm already sick, Connor. What's the difference?"

He stared down at me with a strange look on his face and did something I never thought Connor Black would do. He laid himself down beside me and looked up at the sky. I looked over at him as he struggled to keep his eyes open as the rain pelted him in the face; a small smile crossed my lips.

"Why are you doing this?" he asked as he turned and looked at me.

"Because I can lay here and no one will know I'm crying."

He looked at me for a moment and then back up at the falling rain. We laid there and didn't speak a word. Connor put his hand on top of mine, and that was all the words we needed. Both of us were soaked, and I was starting to get cold. I sat up on my elbows.

"I think it's time to go."

He looked over at me and smiled. "Good, because I can't stand being wet like this."

I lightly laughed as we both got up and started walking out of the park. I suddenly stopped and turned the other way to some nearby bushes. I bent down as the nausea set in, and I began to vomit. Connor waited for me to finish as he put his arms under my legs, picked me up, and carried me to the car. That was all I needed to feel safe again.

He carried me up to the penthouse and into the bedroom. He started to help me undress, but I stopped him.

"I'm fine; you need to get out of those wet clothes. Please go change; I'm going to take a hot bath."

"Do you feel well enough to take a bath by yourself?"

I shot him a look. "If I said no, does that mean you'll get in with me?"

He looked down. "Ellery."

I saw the look on his face, and it was one of pain; almost the same look as the day in the hotel room.

"I was only kidding, Connor. Now, get out of here and go change."

He walked out and left me standing there, feeling like an idiot. I didn't make it to the bathtub. I put on my nightshirt and robe and collapsed onto the bed.

Chapter 28

I woke up four hours later and couldn't move. The part I feared the most hit me; the pain. I started to whimper when I wanted to scream because I didn't want anyone to hear me. My body felt like it had been hacked into a million pieces, starting from the top of my head down to my toes. There wasn't a single bone, joint, or muscle that didn't hurt. I tried to get comfortable, but I couldn't. I slowly got off the bed and wanted to scream when my feet touched the floor. I stood up and made my way to the door; I stepped out into the hallway and dropped to my knees and then onto my side.

I started to cry—more a soft whimper like a puppy. Connor must have been in his office, which was the room next to the staircase, because I could hear him on the phone. I tried to crawl to the bathroom, but the pain was too great. It wasn't too long when I saw Connor running up the stairs, skipping a step in between.

"Ellery, my god, what's wrong?"

At that point, I was shaking uncontrollably. I put my hand up. "Don't touch me; it hurts," I cried.

He yelled for Claire and told her to call the nurse immediately and to get her over to the penthouse. He sat down beside me and touched my hair.

"I need to get back in bed; just pick me up and get it over with," I begged. He stood and picked me up off the ground. He flinched as I screamed. He carefully carried me into the bedroom and laid me on the bed.

"The nurse will be here soon; she'll help you," he said as he gently brushed the hair away from my face.

I looked at him and cried. "I'm sorry, Connor. I never wanted you to see me like this."

He knelt down beside the bed and lightly touched my hand. "You have nothing to be sorry for; I'm the one who is sorry. It kills me to see you in such pain," he said as a single tear fell down his cheek.

I took my thumb and gently wiped the tear from his face as he took my hand and looked at my wrist; the one tattooed with his name. He didn't have a chance to say anything as the nurse came in with her bag. Connor stood up and sat at the edge of the bed while Claire stood in the doorway.

"You're going to be just fine, sweetie," she said as she held up a needle. "I'm going to give you a shot of morphine for the pain."

She injected the shot into my hip and told me to relax. She then asked Connor to step into the hallway. I started to relax as the pain began to subside. Connor walked back into the room and to the other side of the bed, where he sat up with his back against the headboard. I turned on my side to face him.

"It isn't always going to be like this," I said. "The first three days after chemo is the worst, and then I am usually fortunate enough to have a few days where I feel good; well, as good as can be expected on chemo." He didn't say a word; he only sat there, playing with my hair.

"Don't get to use to doing that; it's going to be gone soon."

He flashed me that smile that melts my heart. "I don't care. You'll still be just as beautiful."

I smiled at him, and he kissed me lightly on my forehead. He softly took a hold of both my wrists and looked at them, rubbing the tattoos lightly. I saw the anguish in his eyes.

"I noticed these at the hospital when you were receiving chemo. I've been waiting for you to show me; why, Ellery?" he asked.

I rolled over as the morphine settled through my body, and I was able to step out of bed and slowly walked over to the window. "Because at some point, you have to realize that some people can stay in your heart, but not in your life, and this is my way of keeping you in my heart."

Silence overtook the large room until I felt his arms wrap around me, and he softly whispered in my ear, "Get back in bed and I'll bring you some tea."

I turned around with his arms still wrapped around me as I delicately kissed him on the cheek. He closed his eyes and took in a sharp breath. He released his arms from me and left the room. He came back a few minutes later with a cup of peppermint tea and set it on the nightstand, then climbed on the other side and sat next to me.

"Peyton called me and read me the riot act." He laughed.

"Why would she do that?" I asked.

"She said she's been trying to get a hold of you for a couple of days, and when she didn't have any luck, she called me. When I told her about your chemo and that you were staying here, she started yelling and said to sit tight because she was coming straight over from the airport to kick my ass."

I rolled my eyes. "Oh god, not tonight."

Connor lightly laughed. "No, we're in luck. She'll only be here tomorrow since her flight was cancelled."

I let out a sigh of relief. "Good, because tonight I couldn't deal with her."

I must have drifted to sleep because when I woke up I was under the covers, and Connor was gone. I felt so alone and did the only thing I couldn't control—I cried. As my shoulders were shaking and the sobs were buried deep in my pillow, I felt an overwhelming sense of comfort from behind.

"It's ok, baby, I'm here." Connor wrapped his arms around me and held me the rest of the night.

***

I woke up and patted the empty side where Connor laid and held me last night. I wanted to wake up in his arms, and I wanted him to tell me that he loved me. I'm getting too many mixed signals from him; it's hurting me, and I don't have the strength to fight both the cancer and him at the same time.

I felt like my chemo fog lifted, and I was starting to feel somewhat normal—as if I even knew what normal was anymore. I followed the aroma of coffee down the stairs and into the kitchen where Claire was cooking.

"Good morning, dear." She turned and smiled.

"Good morning, Claire. I'm in desperate need of some coffee."

She walked to the cabinet and grabbed a mug. "One cup coming right up!"

I heard a raised voice coming from over by the living room. I took my coffee and walked towards it when I noticed it was coming from Connor's office. He was on the phone, and he sounded angry.

"It's complicated Ashlyn. Yeah, well I'm sorry about the other night, but something came up! Fuck!" I heard him yell as he threw his phone across his desk. He paced back and forth, rubbing the back of his neck and shook his head. It hurt me to the very core that he still talked to her and still never explained to me who she was and what their relationship was. I heard his footsteps coming towards the door as I darted back into the kitchen.

He walked in and looked at me. "How are you feeling? You look better today." I could see the anguish in his face. He looked tired and weary.

"I'm fine," I said as I looked down.

Then out of nowhere, he went off on a tangent and started yelling, "You always say you're fine, Elle, even when you're not. Are you ever really *fine*? Can you ever just tell me the damn truth for once in your fucking life so that I can stop playing these goddamn guessing games? Can you say something other than 'I'm fine, Connor'? Because you know what, Ellery, it makes me sick."

I stood there, shocked and unable to say anything in my defense. I didn't know this man standing in front of me, and I didn't want to know him at this moment either. He stood with his hands on the counter; his body pushed away from it with his head down. I walked over to him, and as he looked at me, I took my hand and slapped him as hard as I could across his face. There was no emotion in his eyes or on his face—just like that night at the club. I walked out of the kitchen and started up the stairs. I heard something break as Claire looked at me from the living room. Before I made it to my room, I heard the front door slam. My heart was racing, but other than that, I felt nothing at that moment. I couldn't stay in his house another day. He was too affected by my illness, and he didn't deserve to live like this. I packed my bag and left.

I hailed a cab and went back to my cold, lonely apartment. I walked to my room and pulled out a piece of paper from under my mattress. I stared at it for a while, folded it up, and tucked it in my purse. I threw the rest of my clothes, or really what would fit into the bag that was already packed. I grabbed some cash from my drawer, grabbed my laptop, and left. I walked down the street for a bit until I was able to hail a cab. I got in and smiled when I saw Manny looking at me from the front.

"Are you going somewhere, Elle?"

"Yeah, Manny, I'm going somewhere, but I need you to promise me something."

"Of course, anything," he said.

"I need you to take me to the airport, and you can't tell a single person where you took me or that you saw me, please." He looked at me from the rearview mirror. "Yeah, ok, Elle. Don't worry; I never saw you."

I arrived at the airport and was fortunate enough to book the flight that was leaving in 30 minutes for Michigan. I checked my bag and ran to the gate. I handed the man my ticket and boarded the plane. I sat in my seat and took a deep breath. My phone beeped and as I took it out of my pocket; I saw a text message from Connor.

"I want to apologize for my behavior. I'm on my way back to the penthouse, and we need to talk. If you're feeling up to it, we can go out for lunch."

My heart sank as I read his words, but it was too late. I knew what I had to do now; it's probably what I should have done from the start, before Connor Black walked into my life.

Chapter 29

I took a cab to the bank where my father used to do all his banking. I stepped inside and walked over to the teller, handing her the folded piece of paper that I took from my purse. She walked me over to the safety deposit boxes, pulled the number that was indicated on the paper, and led me to a small room.

"Let me know when you're finished." She smiled. I stared at the box and the letter as the memory of my father's death haunted me.

Dear Ellery,

If you're reading this letter, that means one thing; that I've gone to be with your mother. I'm sorry for being such a lousy father to you. I tried to do what's right by you, but the death of your mother was too much for me to handle, and drinking was the only way to kill the pain—at least for me. No matter how bad it got, you always stood by me and took care of me when I should have been the one taking care of you. You had to grow up so fast, and I'm sorry for that. I feel like I stole your childhood from under you. You should have been playing with your friends and having fun, but instead, you were home taking care of your alcoholic father because he wasn't strong enough to help himself. I do know one thing, Ellery; I know that you grew into a strong young lady. I know you've endured a lot of heartache through the years and then having to fight cancer was unfair, but you did it, baby, and I'm so proud of you. If I don't or didn't get the chance to tell you that, I am now. I am so proud of my little girl. Your mother gave me the attached instructions before she died and asked me to hold it until you were 18. It's the number of a safety deposit box that your mother had kept for you. I've been adding to it every year since your mother passed. When you're ready, go and open the box and remember how much you're loved.

Love always,

Dad.

My Aunt, Diane, gave me the letter a couple of days after my dad had died. She told me he gave it to her for safe keeping, and if anything should happen to him before my 18th birthday, she was to give it to me. I held onto the letter all these years because I was never ready to open that box.

I carefully slipped my fingers around the edge of the top and lifted it slowly until it stopped. I looked down into the box with the black felt lining and pulled out a wad of cash that was sitting on top in a white envelope. I set it down on the table and pulled out a silver heart locket with an inscription on the back, "Happy 18th Birthday, Love Mom. I covered my mouth as the tears poured from my eyes. I opened the locket, and there was a picture of my mother one side, and me as a child on the other. I wiped my eyes as I pulled out a video cassette tape that was labeled, "To my darling daughter." Lying at the bottom of the box was a stack of bonds with my name on them. I took a deep breath and composed myself before closing the lid on the box and leaving the room.

My phone chimed. I reached in my pocket and pulled it out; there was another text from Connor.

"Where are you, Ellery?"

I looked at his words; my heart aching, and I didn't want him to worry, so I replied.

"Connor, I had to leave. My being at your place was hurting you as bad as it was hurting me. The only thing I can tell you is I'm ok, and please don't worry about me. I have a few things that I

need to do, and I don't know when I'll be back."

I grabbed my things and handed the teller the safety deposit box and the bonds. As I was waiting for her to return, a text from Connor came through.

"What do you mean you don't know when you'll be back? Where the fuck are you going? You have treatments to finish; you better get the hell back here, right NOW!"

I lightly laughed because even over text he was yelling at me, but I loved him, and I was doing this for him—for us. A few moments later another text came through.

"I will find you, Ellery Lane, even if I have to travel to the ends of the earth; make no mistake that I will find you."

I smiled and quickly replied, *"I know you will my stalker."* I shut my phone off and took the money the teller handed me from my bonds. Combined with the cash in the envelope and with the money from the sale of my paintings, I had a little over one hundred thousand dollars.

I called a cab and had the driver take me to the airport. I stepped up to the ticket counter and booked a one way flight to California. The flight didn't leave for a couple of hours, so I sat down and turned on my phone. I dialed Peyton's number, and she answered on the first ring.

"Ellery, where are you? I've been so worried; we've *all* been worried."

"Peyton, stop and calm down. I need you to listen to me; you're the only one I'm telling this to, so whatever you do, don't you dare let Connor or Henry know, please."

She hesitated. "Ok; anything."

I took a deep breath. "I'm flying out to California for a while, and I need you to throw Connor off my trail. I need you to talk to him every day and find out what he's learned. I need to buy some time before he finds me."

"Do you want him to find you?" she whispered.

"Yeah, I do want him to find me, because if he does, then I know we were meant to be together and everything I'm doing would be for something."

"He's pissed, Ellery; he was throwing things and swearing. You should have heard the things he was saying."

"He's angry, and he'll get over it. Just try to be a friend to him. I have to go; love you." I hung up and threw my phone in the trash.

Chapter 30

I stepped onto the pavement of Los Angeles, California a nervous wreck. I couldn't believe I was here, alone in a strange city. The air was much warmer than New York, and it felt like the sun shined brighter. I put on my sunglasses and hailed a cab. I handed the driver a piece of scrap paper from the airport in Michigan and told him to take me to that address. He pulled up to the building, and as he drove away, I stood there, examining my surroundings. I walked around the side of the rental office where I met Mason, the manager of the apartment building.

"Hi, I'm Mason Grant; I manage these wonderful apartments. You must be Ellery?"

I extended my hand to greet his. "Yes, I am."

"Fabulous," he said as he turned and grabbed a key off the board.

We walked over to the next building, and he took me up to the third floor apartment. He inserted the key and opened the door. I walked in and looked around. It was fully furnished and clean, and that's all I needed. Before I agreed to rent it, I needed to talk to Mason first. I asked him to sit at the table. He looked at me awkwardly as he sat down.

"Let me guess, you're running from the law?"

"No, it's not like that." I laughed. "I can't leave a paper trail because it'll make it easier for someone to find me."

He leaned in closer. "Oh, now you have me intrigued; please continue."

I continued with the story about why I was here and all about Connor. I went as far as to show him my tattoos. He grabbed my wrists and stared at them. Then he looked at me with a tear in his eye. "You had me at hi." I laughed, and he reached over and hugged me. We came to the agreement that I wouldn't sign a lease and that I would pay cash every month for as long as I needed to stay, but I had to promise one thing; I had to come to his place for dinner and meet his partner, Landon. I agreed and hugged him as he handed me the keys to my new apartment.

I looked around. It was bigger than my box back in New York. The thing that excited me most was the fireplace in the living room. The kitchen was much more spacious with its white cabinets and black granite countertops. This place had everything I needed right down to the BUNN coffee maker. I walked to the bedroom and set my bag on the bed. The first thing I had to do was go get a new cell phone.

I walked down the street to the shopping center and slipped inside the wireless store. I glanced at the wall that indicated "PREPAID PHONES." I picked the phone, paid, and headed to the little grocery store at the end of the strip. I picked up some essentials and carried my bags back to the apartment. I was exhausted by the time I got back. I put my food away, sat on my couch, and text-messaged Peyton.

"DO NOT store my name in your phone, and delete these texts after you read them."

"Are you some secret agent now?"

"Very funny; what's going on?"

"All is quiet on the home front so far; Connor did ask me to let him know if I hear from you. Are you sure you know what

you're doing?"

"Yes, I have to go; remember to delete."

I unpacked my bag and put everything away in the dresser and closet. The one thing I was missing that I needed was an easel and paint. I walked downstairs to Mason's apartment and knocked on the door.

"Hello, *fabulous*," he answered exuberantly, "Come in." I walked into his beautifully decorated apartment that was bigger than mine.

"Do you know where there's an art store close by?"

He looked at me and cocked his head. "An art store? As in completed paintings, or artsy supply stuff?"

I laughed. "Artsy supply stuff."

He turned his head and yelled, "Landon, come meet our new tenant that lives upstairs!"

Landon, who looked like he just stepped out of the pages of a GQ magazine, strutted across the floor with his hand held out.

"Nice to meet you, Ellery." He smiled as he kissed my hand.

"Miss *fabulous* wants to go to the artsy supply store, so I say, let's take her."

"Oh no, that's ok. If you'll just tell me where it is, I can go myself."

Mason and Landon laughed. "Don't be silly, we'll take you; someone has to show you around L.A."

I got into the back seat of their 2009 Volvo as the boys drove me to the art store. I knew exactly what I needed, so I wasn't in there very long. I picked up an easel, a variety of paint colors, canvases, and brushes.

"I'm so excited to see what you're going to paint," Landon said as he carried my easel up the stairs for me. There was a perfect spot in the corner between two windows where it fit perfectly. I was exhausted, and it was already 12:00 am California time, and I was still on New York time. I needed sleep badly; I had an early appointment in the morning that I couldn't miss. I slid into my new queen size bed and was surprised at how fast I drifted to sleep.

***

I opened my eyes and had to remember I wasn't in New York anymore. I still couldn't believe I was in California. I took a shower and put on a cute little beige sundress and flip-flops. I pulled my hair to a side braid and headed out the door. One of the main reasons I took the apartment was because it was within walking distance of the place I would be visiting frequently.

When I reached my destination, I stood in front of the infamous Cedars Sinai Grace Hospital. I met with Dr. Danielle Murphy, who was the head of the new cancer clinical trial involving cancer treatment injections and immunotherapy.

"Nice to meet you, Ellery," Dr. Murphy said as she motioned for me to sit down. "So, you were first diagnosed with leukemia at age 16?" she asked as she looked at me. I nodded.

"You had 24 chemotherapy treatments and went into remission, and now at 23 years old, the leukemia came back."

"Yes," I said as I looked down at my hands.

"First of all, let me tell you that I'm sorry you did and are going through that again, but I was very pleased when I got your email because I think you're the perfect candidate for our clinical trial." I sat there listening to her with enthusiasm in her voice.

"You've had one chemo treatment which was almost two weeks ago, correct?" I nodded my head. She closed my file and threw it on the desk.

"Ellery, look at me. You're in the trial, and this is how it's going to work. I'm going to send you home with some immunotherapy pills; it's a cocktail, like chemo, but with less side effects, and you are to take them every day you're in this trial. Then, you come here once a month for three injections over the span of three months. Once you receive your last injection, we'll do all the necessary testing to see if you're cancer free. If the cancer is still there, but you're getting better, then we will continue treatment for another three months. I see here in your medical file that you had stem cells removed before you received treatment when you were 16."

I narrowed my eyes at her. "I had forgotten about that."

She crossed her arms and ankles and leaned back on the desk. "Well, it's a good thing you had it done because my recommendation is that you undergo a stem cell transplant once you're better to prevent this disease from coming back later in life. Now, sit tight while I get your pills and then you're free to go," she said as she patted me on the shoulder.

I pulled out my phone and text-messaged Peyton, *"What's the low down on Mr. B?*

"Mr. B isn't talking. He says he hasn't heard from you, but he'd let me know if he did. Elle, he's weird; he's acting normal. I'm so sorry."

There was one piece of my heart that started to heal when he took care of me after my chemo treatment. Now, that piece shattered into even more pieces than before. Tears started to sting my eyes as Dr. Murphy came back and handed me a bag full of pills.

"Here you go, Ellery. You are to take these pills first thing in the morning before you eat, and I'm scheduling your first round of injections two weeks from today."

I managed a half-smile as I thanked her and walked out the door. The minute the warm California air hit my skin, the tears began to flow freely. I barely made it home before my legs started to shake. I made it up to my apartment and fell to the floor, sobbing into my hands. A loud knock startled me.

"Elle, it's Mason. Please open up; I can hear you crying."

I turned around, still on the floor, and reached up to open the door. Mason looked down and met me on the floor.

"What's wrong?" he asked as he hugged me. My shoulders moved up and down as I tried to talk.

"I'm pretty sure Connor gave up on me."

"Sweetie, you don't know that for sure." He pulled me closer. He sat with me on the floor while I cried. "Maybe he's just giving the two of you some space."

"I don't know. Peyton said he's acting normal. How the fuck can he act normal when I'm a total mess?"

"Guys are different, Elle; they don't wear their heart on their sleeves like women do. Give him some time; I'm sure he's just as upset but not letting Peyton know it." I shook my head and got up from the floor.

"Thanks, Mason, I appreciate it." He hugged me tight and left to go back to his apartment.

I spent the rest of the day, painting a vision that I had in my mind of a Cape Cod style house that sat surrounded by grass. I envisioned a short stone wall that went around the property, and an archway that led to steps going down to a small private beach with a boat and a lighthouse. I was going to paint two versions; one day, and one night. I had nothing but time on my hands, and painting was my escape from this reality into another with peace and tranquility.

Chapter 31

I took my 15 pills every morning, and every night, my body shook for an hour straight. So far, that was the only side effect I had, and after what chemo did to me, that was a piece of cake. I occupied the last couple of weeks by absorbing myself in my artwork and spending time with Mason and Landon. They quickly became my best friends in California. Even though I tried to keep myself busy, I thought about Connor every day and night. Peyton kept me updated, and nothing had changed; he wasn't doing anything to find me.

The loneliness I felt was beyond anything I've ever experienced before. When we were apart in New York, I had the comfort of knowing he was in the same city and that we would eventually run into each other; but he's not here in California, and the loneliness factor is 10 times worse now. I checked my email every day, hoping he would send me one, but he didn't, and I didn't send one because it was obvious he was over me. I would pull his picture up online and put my wrist over my heart. Sometimes, just seeing a picture of him eased the pain, but most of the time, it made it worse.

***

In two days, I get my first set of injections. I was nervous not knowing what effects they'll have on me, so I decided to take the morning to run to the store. I needed to stock up on some things in case I couldn't leave the apartment. I put on my khaki shorts, a black tank top, and a pair of black strappy sandals that I picked up on sale when I first moved here. I stopped by Mason and Landon's apartment to ask if they needed me to pick up anything; they graciously said no but appreciated the thought. I walked down the street and around the corner to Trader Joes and picked up some things to stock my refrigerator. I took in the warmth of the California sun as I headed back to the apartment.

I reached down in my bag and pulled out the Twix bar I desperately craved. I looked up as I almost reached the building and came to a standstill when I saw *him* leaning against the side of a black convertible Porsche. He looked at me and smiled.

"You're a hard woman to find, Miss Lane."

It felt like life was breathed into me again as my heart started racing. I let my bags fall to the ground and ran to him as fast as I could. He was no longer leaning against the car when I jumped up and wrapped my legs and arms around him. He caught me by wrapping his arms around me and holding me tight.

"I've missed you so much," he whispered in my ear.

"I missed you, and I'm so sorry."

"Shh...no apologies; the only thing that matters is I found you, and you're safe."

I lifted my head up, cupped his face in my hands, and kissed him passionately. Our tongues met with excitement and exhilaration as our long-lost kiss left us breathless. Tears started running down my face as he put me down and softly wiped my cheeks with his thumb.

"Let me look at you," he said as he spun me around. He grabbed me and held me tight. "You look just as beautiful as when you left."

Mason and Landon emerged from their apartment, clapping. I turned my head and smiled. "Guys this is—"

Mason held up his hand. "We already met this gorgeous man, Elle." I looked at them and then at Connor.

"What? How?"

"Your hot, sexy boy toy came to the rental office and wanted to know if you were renting an apartment here, and we said YES! We told him you ran to the store but that you'd be right back."

Connor kissed the top of my head. "You have some great friends here."

I hugged him again as Mason and Landon walked over and picked up the bags that I'd dropped on the cement. Connor put his arm around me as we walked up to the building.

"See, no private entrance." I smiled.

"You're learning." He lightly laughed.

I took him up to my apartment. Mason and Landon stepped inside, put the bags on the counter, and quickly left as Landon gave me a wink. Connor turned and ran his finger along my jaw line and over my lips.

"You have a lot of explaining to do, but first, I'm going to make love to you."

I gasped as my body quivered. He lightly brushed his lips against mine as his tongue trailed down my neck. "You taste so good. It's been too long, Ellery; I need you. I need to be inside you."

His words sounded desperate as was my body, begging him to take me. He picked me up and carried me to the bedroom, his lips never leaving mine. He set me down in front of the bed and lifted my shirt over my head, tossing it to the side. His hands ran up and down my sides and over my hips as he let out a light moan. He unhooked my bra and let it fell to the floor. His hands were cupping my breasts and fingering my nipples as his tongue explored my navel. He found his way up to my breasts, lightly biting my nipple while removing my shorts. My body was on fire, and the ache I felt for him was an ache much stronger than before. He didn't even need to touch me; my body was in a constant state of ache whenever he was near me.

I brought his face to mine and kissed him, letting him know how much I needed and wanted him. He groaned as my hands took off his shirt, and my nails lightly dug into his back. He broke from me as he kicked off his shoes and took down his pants. I stared at his masculine body as the fire in my body raged. He put his arms around me as he gently laid me onto the bed, hovering over me and staring into my eyes.

"You make me feel alive like no one ever has."

I ran my hands through his perfect tousled hair and brought him in for a kiss. His hands traveled from my breasts down to the edge of my panties. He pressed his erection into me as I arched my back, begging for more. He slid his hand down to the front of my panties and moaned, "Ellery, you're so wet."

"This is what you do to me, Connor. Feel every bit of it."

He slid his fingers inside me and gently worked them around as his thumb circled around me, arousing me more than I already was. The ache was getting unbearable.

"I want you to come now, Ellery, while my fingers are inside of you and pleasuring you." His words sent me into oblivion as I screamed out from the amazing orgasm this man gave me. "That's my girl." He smiled.

With him still hovering over me and his tongue circling my nipple, I reached down and grabbed his erection, gently stroking it and feeling the wetness as I lightly moved my thumb over the tip. He groaned. "Oh god."

His lips moved to mine as I pushed him off me and got on top. He smiled and bit his bottom lip. I wanted to take control of him; I wanted to pleasure him as much as he pleasured me. I straddled him as I took him inside me, gently moving up and down. His hands traveled over my breasts as he took my nipples between his fingers.

"You're so beautiful, especially when I see you like this." He groaned.

I was swelling as I moved back and forth, preparing for my next release. My hands were planted firmly on his chest as his were planted on my hips, moving me up and down.

"Look at me, Ellery; I need to see you come."

I looked directly in his eyes as our breathing was heavy, and I moved up and down, back and forth, faster and faster. His moans grew louder, and his eyes never left mine.

"Don't come yet, baby. I want us to come together," he panted.

He flexed his hips under me so he was deeper inside; I didn't think it was possible, but it was. He moved up and down with me as our bodies became one.

"Ellery, come with me, baby. I want us to come together, and I want to hear what I do to you."

That sent me over the top as I couldn't hold back anymore and neither could he; one final thrust as we both came together, never taking our eyes off one another.

I collapsed onto his chest and buried my head into his neck. I laid there as he rubbed his hands up and down my back, and I lightly kissed his neck, taking in his incredible scent. Our heart rates slowed, as did our breathing. He rolled me off of him and onto my side as he faced me, pushing my hair back behind my ear without saying a word. He didn't need to say anything; I knew exactly what he was feeling just by his stare and his touch. I never wanted to leave this position; I wanted to stay like this forever.

"Tell me what you're thinking," he said. I took his hand and brought it up to my mouth.

"I was thinking about how happy I am that you found me." He smiled in the way that made me ache for him.

"I told you that I'd find you; remember I'm a stalker." I laughed and ran my fingers up and down his arm.

"You can stalk me any day, Mr. Black."

He sat up and pulled me closer so that my head was resting on his chest.

"How did you find me?" I asked.

He kissed me on the top of my head. "We'll discuss everything later while we go grab something to eat; I'm starving."

I lifted my head and frowned at him. "You mean we have to leave this bed?"

"Yes darling, but trust me, we'll be back in it soon enough."

I reached up and kissed him on the lips, and we got out of bed. We redressed ourselves and headed to the main room of the apartment.

"This apartment's really nice, better than the one in New York." I hit him on the arm as I walked past.

"Hey, I like my little box in New York."

He smiled and walked to the kitchen. He stopped as he stared at the 15 bottles of pills all lined up in a row on the counter. He picked up one of the bottles and starting reading the label.

"Care to explain what these are?" he asked as he gave me a pained look. I took his hands and led him over to the couch.

"I'm in a clinical trial study, that's why I came out here." He started to interrupt as I put my finger over his mouth. "Let me finish."

He smiled as he took my finger in his mouth and sucked on it. I giggled and removed it as I continued, "I have to take these pills every day. Once a month, I go to the hospital and get a set of three injections. It's called some type of 'Immunotherapy'. I have to do this for a period of three months. Once I complete the three months, the doctor will test my blood to see if the cancer is gone; if not, then I will continue for another three months. I don't even know if it's going to work," I said as I looked down.

He lifted my chin so I was looking at him. "It will work; it has to work."

"It's only a trial, Connor; it's the first time it's been done on humans, so right now, I don't know what to think."

"You're strong, Elle. You're the strongest and most stubborn person I've ever met in my life, and if anybody can pull through this, it's you, but you have to stop running away from me." I took his hand that was stroking my cheek.

"I know; I'm just so scared."

He grabbed my hands and turned them over as he looked at my tattoos and lightly kissed each one. "Don't be scared. I'm here, and I'm going to help you through this. Even if this trial doesn't work, it doesn't matter because I will fly you around the world and find you the treatment that will work because…" He took in a deep breath and said, "I love you, Ellery Lane, and I will protect you."

Tears streamed down my face as I heard the words that he never spoke to anyone before. I hugged him as tight as I could and whispered into his ear, "I love you too." His fingers wrapped around the bottom of my shirt as he gently lifted it off me. My heart started racing as he leaned me back on the couch, and we made love.

Chapter 32

Connor emerged from the bathroom as I was putting my shoes on. "Nice touch by the way." I spun around and looked at him.

"Nice touch?" I asked.

"Yes, throwing your phone in the trash at the airport in Michigan."

I crinkled my nose. "Yeah, I knew you would trace it, so I had to get rid of it. By the way, how did you find me? And why did it take you so long?"

He smiled. "Do you want the truth or do you want me to tell you what YOU want to hear?"

I looked at him from across the room and cocked my head. "Huh? I want the truth."

He laughed. "Ok, but you need to promise me you won't get mad at me," he said as he walked towards me but kept a distance.

I bit my bottom lip and narrowed my eyes. "Ok, I promise."

"I actually found you in less than a week." He could see the anger brewing as I clenched my jaw and moved it back and forth.

"Hey, you promised."

I swallowed hard. "Continue."

"You need to remember, Ellery, with the kind of money I have, I can do and find out just about anything. I'll hand it to you though, I loved the way you paid off the girl at the ticket counter to put your ticket under a different name, but unfortunately, she liked my money more."

"Ugh, you sneak."

He laughed. "Shall I continue?" I shook my head and crossed my arms.

"Don't get mad at me for what I'm about to tell you," he nervously said as he ran his hands through his hair. "I had my tech guy hack into your computer through your IP address."

My breathing became heavy as my eyes widened in disbelief. "That's when I saw you were looking up a Dr. Murphy, so I did some research, and that's what led me here."

I clenched my fists and walked towards him. He put his hands up in front of him. "You promised you wouldn't get mad."

"That was before I knew you hacked into my computer, you stalker."

He grabbed my wrists as I approached him and held me back. "I really don't want you slapping me again; that really hurt."

"Oh, you don't have to worry about me slapping you; I'm going to punch you instead." He laughed, kissed my fists, and wrapped his arms around me.

"Tell me one more thing," I asked.

"What do you want to know, baby?"

"If you knew in less than a week that I was here, why did you wait so long to come?" The pain in my voice was apparent, and he knew it as he sighed and looked at me.

"You didn't want to be found so quickly, so I was giving you time; did you really think I'd let you spend your birthday alone?"

I looked at him and smiled as I buried my head in his chest. Tomorrow was my 24th birthday.

We walked hand in hand to the beach as he spread out the blanket over the warm sand, and I set the basket on it.

"You know, we could have just gone to a restaurant?"

I smacked his arm. "I love the beach and nothing is more romantic than having a picnic here."

He smiled as he put his arm around me. "Sex on the beach is just as romantic; can we do that too?"

My skin ignited when he said that as that familiar ache appeared. "Look around the area, my dear; there are children around." He laughed and opened up the picnic basket, took out a strawberry, and seductively fed it to me. I moaned as I bit into it.

"If you keep doing that, it's not going to matter if there's people around here, I'm going to take you right here and now," he whispered.

I smiled and bit my lip. "Down boy, there's plenty of time for that."

We ate, talked, and enjoyed the warmth of the sun. I leaned over to kiss Connor when a little girl, about five years old, came and tapped me on the shoulder. "I can't find my mommy," she whined.

"What does your mommy look like?" I asked her. She rubbed her eyes with her small hands. "Her hair's like yours."

"Well, that certainly narrows it down," Connor said. I shot him a look, and he shrugged his shoulders.

"Come on, sweetie; let's see if we can find her, but first, what is your name?"

She tilted her head and closed one eye. "It's Chloe."

"It's nice to meet you, Chloe. I'm Ellery, and this is my friend Connor," I said as I shook her little hand. Connor looked at me and then at her small hand that extended out to him.

"It's nice to meet you, Chloe." He smiled.

The way he shook her hand made me melt inside, so gentle and pure. I got up and took her by the hand and motioned for Connor to do the same. He got up and took her other hand as we walked her up and down the beach. I heard a woman yell Chloe's name. Connor and I turned around as the small woman with blonde wavy hair came running up to her and hugging her tight.

"Chloe, you scared me!"

She stood up and looked at me and Connor. "Thank you so much for taking care of her."

I was surprised when Connor spoke out. "No problem, but you need to keep a closer eye on her." She shot him a look, took Chloe by the hand, and walked away.

"Connor, that wasn't very nice."

He sighed. "Look at her, she looks all of what 19 or 20? She shouldn't even have a kid; she's still a kid herself."

I wasn't sure where that came from, but I had a suspicion it had something to do with his sister. We walked back to the blanket; he spread his legs and pulled me in between them as my back laid into his firm chest.

"The very last memory I have of my mom was at the beach. I

think that's why I love it so much; I feel closer to her when I'm here," I softly said as I stared out into the blue ocean.

Connor tightened his grip around me and kissed the top of my head. "Tell me about your memory." I lifted my head back as he leaned down and kissed my lips.

"It was our last vacation before she died. My dad took us to the beach because she wanted to see the sunset over the water. I remember her sitting in a lounge chair with a big floppy straw hat on and big white sunglasses. I was building a sand castle, and just as the sun was starting to set, she called me over to her and had me sit on her lap. She pointed to the sunset and said, 'See that Ellery, there's nothing more beautiful than the sun setting over the ocean water. I want you to remember something for me, if you ever feel sad or lonely or need to talk to me, come here and wait for the sun to set, and I'll be here with you.'"

Connor lifted me up and turned me around so that I was facing him. He stroked my face with the back of one hand while the other was around my waist. "Memories are our way of holding onto the things we love, and I plan on making the most beautiful memories with you."

I stared into his enchanting eyes as I leaned over and softly kissed his moist lips. I could feel him harden beneath my thighs. "I love you, Connor Black," I whispered.

He hardened our kiss as he ran his hands through my hair. "I love you too."

I jumped up and took his hand, pulling him behind me. "Where are we going?" he asked as he adjusted himself.

"You'll see," I said.

I took him to a lighthouse I noticed earlier in the day at the end of the beach. I prayed the door would be unlocked as I turned the handle and it opened. I turned to Connor and smiled.

"Ellery, what are you doing?"

I shut the door and pulled him by his shirt into me, kissing him passionately.

"You said you wanted beach sex. Well, this is the best I can give you right now. We'll call it 'sex in a lighthouse on the beach.'"

He growled and then his face lit up. "You kinky girl," he said as he pushed me up against the wall.

His hands moved up my shirt and to my breasts as his tongue explored my neck. I unbuttoned his pants and took him in my hand. He moaned as I ran my hand up and down the length of him. He easily took down my shorts and panties and slid his fingers inside me to make sure I was ready for him. He wasted no time as he grabbed himself and entered me, not gently, but rough and with such force it made me scream. He moved in and out of me at what seemed like at the speed of light as he savagely kissed me. He grabbed my wrists and pinned them above my head with one hand as he took the other hand and pulled my leg up to his waist. His roughness was something that I had never experienced before, and it made me wonder if this is what sex was to him with other women. My body shot up in flames as he brought me to the point of no return.

I moaned his name as he commanded, "Tell me you want me to fuck you; I want to hear you say it."

I obliged by telling him what he wanted to hear. He gave one last hard thrust as we both moaned and came together. He buried his head in my neck as he let go of my wrists, and I held him tight. As our breathing slowed, he lifted his head and brought it to mine.

"You never cease to amaze me."

I smiled. "Let's get out of here and go home."

Chapter 33

Home; referring to us going home is bittersweet. Connor walked over to the easel and looked intrigued by my painting.

"I have to say, Ellery, you are a very talented artist; this painting is stunning."

I walked over and slipped my hands in his back pockets and put my chin on his shoulder.

"Thank you. This is a glimpse of my future; it looks so peaceful there."

"It's very beautiful. I suggest you keep it and don't sell it," he said.

I kissed him on the cheek. "Maybe I will."

I paused for a moment as I looked into the depth of my painting, "I was going to tell you, you know."

He reached for my hands and brought my arms around his waist. "Tell me what?"

I took in a sharp breath. "About coming here and seeing Dr. Murphy. I wanted to talk to you about it that day, but you were so angry; I heard you on the phone, in your office, with Ashlyn."

He looked down. "I'm sorry, Ellery. I never should have said those things to you; I was..." He couldn't find the words he needed to say, so I interrupted him.

"You need to tell me about her, Connor. We can never move forward if you don't, and I think I have a right to know."

He turned around so that he was facing me and pressed his

forehead against mine. "I know, and I will; just not tonight."

I was starting to wonder if he was ever going to tell me, because if not, I would have to find out for myself, and that was something I didn't want to have to do. I sighed as we headed to the bedroom.

***

I awoke the next day to the sensation of my neck being covered in small, light kisses. I smiled as I rolled over to view the sexy man who was sending, shivers throughout my body.

"Happy Birthday, baby," he smiled as he lightly kissed my lips.

I interlaced our fingers and nestled into his chest. "Thank you."

It amazed me how fast things changed. I was dreading this day not too long ago for the fear of celebrating alone. Not that I would celebrate because it was just eight short years ago that I was diagnosed with cancer the first time, and here I am facing it again, but Connor being here made things better; he made me feel safe and happy.

"Don't move," he said as he swiftly got off the bed. I bit my lower lip, anxiously waiting for his return.

Wearing only dark gray pajama bottoms, he strutted into the bedroom holding a tray. I could do nothing short of holding my breath as I looked at his perfectly chiseled chest and his exposed hips as his bottoms hung so perfectly below them. Connor Black knew he was a sexy man, and he didn't have any trouble letting me know. He sat the tray across my legs and sat down next to me. With a grin that went from ear to ear, I looked down at the scrambled eggs, bagel, fruit, and bacon that sat before me.

"How? When? Where?"

He laughed as he took my fork and stabbed the eggs. "Since you didn't have anything besides eggs, I headed down the street to the café."

He smiled as he opened his hand and handed me my daily dose of 15 pills; needless to say, I rolled my eyes. He picked up the fork and brought it to my mouth as I graciously removed the eggs from it.

"You're amazing." I smiled.

I grabbed the fork from his hand and shared my eggs and bacon with him. A happiness grew inside me that I never thought could exist. I was too happy, and it scared me; it scared me to death because all I kept thinking was that nothing lasts forever, and I never wanted this feeling to end.

"Present time!" He smiled as he reached one arm under the bed. He pulled out three beautifully wrapped boxes and then removed the tray from my lap.

"I love presents!" I squealed.

The expression on his face was pure bliss. He was just as happy in this moment as I was. He handed me the first box, and I carefully unwrapped it. My mouth dropped as I pulled a new iPhone out of the box.

"Your phone number is the same as your old phone; you know the one you threw away?" He smirked. "Who just throws away their phone?" He shook his head.

I playfully smacked him on his arm. "I'm crazy, remember?"

He laughed and kissed me on the head. I turned the phone on, and instantly, there were text messages from all my friends wishing me a happy birthday.

A text from Peyton read, *"Happy Birthday bitch! Nah, you know I love you. Call me soon; we have a lot to catch up on. By the way, have lots of birthday sex; you deserve it."*

I shook my head and laughed. Connor knew how Peyton was, so he didn't even ask what she said, he could just tell by my reaction.

He took the phone from my hand and set it on the bed while he handed me the next box. I smiled as I bit my bottom lip, anxiously unwrapping and excited like a child on Christmas morning, the perfect silver square box. I removed the top and inside sat a stunning silver bracelet with the infinity symbol encased in diamonds. I gasped as I ran my finger along the diamonds.

"Connor, I...I love it! This is the most beautiful gift that anyone has ever given me."

He took the box from my hand and took out the bracelet. He unclasped it and put it on my wrist. "I love you, Eller. Not only for who you are, but for the person I've become because of you. This is my forever to you."

The uncontrollable tears that seemed to plague my face recently started their trail down my cheeks, but they were quickly stopped by Connors response.

"Oh no, you don't! There will be no tears on your birthday, whether they're good tears or not; I forbid it. Do you understand, Miss Lane?" I couldn't help but break into laughter at his commanding voice.

I wrapped my arms around him as tight as I could and met his mouth with mine. He responded, but quickly broke our kiss. "You still have one more present to open."

I smiled as I leaned back on my pillow. "You spoil me."

He handed me the long box as he smiled. I took the box, and with the same finesse, I un-wrapped it like the others. I took off the top and stared at the voucher inside. I looked at Connor as my eyes started to swell.

"Don't do it; no tears."

I couldn't help it this time; my emotions were too far fallen for inside the box were two tickets to Paris. As he looked at me, he gently wiped the tears from under my eyes.

"I know your dream is to go to Paris; I saw it on that list you hid in your desk, and as soon as the doctor says it's ok to go, we'll be on the first flight there for however long you want to stay."

I couldn't believe he remembered what was on my bucket list from that brief minute he looked at it. I was overwhelmed by the love I was receiving from this man, who not too long ago, couldn't bring himself to love anyone. I straddled him and cupped his face in my hands.

"Thank you for everything. I love you, Connor Black," I said as I kissed him and showed him for the next two hours how grateful I was.

The day was perfect. All days were perfect when I spent them with Connor. It didn't matter if we were held up in a cave in the middle of nowhere, it would still be perfect. Mason and Landon were taking us to a swank bar in downtown Los Angeles for my birthday. They had it planned before we knew Connor would be here, but he was game and said it sounded like fun.

Chapter 34

We entered the bar as Mason pulled us through the crowd of people to a booth in the back. The side we sat on was the one with the stage and a piano; it's the stage where the local bands perform. But there was no band playing tonight; it was a free for all for any patron who wanted to show off their talent on stage.

We sat in the round booth, Connor on one side of me and Landon on the other. A redheaded waitress, dressed in a tiny black skirt that barely covered her ass and a tank top that was exposing her entire breasts, came over to our table to take our drink orders. Landon and Mason ordered a couple of martinis each, and Connor ordered a scotch. I could tell Connor was uncomfortable because she was eyeing him up and down instead of taking my order, and he was afraid of another comment like the one at the seafood restaurant. He looked at me and could see me gearing up to say something, so he stepped in and put his arm around me.

"My girlfriend will have a glass of white wine." He smiled at her. She looked me up and down.

"Oh, I thought she was with one of them."

I shifted in my seat as Landon pulled me in closer to him. "Sweetheart, she's with all three of us, and you should see the things she can do to us at the same time; oh my god, it's incredible."

She gave him a dirty look and walked away as the three of us did a high-five in the air, and Connor sat there shaking his head. I leaned over and snuggled into him, taking in his scent that was already making me ache.

"Don't be jealous, sweetheart; you know I love you more."

He laughed as he took his hand that was resting on his lap, placed it on my bare thigh, and slowly moved it up my skirt, stopping as soon as his fingers reached the lace on my panties. My body shook and shivered as he grinned. The waitress brought our drinks and never took her eyes off me as she set them down on the table.

Mason leaned over. "I think she likes you." I laughed and took a sip of my wine.

"Just stick to one glass tonight. I don't think you should be drinking while taking that medication. Plus, you have your injections in the morning," Connor said as he moved his fingers passed the lace and was now touching bare skin. I jumped at his touch.

"Thank you for your concern. I will take that under advisement," I said with gritted teeth.

Mason and Landon excused themselves as they saw a couple of friends across the bar. Connor smiled as they walked by, then took my chin in his hand and turned it toward him. "Do you want me to stop?" he asked seductively. My breathing started to increase as he lightly rubbed the area that was now pulsating for him.

"What are you going to make me do? Come right here in the bar in front of everyone?" I asked almost breathlessly.

He gave me that seductive smile and twisted my hips so that I was sitting sideways facing him in the booth.

"That was my plan, but you have to act like nothing's happening."

He gently inserted his finger as I bit my bottom lip. I looked around the bar to see if anyone was paying attention, but everyone was drinking, dancing, and carrying on conversations. My skin ignited, and my heart raced as he inserted another finger and began rubbing my aching spot with his thumb. "Oh fuck," I said as I buried my head into his neck.

I wrapped my arm around him to make it look like I was hugging him as he moved his fingers in and out. "Why are you doing this to me?" I asked as he was starting to bring me to orgasm.

He brought his lips to my ear. "Because I like pleasuring you, and I know you want it. You're so wet, Ellery."

My body was preparing to enter oblivion, and he knew it; he could feel it. "Remember, you need to be quiet."

It was easy for him to say. He's not the one getting off in a public place, and it's not so easy to keep quiet when Connor Black is bringing you to the edge of an orgasm. I tightened my hand around the back of his neck, digging my fingers into his delicate skin. My mouth was on his neck lightly nipping at it with my teeth; he started to groan. Game on, it was payback time.

My body reached the point of no return as I squeezed my eyes shut and buried my mouth deep into his neck and released over his fingers. I nipped on his ear lobe which sent him over the edge. As soon as he was sure my orgasm was over, he grabbed my hand and slid out of the seat.

"What are you doing? Where are we going?" I laughed as my legs were shaking uncontrollably.

He led me down a narrow hallway and opened a door that led to a closet. He led me inside and then closed the door. The room was dark, and the only light that I could see was the light coming from underneath the door. He lifted up my skirt and pulled down my panties. I reached for his pants as he already had them halfway down. My back was pushed against the door as he went down and joyfully licked my aching area. I ran my hands through his hair as he kept going around with his tongue, licking and sucking, making it unbearable to control myself. He stopped and inserted himself inside me as he positioned his hands on each side of me against the door and quickly moved in and out of me until he released and filled my insides full of his come.

"Happy Birthday, baby," he panted in my ear.

"You have control issues," I whispered as I caught my breath. I heard him chuckle.

"You're the one who took me into the lighthouse; now, I'm returning the favor."

"In a closet, Connor?" I laughed.

"Hey, anywhere we can get it, right?"

I carefully opened the door as he looked out to make sure no one was coming. We left the closet and casually walked down the hallway as if nothing happened. We walked back to the table where Mason and Landon were seated.

They looked at us as Landon started to speak. "Where did you guys—" and then was interrupted by Mason yelling, "oh my god, they have sex hair! They just had sex somewhere!" I didn't say anything, but the smile on both mine and Connors face answered their question.

Mason and Landon asked if we were ready to leave because they had a birthday cake waiting at home for me. I smiled as Connor motioned for the waitress to stop over and give him the bill. I excused myself to the bathroom to fix my hair and makeup. I was walking back to the table and noticed the waitress was there, bending over with her cleavage in Connors face. I could see his eyes fixated on me and the panic in them as he was wondering what I was thinking. I walked up to the table and tapped the waitress on the shoulder.

"Excuse me, lady; what the fuck do you think you're doing?"

She turned around and looked at me. "Listen, bitch; if you're doing all three of them, then there's no harm in letting me have a taste of this juicy one." She smiled at Connor.

The look on his face was sheer panic as he wouldn't take his eyes off me. "Who are you calling a bitch?!" I yelled at her.

Connor stepped out of the booth and put his arm around me. "Come on, let's go." He quickly led me out of the bar as Mason and Landon were laughing. "Oh my god, Elle, have you retracted your claws yet?" Mason laughed.

Connor kissed me on the side of my head. "I can't take you anywhere."

I looked sternly at him. "It's not me; it's you and these damn women you attract. He laughed as he picked me up and carried me to the car.

Chapter 35
CONNOR

Celebrating her birthday with her was the best day of my life, except for the day I found her standing in my kitchen. I walked into the room with a 12 inch round cake, beautifully lit up with 24 burning candles. I set it in front of her and watched her smile as she closed her eyes, made a wish, and blew them out. Her sweetness and innocence swept me off my feet and left me with a feeling that I never knew I was capable of. Her smile, her laughter, and the way she played with her hair when she was nervous were some of the things I loved most about her.

I handed her the knife to cut the first piece of cake, and she took it from my hand with her delicate fingers. I stood there and stared at her as she cut each piece with finesse. She looked at me with her ice blue eye; eyes that were mesmerizing and full of life.

"What are you thinking about?" she asked.

A smile fell upon my face as I answered, "I was just thinking about how much I love you." The words I was never able to say before, now flowed freely from my lips as easy as loving her did. She leaned over, put a dab of icing on the tip of my nose, and laughed. She wiped it off and held her finger to my mouth as I took it inside and licked it slowly. I saw the fire in her eyes like I do every time she looks at me.

I can't extinguish the fear that resides in my heart with her illness. I don't want to believe that she won't get better, but there's a tiny part of me that is scared shitless that she won't. I put on a brave front for her because she needs me. She needs me to be her rock, and I won't let her down.

I laid there in bed, checking my emails while waiting for her to come out of the bathroom. She opened the door and walked into the bedroom while brushing her teeth, frantically looking for something. "What's wrong, baby?" I asked. She mumbled something; I couldn't understand her between the toothbrush and the foam. She held up her free hand against her ear.

"Are you looking for your phone?"

She nodded her head. I smiled as I pulled it from between the sheets. She smiled at me and gave me thumbs up as she went back into the bathroom and spit in the sink.

"Thanks, baby!" she yelled. She walked towards the bed and looked at her phone, checking her messages before she pulled back the covers and climbed in. She snuggled into my chest as I put my arm around her. This was right, too right, as she softly kissed my chest and slowly drifted to sleep.

Chapter 36

ELLERY

I chewed my bottom lip as we walked through the doors of Sinai Grace Hospital. I tightened the grip on Connor's hand.

"It's going to be ok, Elle; I'm here with you," he sympathetically said.

"I know; I'm just a little nervous." I pouted.

He put his arm around me and pulled me into him, giving me the only safety I've known. We stepped into the waiting room of Dr. Murphy's office as the leggy blonde receptionist told us to take a seat. Not too long after, the leggy blonde called my name and took us back to a small room. She handed me a gown and told me to change into it as she was eyeing my boyfriend up and down, giving him suggestive looks. He turned away so not to face her while looking down at my hands wondering if I'm going to get up and bitch-slap her. She saw the look on my face and exited the room quickly.

Dr. Murphy walked in with three large needles on a silver tray. "Good morning, Ellery. Are you ready for your first set of injections?"

"I guess as much as I'll ever be," I nervously answered.

She was flipping through my chart and then looked at me with concerning eyes.

"Tell me how you're feeling right now, at this moment."

I narrowed my eyes at her. "I'm scared and unsure; that's how I'm feeling."

She took hold of my hand. "I know you're scared, but this will be a walk in the park compared to chemotherapy, I promise. The others who have recently received these injections have not had any side effects."

"That's great, Dr. Murphy, but you don't even know if the injections are working." She pursed her lips together as Connor walked over and put his hands on my shoulders.

"I'm confident it's going to work; have faith, Ellery." I managed a small smile as she asked me to lie down on the bed. She looked over to Connor.

"She's going to need you; I would suggest holding her hands." I looked at Dr. Murphy alarmed.

"Why?" I asked.

She heavily sighed. "Ellery, I'm not going to lie to you, these injections are very painful; you are going to feel like someone lit your body on fire, but it's only temporary, and we need to keep you here under observation for a couple of hours to make sure there aren't any side effects."

Connor sat on the side of the bed as I turned on my side to face him. Dr. Murphy called her nurse in and held up the first needle. Connor grabbed my hands as he stared directly in my eyes. "Just look at me, baby, and focus on nothing but me, ok?" I nodded my head as Dr. Murphy inserted the first needle. I shrieked at its sting as tears swelled in my eyes. It didn't take long for the fiery pain to start blazing through my body.

"Ok, Ellery, I'm going to give injection number two," Dr. Murphy said as she pierced my skin with the needle.

I let out a louder cry this time for the burning intensified. I let go of Connor and clutched his shirt with both hands as he moved in closer and wrapped his arms around me. I screamed in his chest as the last needle entered my body.

"Please, Dr. Murphy; isn't there anything we can do for her?" Connor desperately asked.

"I'm sorry, Mr. Black. We have to let it run its course, but it's only temporary. I'll be back in an hour to see how she's doing; if you need anything, or she's having a reaction, you are to push this button immediately."

He nodded his head as she walked out of the room. My body felt like it was engulfed in flames, and my soul was trying to escape.

"It's ok, baby. Just hold onto me," Connor kept saying as he held me, and I shook in his arms. At that point, I didn't know which was worse, this or chemotherapy.

***

A couple of days had passed, and we mostly stayed in. We cooked together, had lots of sex, and watched movies. When Connor had to do work, I would sit in front of my easel and paint. I smiled at Connor who was sitting at the table on his laptop, conducting business meetings with his employees. I was happy, and it felt right. For the first time in a long time, I had hope that I would have a future, and this man would be a part of it.

The next morning, I didn't feel like getting out of bed, so I laid there, and I tried to sleep, but I could hear Connor talking to someone on the phone.

"Yes mom, I'm coming and I'm bringing someone with me; she's very special, and I want you to meet her."

It was then I realized that next week was Thanksgiving.

Connor came walking into the room as I opened my eyes and saw him staring at me. He smiled as he walked over and sat on the edge of the bed. "How are you feeling?" he asked as his finger ran down my jaw line.

"I'm feeling ok. I heard you on the phone."

"I was talking to my mother. I'm taking you home for Thanksgiving."

As much as I wanted to meet his family, I was a hot mess of a cancer patient, and I didn't know how they would react to that.

"Did you tell your mom about me?"

"Of course I did, and she's looking forward to meeting you. She's going to love you."

I licked the bottom of my dry lip. "I meant, did you tell her I have cancer?"

He sat there and looked at me, and I could see the pain in his eyes which told me he didn't.

"Why didn't you tell her, Connor?"

His eyes traveled to the window. "I haven't had the chance, and it's not something I want to do over the phone, Elle. I think that needs to be done in person."

"So, what you're saying is that you want me to spring it on her on Thanksgiving? Hi Black family! I'm Ellery Lane, your son's girlfriend who has cancer for the second time in her 24 years of life and is nothing but a walking cancer disaster."

He got up from the bed. "Wow, Elle, you really know how to ruin a moment."

I felt an argument coming on, but I didn't care, I was angry at him for not telling his mother.

"I will tell her before Thanksgiving; end of discussion."

His authoritative tone burned my blood. "No, Connor. It's not the end of the discussion, and don't you dare take that tone with me!"

He turned away from the window and looked at me. "Are you looking to start an argument?"

"All you have to do is tell me why you didn't tell her yet."

His eyes turned dark as he glared at me. I could see anger in them. "You want to know why?! I haven't been able to do anything because I'm stuck here taking care of you!"

Did I just hear this bastard right? Did he just say he's *stuck* here taking care of me? I felt my blood pressure rise as my heart felt like it had been stabbed with a knife. He realized what he said because he turned towards the window again and ran his hands through his hair.

"Stuck? You're not stuck here, Connor. I didn't fucking ask you to come here, and I sure as hell didn't ask you to take care of me."

He turned towards me. "Baby, I didn't mean it like that."

The only thoughts running through my insane mind were that he felt trapped. "Get out of here!" I screamed as I picked up a glass and threw it at him. He ducked and shook his head.

"Fine, if that's what you want!"

He turned just like that and walked out, and I flinched when I heard the apartment door slam shut. My phone quickly signaled a text message from Mason, *"Everything ok? We just saw Connor storm out."*

My fingers typed frantically. *"I'm fine; we'll talk tomorrow."*

I dialed Peyton and let out a sigh of relief when she answered, "Hi, Elle."

I couldn't even get the words hello out first. "Connor and I got into an argument, and he stormed out." I started to cry.

She asked what we argued about, and I told her the stuck comment he made. I was appalled how quickly she proceeded to yell at me.

"You know I love you, Elle, but I'm telling you this for your own good. You need to get your head out of your ass and start thinking about someone else! I know you're sick, and I'm sorry for that; in fact, I hate that I'm not there with you, but you need to step out of your—oh pity me—self, and think about what Connor's going through. You think it's easy for him to watch the only woman he's ever loved go through cancer? He needs to vent too, you know; you're not the only one who gets to scream and be pissed off at the world!"

I couldn't speak. I was frozen with the reality that Peyton was right.

"Elle, are you still there?"

I sighed. "Yes, and thank you. As always you're right." I could feel her smile over the phone.

"You're welcome, and that's what best friends are for. Now cut that man some slack and think about his feelings."

I hung up and climbed out of bed. I walked over to the shattered glass, sat on my knees, and started picking up the pieces. How could I not realize Connor's feelings? How could I not stop wallowing in my own pity for just a minute and see how hard this was for him? I sat there, staring at the pieces of glass as he took my hand.

"Stop, you're going to cut yourself," he whispered.

I took in a deep breath and slowly turned my head so that I was looking at him. "I'm sorry, I just…"

He took my face in his hands. "I know, baby, and it's ok."

"No, it's not, Connor. I know this is hard for you, and I'm so sorry." His soft lips brushed against mine.

"It's ok, baby. I didn't mean what I said; it came out wrong."

I melted into his arms as he wrapped them around me.

"I know you didn't, and I overreacted." He kissed the top my head. I looked up at him with pleading eyes and a pouty mouth.

"Where did you go?"

He smiled at my lips and lightly nipped them. "I bought you something."

He stood and helped me up. He walked to the dresser and handed me a brown bag. I smiled excitedly as I opened the bag and peeked inside. I looked up at him and his big smile as he took my hand and led me to the bed. I dumped the brown bag in the middle and stared at the pile of chocolate that looked up at me.

"I figured this would make you feel better," he said with caution.

"You are amazing and absolutely perfect! I love you," I said as I wrapped my arms around him and pulled him on top of me. "I know something else that will make me feel better." I smiled as he hovered over me.

He bit his bottom lip. "Are you sure you're up for it?" I lifted my head and kissed him passionately; that was the only sign he needed.

Chapter 37

I got out of bed the next morning and stumbled into the kitchen for some already brewed coffee. Connor was sitting on the couch with his cup and typing something into his phone.

"Hey, babe, I hope I didn't wake you?" he said.

"Nope, not at all; what are you doing?"

"We need to talk; come here and sit down."

My stomach got all panicky as his tone was serious. I sat down next to him and kissed him on his cheek. He smiled and put his phone down on the table.

"I have to go back to New York today for a meeting regarding the acquisition of a company that I've been interested in. I want you to come back with me."

I stared at him and twisted my face. "Can I?"

"Why not; you don't get your next set of injections until next month. We'll go back today, stay through Thanksgiving, and come back before your next treatment."

A smile grew across my face. "I'll get to see Peyton; she'll be so excited! And I'll see my apartment."

Connor frowned. "You're not staying in that box you call an apartment; you're living with me."

I gave him a pouty look. "Do I have to stay in the guest bedroom?"

He laughed as he touched my cheek. "There's no way you're staying in the guest bedroom; I want you in *my* bed."

We took his private jet back to New York. I ran to Denny as I saw him leaning up against the black limo. I threw my arms around him.

"Denny, I've missed you! How are you?"

He smiled and twirled me around. "Look at you, Elle; you look great."

I saw Connor smirking as he put our bags in the trunk. "I'm sorry, Mr. Black, let me get those."

"No Denny, its ok. She's been dying to see you; she missed you."

Denny looked at me and gave me a hug. "I've missed you too, and it's nice to see your bright smiling face here again."

I slid into the back of the limo and Connor followed, interlacing our fingers.

"I called Peyton and told her I was back in town and that I needed her help with something for you, so she's coming by the penthouse around 7:00 pm tonight."

"You didn't tell her I was here?"

He tightened the grip on my hand. "No, I was going to let you surprise her."

I rested my head on his shoulder. "I love you."

We arrived back at the penthouse around 5:00 pm. Connor took our bags to the bedroom while I went to the kitchen to get some water. I went up the stairs and headed straight to his room.

I've only been in his room one time, and that was when I brought him home from the club. The door was open, so I walked in; I gasped at what I saw. Connor turned around and looked at me.

"Oh, I forgot you haven't been in here."

My eyes glanced to the right, then above the bed, and then to the left side of the room. Each wall was displayed with my paintings from the art gallery.

"You were the one who bought my paintings?"

He held his hands up. "Please tell me that you aren't mad."

I looked at the painting that hung over his bed, the one of the man and woman dancing under the stars.

"I'm not mad; I just want to know why."

He sighed. "Look at them, Elle. They're beautiful. It was my way of being able to be close to you when you weren't around."

I walked over to him and wrapped my arms around his waist. "Thank you, it means a lot." He let out a sigh as if he was relieved there wasn't going to be a battle.

I walked over to his bed and slightly giggled, remembering the night I struggled to get his clothes off.

"What's so funny?"

"I was just remembering the night you were passed out on this bed, and I was straddled over you, taking off your clothes."

His sexy smile captivated me as he laid himself down on the bed and spread out.

"What are you doing?" I laughed.

"I don't remember you doing that, and I want to, so I thought you could reenact it for me."

I bit my lip as I pulled my shirt over my head and threw it on the floor.

"Um, I don't think you did that."

I seductively smiled, "No, I didn't, but I'm going to make it a little more interesting this time." I unbuttoned my pants and took them off, throwing them on top of my shirt. I straddled him and slowly unbuttoned his shirt.

"Fuck it; I need you now," he said. Before I knew it, I was lying on my back and he was on top of me.

***

I stayed in the kitchen while Connor went to the elevator and greeted Peyton.

"Ok Connor, what's so important that you need my help with?"

I stepped from the kitchen. "That would be me!" I exclaimed.

Peyton shrieked as she ran to me, and we hugged, jumping up and down.

"Oh my god, Elle! I'm so happy you're here!"

Connor smiled. "I'll let you two catch up. I'll be in my office if you need anything."

I took Peyton to the kitchen and poured us each a glass of wine. We moved ourselves to the comfort of the couch in the living room.

"So, tell me what's going on with you and Henry?"

She smiled her big Peyton smile and told me they were doing great, and she thought he was going to propose at Christmas. We talked for a few hours before Henry called her and asked her when she was coming home. She took my hands and held them in front of her as I noticed her eyes start to tear.

"You're my best friend, and I hate that you have to fight cancer again. I want you to know that I will always be here for you no matter what. You will beat this, Ellery Lane, or I will kick your ass; do you understand me?" I hugged her and smiled.

"Yes, Peyton, I will beat this because you scare me." She let out a laugh and walked out the door.

I walked upstairs to find Connor in bed sound asleep. I changed into my nightshirt and climbed into his king size bed. I watched his chest slowly rise and fall with each peaceful breath. I envisioned this being my future. I laid myself down and snuggled against him. He stirred and put his arm around me, bringing me in closer to him. It was the perfect end to the perfect day.

***

The week went by rather quickly as I visited the soup kitchen and the art gallery. Connor took me shopping and bought me some new clothes. I insisted on paying for them myself, but he just laughed and told me to stop being silly.

While Connor was at the office, I would occupy my time, painting and hanging out with Peyton. Sal called me to let me know that two of my paintings sold and that I needed to paint more. I asked Connor if he bought them, and he just laughed. Before we knew it, Thanksgiving was here, and I was a nervous wreck to meet his family.

Chapter 38

We pulled up the long winding driveway to the Black family home in Hoboken, New Jersey. I bit my bottom lip as Connor put the Range Rover in park. He put his hand on top of mine.

"Don't be nervous; my family will love you."

I smiled and took Connor's arm as we walked up the steps to the grand house. He opened the front door, and we stepped inside. The smell of turkey and stuffing filled the elegantly decorated home. There was laughter coming from the other room as a brown-haired boy peeked around the corner of the wall. He took one look at Connor and ran to him, jumping into his arms.

"Hey, buddy, how are you?" Connor smiled. The boy hugged him tight. "Camden, this is my special friend, Ellery." Camden looked at me with his blue eyes and just stared.

"Hello, Camden." I smiled and held out my hand. He continued to stare, unsure of me, and then looked back at Connor. He put both hands on Connor's cheeks and smiled. My heart melted at that moment; it was obvious this boy loved him.

"It's ok, Camden, you can touch Ellery." He looked back at me and slowly put his hand in mine as I gently shook it.

"Connor, darling." A woman emerged from the other room.

"Mother, this is Ellery."

She looked at me and took my hands. "You're just as beautiful as Connor said you were."

I blushed. "Thank you, it's nice to meet you, Mrs. Black."

"Call me Jenny, dear." She smiled.

Jenny was a beautiful woman who Connor resembled a great deal. She was tall and thin, and with her light brown bob style hair and green eyes, she didn't look her age; she looked much younger.

Camden was struggling to be put down as Connor and I walked towards the living room. Everyone in the room stopped talking and turned to stare at us as we walked in. Connor put down Camden as he ran over to a young woman. I felt like I was on display the way everyone was staring at me. The young woman jumped up and gave Connor a big hug. "Happy Thanksgiving, brother."

He smiled and kissed her on the cheek. "Cassidy, this is Ellery."

She turned and hugged me. "I'm so happy to finally meet you."

I smiled and hugged her back. Her smile was big, and her green eyes were full of light. She was exactly my height, and she wore her black hair short and stylish. Connor took me around the room and introduced me to the rest of his family and friends.

Cassidy took my hand. "Come on, let's see if mom needs help in the kitchen."

I looked at Connor, and he nodded for me to go with a big smile on his face that made me miss him already. It surprised me to find Mrs. Black in the kitchen cooking Thanksgiving dinner; usually the rich have their own personal chefs to do that for them.

"So, Ellery, Connor says you're an artist," Jenny said as she basted the turkey.

"Yes, I paint pictures for a small art gallery in New York."

Cassidy smiled. "I bought one, but I didn't know my brother was dating the artist. You paint beautiful pictures, Ellery; you're very talented."

I was starting to feel more relaxed as she handed me a glass of red wine. As Jenny pushed the turkey back in the oven, she turned to me.

"Connor hasn't really told us anything about you, so why don't you fill us in."

Panic started to set in; how could I tell these people, whom I just met less than 30 minutes ago, about my past and present life.

"You have to excuse my mother," Cassidy said. "It's just that you're the first girl Connor has ever brought home, and we just want to get to know the woman who finally managed to steal his heart."

I smiled as I took a sip of wine. Just as I was about to say something, an older woman walked into the kitchen. She was in her late sixties with black hair and gray streaks running through it. Cassidy ran to her and hugged her tight. "Aunt Sadie, you made it!"

"Of course I did; I couldn't wait to see my favorite niece."

"I'm your only niece, Aunt Sadie." Cassidy frowned.

"And that's why you're my favorite," Sadie smiled.

She turned to me. "Now, who might this young pretty woman be?"

"Her name is Ellery, and she's Connors girlfriend," Jenny spoke.

She smiled and gently hugged me. "It's nice to meet you, dear."

She pulled away and looked at me with serious eyes—like she was looking into my soul. "You're sick," she said. My eyes widened, and fear started running through my body. What did she mean by that?

Jenny looked at her sister. "Sadie, that's rude." Sadie looked at me and grabbed my hands, turning my wrists over and staring at my tattoos.

"Forgive my sister, Ellery; she has a bit of a gift, and sometimes, she can be very bold with it."

"Are you sick, Ellery? D you have a cold or something?" Cassidy asked.

"It's more than a cold," Sadie answered.

Oh god, here we go, and thank you Connor for not telling your family ahead of time and for not telling me that Aunt Sadie has a gift. I took another sip of my wine and looked at them.

"I have cancer," I blurted out. Just like that, without hesitation, I just let the words fall out. They stood there and stared at me; I couldn't have been placed in a more awkward position even if I tried. Sadie finally spoke up to break the tension.

"This isn't your first bout with it, is it?" Holy mother of pearl, I bet she's going to bring up my suicide attempt next; great first impression.

I heavily sighed. "No, it isn't. I was first diagnosed with cancer when I was 16."

At that point Connor decided to make an appearance. He heard what I said as he came from behind and wrapped his arms around my waist.

"Her cancer came back recently, but she's in a clinical trial in California, so everything is good at the moment. She's doing fine, and she's going to be fine, so there's nothing more to discuss."

His tone was commanding and everyone knew it. I smiled as I pulled him out of the kitchen and into the hallway.

"How could you not tell me about Aunt Sadie?" I asked furiously as I hit him in the chest.

"Ouch, Elle, that hurt."

"That's not the only thing that's going to hurt, Connor Black."

A smug smirk blew across his face as he looked at me "Promise, baby?"

"Ugh, you make me so mad!" I whispered as I turned the opposite way.

He wrapped his arms around me and whispered. "I'm sorry; I never took much stock in what Aunt Sadie had to say. I always thought she was kind of crazy."

"Your family must think I'm a walking disaster of a human being, and they are probably wondering what the hell you're doing with me."

He squeezed me tight, "They love you; I can tell, and it doesn't matter what they think about our relationship. I love you for all that you are, nothing less, and for the record, I think you're a beautiful disaster."

I laid my head back on his chest and looked up as he leaned

down to kiss me. I bit his lip for that 'beautiful disaster' comment.

"Ouch, you really need to save this shit for the bedroom, Ellery; you have no idea how much you're turning me on with all your hitting and biting." I couldn't help but laugh and turned around to gently lick his bitten lip.

Dinner was exceptional and the rest of the day went smooth. Cassidy and I talked about our jobs while Connor sat on the floor and played with Camden. We both stared at them as Camden was teaching Connor how to stack the blocks.

"I've never seen my brother as happy as he is right now," she said to me.

I smiled and looked over at him. "He's a very special man."

Just then, Jenny interrupted, "Ellery how did you and my son meet?"

A smile spread across my face as Connor looked at me with fear in his eyes. I decided to spare him the embarrassment and replied, "We met at a club."

She smiled. "Well, lucky for him you were there." I smiled back and looked at the relief that washed over his face.

Chapter 39

I was leaning over the bathroom sink, washing my face as Connor was getting undressed. "I loved watching you with Camden today; it was so special and sweet."

"Yeah, well he's a pretty special kid."

I folded the wash cloth and put it on the sink. "Watching you with him made me think of some things."

We walked out of the bathroom, and I opened the drawer to take out my nightshirt.

"What things?" he asked hesitantly.

"I don't know; just how good you are with him and…"

Instantly he cut me off, "I can't have children, Elle; I took care of that many years ago."

My back was turned to him, and his words shredded their way through my body. I took in a deep breath and continued to undress and get into my nightshirt. The air that surrounded us changed.

"Aren't you going to respond to that?" he asked.

I turned around. "Ok, why didn't you tell me that before?" I was feeling a little betrayed that he wouldn't have told me that sooner in our relationship. Maybe he thought it wasn't necessary because I was going to die anyway.

"I don't know, Elle. It just didn't seem to ever be appropriate."

Then it came; the words only my mouth would say, "Was it because you thought I was going to die, and it didn't matter if I never knew?"

The look on his face broke, and anguish washed over him. "How could you say that?"

I turned to face the window. "I'm sorry, I didn't mean it, and anyway, I don't want kids. With my fucked up family genes the kid wouldn't stand a chance."

He walked over to me, put his arms around me, and pulled me into him. "Don't say things like that."

"It's the truth. My mother died of cancer, father was an alcoholic, and now me having cancer for the second time; think about it, Connor, the child would be doomed the minute it was conceived." It killed me to say those words, but it was the truth, and I was being honest with him.

"You're wrong, and I don't want you talking like that ever again."

I loosened myself from his grip. "Well, it doesn't matter anyway because neither of us wants kids, so end of discussion." I walked across the room over to the dresser and grabbed the lotion bottle.

"Does it bother you that I can't have children?"

"No, and like I said, it's for the best anyway."

I was lying; it did bother me, and it bothered me that he didn't tell me. I braced myself as I asked the next question.

"Why did you do it, Connor?"

He took in a sharp breath. "Do you really want to hear the answer to that, Elle?"

I didn't, but I did. I needed to hear him say it. "Yes, I do, since

270

we're being honest and not keeping secrets."

He swallowed hard and didn't say anything; I didn't think the words would come out of his mouth, but my mouth had no problems at all.

"Since you can't say anything, let me say it for you. You were never going to fall in love, and that meant never having kids, so why torture yourself with only experiencing half pleasure every time you fucked a woman when you could experience the whole natural pleasure and not have a worry in the world, except being ignorant about STD's."

His face fell and anger grew in his eyes. He was genuinely pissed at what I said.

"I'm not even going to respond to something as fucked up as that!" he yelled. He continued his rant. "You're pissed that I can't have kids? Aren't you the one who said she doesn't believe in happily ever after and fairytale romances?!"

All I could think about as he was yelling at me was how since meeting him he's changed all that for me, but obviously, I didn't do the same for him. I walked over to the floor where I left my pants and pulled them on.

"What the hell do you think you're doing?!" he yelled.

"I'm not staying here tonight; you're a dick, and I don't want to be near you right now."

"I'm a dick?" He laughed.

"You're the one being a bitch and overreacting about me not being able to have kids."

Did he just call me a bitch? I spun around. "I'm a bitch

because you didn't tell me about this sooner?!"

The anger and darkness now consumed his eyes. "You really want to go there, Ellery, about not telling each other things?" He was now bringing up the cancer, and he was hitting below the belt.

"I regretted that from day one, and you know it!" my voice was yelling. "How dare you throw that in my face?!"

"Then, I guess we're even!" he yelled.

Oh, he shouldn't have said that. My blood was boiling, and my veins were pulsating full of anger.

"Maybe it's best you stay in the guest room tonight, till we both cool off."

I spun around and pointed my finger at him. "I'm not staying in the guest room; I'm going home to my apartment that you so graciously call a box."

"Really, Ellery, you're going to run?" He waved his hand. "Why not; it's what you do best anyway."

Tears filled my eyes at his cold words as I stormed out of the bedroom and out of his penthouse. He didn't come after me, which told me he was really pissed off.

The night air was cold as I looked around the crowded streets of New York. I realized I didn't have my keys, so going back to my apartment wasn't an option. I waited for a text or call or even for him to tell me that he was sorry and take me back upstairs with him, but he didn't. I hailed a cab and had him take me to the nearest hotel. I was weak and exhausted as I laid myself on the bed. I looked at my phone, hoping if I stared at it long enough that he'd call me and tell me he's sorry.

I fell asleep, sprawled across the bed.

***

The next morning, I was rudely awoken from an incoming text. *"Where the hell are you?! I went to your apartment, and you weren't there."*

I rolled my eyes and quickly typed my response. *"It's none of your business where I am; remember I'm doing what I do best."*

Within seconds I received another text, *"You are behaving like a child, and I don't like it; now get your ass back to my penthouse."*

Shit, you talk about adding fuel to the fire; he was sure doing an exceptional job at it. I responded, *"I think we need time apart to think about what each of us said last night."*

A sudden reply that broke my heart came through. *"I agree, and when you stop behaving like a selfish child, call me so we can talk like adults."*

I did the only thing I normally do, I threw my phone against the wall, and it shattered. I sighed and took a hot shower, sobbing as the water ran down my body.

I bent down to pick up the broken pieces that were once my phone. I really need to get that under control and stop throwing things. I walked to the cellular store and purchased the same phone with my same number. I can't say I didn't care about my phone, because I did, and what if Peyton needed me, or what if Connor needed me?

Chapter 40

A few days passed, and I barely left the hotel room. I read and drew pictures of things that I wanted to eventually paint on a canvas. Connor didn't attempt to make any contact with me, and it hurt. I was too stubborn to make the first move; his words stilled burned in my heart. I sat and thought maybe I should just book a flight and go back to California. My next treatment was next week, so I needed to get back anyway. I didn't want to leave him, and this time apart was killing me. I hated how I grew so dependent on him. I needed to talk to him and apologize. I was out of line and shouldn't have gotten so angry. We could have talked things out, but instead, I ran. Connor was right; it's what I do best. I swallowed my pride and walked to his penthouse that was right on the next block.

I put my key in the elevator and took it up to the penthouse. The door opened, and I stepped out, looking for Connor. I didn't see him in the kitchen, but I heard the sound of two people talking coming from his office. I slowly took steps towards his office and gasped for air at what I saw; Ashlyn had her mouth on his. Connor pushed her away and was startled when he saw me standing there. The fear in his eyes was a fear I had never seen before.

"Ellery, this isn't what it looks like."

I put my hand up and turned to walk away. I couldn't breathe; my chest felt constricted, and I was starting to panic. That was until I heard her say, "See, Connor, I told you she doesn't love you like I can."

Suddenly, rage replaced panic, and it grew inside me at a rapid pace. I turned around and walked towards her.

"Oh shit," Connor said because he was all too familiar with the look I was displaying.

Ashlyn stood there with her arms crossed, glaring at me as I approached her.

"I don't think we've officially met. I'm Ellery, Connor's girlfriend." She eyed me up and down and refused to shake my hand.

"Funny, Connor said he didn't have a girlfriend anymore when he had his hands all over me."

I looked at Connor as he stood there speechless; his only movement was the slight shaking of his head to let me know she was lying.

"He said that?"

"Yeah, he did, after he kissed me and told me that it was me he loved all along, and you were just a charity case that he felt sorry for."

Oh no, she didn't!

Connor's eyes grew wide as he took a step back. Before I knew it, my fist left my side and ended up right across her jaw line. She fell back on her ass and held her jaw, staring at me like I was a lunatic. I bent down until I was right in her face.

"My advice to you is to crawl back into the whore hole you crawled out from and to never look at me or him again. If I even catch you looking in either of our directions, I will pound my fist into you so hard that even a plastic surgeon wouldn't be able to fix you." I turned on my heels and started to walk away.

"You're a crazy bitch; do you know that?!" she screamed.

Connor came chasing after me and grabbed my arm. "Don't you dare take another step."

Was he stupid or something? Did he really want to do this now when I was so full of rage?

"Let go of me, Connor, right now before you suffer the same fate as your whore over there." Me and my mouth; shit, did I just say that?

He let go of my arm. "You're angry right now, so I'll forgive that last statement, but what I will not forgive is you taking another step and walking out that door."

"I'm sorry, Connor, but I can't stay, especially now."

Connor pulled out his phone and called Denny to come and get Ashlyn out of the penthouse. I started to walk away as he came up from behind me, grabbed me as tight as he could and carried me upstairs to his bedroom, slamming the door shut.

"Now, sit down on that bed, and listen to me, Ellery. I'm not playing games with you anymore, and I know what you just saw hurt you more than anything else. You're going to sit there, and you're going listen to me!"

I sat there as I swallowed hard, silently trying to plan my escape.

"Go on then, explain to me who Ashlyn is, and why you've been keeping your relationship such a secret."

He paced back and forth across the room while running his hands through his hair. "Ashlyn is Amanda's twin sister."

I looked at him and shook my head. "Who the hell is

Amanda?"

He took in a sharp breath. "Amanda's the girl who committed suicide after I broke up with her."

My mouth fell open, and I felt sick to my stomach. A thousand thoughts ran through my mind. He was coming clean about her, and I owed him that chance.

"Keep talking, Connor; I'm listening."

"Ashlyn sought me out and came to my office about a year ago. She told me she had been kicked out of her house, and she didn't have any money or any place to go. She said that I owed her because it was my fault her sister killed herself."

I closed my eyes. I could hear the pain in his voice. How dare that woman do that to him? I wanted to reach out to him, but I had to let him finish telling me about her.

"I took her to dinner. We talked, drank a lot, and we had sex. You have no idea how bad I regret that day." He stood there, shaking his head and looking down as if he was ashamed for telling me.

I got up from the bed and walked over to him. "Why didn't you stop it after that night, Connor?"

He sighed. "She kept talking about Amanda, and making me feel guilty for what had happened. I gave her a job at my company, and we had an arrangement that we would meet three times a week after work for sex, with no strings attached."

"Wait, let me guess; she started falling for you, and she wanted more."

He nodded his head. "Yes, she wanted me to stop seeing other woman and to enter into an exclusive relationship with her. I told her time and time again that I wasn't interested, and that our arrangement was staying the way it was." He turned his back to me and took in a deep breath.

"She threatened to do what her sister did if I didn't succumb to her wants and needs. It was that night at the club; the night you brought me home, that I told her there was never going to be anything more than sex between us."

"Damn it, Connor. Why the hell didn't you just stop seeing her?!" I yelled.

He turned to face me. "The next morning, she called and apologized. She said she would be happy to keep our arrangement the way it was as long as I doubled her pay."

I shook my head in disbelief as the sickness settled into the pit of my stomach, and I had to sit back down on the bed.

"Are you ok?" he asked as he took a few steps towards me.

I put my hand up. "Don't take another step, and I mean it."

I closed my eyes for a moment to try and calm the clusterfuck that was going on inside my head.

"I have one question for you, and I want you to be honest. When was the last time you slept with her?"

There was no hesitation when he answered. "It was the night before I met you. I tried to break things off with her several times since you and I met."

"What was she doing here, and why were her lips on you?"

"I called her and asked her to come over so that I could tell her to never contact me again and that what we had was long over. I told her that I was in love with you. I was paying her to stay out of our lives. That, of course, pissed her off, and she was going to try whatever she could to keep me. You just happened to walk in when she was throwing herself at me."

I got up from the bed and headed for the door. "I can't listen to any more of this, Connor, I'm sorry."

"Ellery, please, we need to talk about everything," he pleaded.

"Why bother? So we can hurt each other again with our words?"

He put his hand on my face as I backed away. "My illness is tearing us apart. You can't handle your emotions, and neither can I. We just end up hurting each other more often than not. I have a question for you, and I want you to be totally honest with me. Are you trying to save me to erase the guilt you've harbored over the years about your ex-girlfriend?"

Fuckity fuck—I couldn't believe I just asked him that. He stared into my eyes with his cold eyes, like all the love he felt for me had just been erased, as if it never existed.

He closed his eyes. "I think it's best if you go back to California, and that I remain here."

He turned around so that he didn't have to look at me. He gave up, and it was my fault; I pushed him to this point. Tears streamed down my face as I turned around and walked out the door.

I walked back to the hotel and grabbed my bag. As I was walking out, a text from Connor came through. *"My private plane is waiting for you to take you back to California. Text Denny your location, and he will pick you up."*

The heart-wrenching pain reared its ugly head again as I didn't respond back. I called Denny, and within five minutes, he was at the hotel picking me up. I slid into the back seat. He turned around and looked at me.

"I'm sorry, Miss Lane, but I'm going to tell you what I told Mr. Black. You two are the most stubborn people on the face of this earth, and you couldn't be more perfect for each other."

I gave a small smile. "We are a disaster together, aren't we?"

He pulled up to the private landing strip where Connor's plane was waiting for me. He opened the door and helped me with my bags.

"Do not let your fear sabotage your relationship with Mr. Black, Ellery. It's not fair to either of you." I kissed him on the cheek and entered the plane.

***

"Ellery!" Mason smiled as he met me outside with a big hug. "How are you? We missed you!" He knew the minute he saw the sadness in my eyes that things were bad. "Not again." He frowned. He walked me upstairs to my apartment. Peyton was calling, so Mason went back downstairs.

"Hi, Peyton," I said.

"What the fuck, Elle? What is going on with you two? And why didn't you call me?"

"I was going to. I wanted to get back to California first. I'm sorry, Peyton, I just can't talk about it right now. How did you know?"

She sighed. "I went to Connor's place to give you something, and he went off on a tangent about you. I looked over and that driver of his was escorting some chick out as she was holding her mouth yelling something about you and telling Connor never to speak to her again. He told me you punched her; is that true?"

"Yeah, I did punch that bitch square in the jaw, and she deserved it."

"That's my girl!" Peyton shouted. "Make things right with Connor, Elle. He loves you, and you love him, and sometimes, people do stupid stuff."

"I know, Peyton, but I'm not sure we're good together as long as I'm sick."

"Elle, you're over thinking things again. You don't want things to be right because you're scared, and I get that, but he's scared too, and it seems to me that you two don't get that."

"It seems like every day I find out something new about him, and it's driving me crazy, Peyton."

"I understand that, Elle, but you need to realize that maybe he keeps some things from you because he doesn't want to hurt you."

"But not telling me hurts me even more."

"Then fucking tell him that; talk to him instead of yelling at him and storming out."

"Peyton, I have to go; we'll talk later."

I crawled into my bed and cried myself to sleep—again.

Chapter 41

The days passed slowly as I threw myself into my paintings. One night, I was putting the final touches on my painting, and I was on my fourth glass of wine when I decided I was going to call Connor. I missed him, and I missed hearing his voice, and I wasn't sure if we were even still together. I hit Connor's name on my phone and sat nervously as it rang. After the third ring it went to voicemail. I was just going to hang up, but as soon as the beep sounded, I left him a message, "Hi Connor, it's Elle. I just called to see how you're doing and how things are going. I guess you're busy, so I'll talk to you soon; bye."

I poured another glass of wine and took a sip. I didn't expect him to call me back. When my phone started ringing and Connor's name appeared on my screen, my stomach twisted itself up, and my heart started racing. "Hello?" I answered. His voice was deep and low.

"Hey, Elle, I just got your message." Hearing his voice made me feel less alone. I grabbed my wine and climbed on the bed.

"Hi, Connor, I was just wondering how you were doing."

"I'm ok, and how are you?"

"I'm ok; I was just finishing up a new painting."

"I'm sure it's beautiful."

I smiled. "I could take a picture and send it to you if you want."

"That would be great, thanks. I'd like to see it."

I decided to go for it and try to carry on a normal, full on conversation.

"So, what have you been up to?" I asked, not fully aware if I wanted to know the answer.

"Not much, really; I've been working a lot. What have you been up to?" he asked me.

"Nothing really, I've been doing a lot of painting."

"How are you feeling?" he asked.

"I'm ok, I guess." What I really wanted to say was that I was feeling like fucking shit because I miss him so much.

"I'm sorry, Elle, but I have to get going; Cassidy and Camden are in the city, and I'm taking them to dinner. They should be here any minute."

"Oh ok. Please tell Cassidy that I said hi, and give Camden a big hug for me."

"I sure will, Elle. Thanks for calling."

"Sure, no problem; I'll talk to you soon. Bye, Connor."

"Bye, Elle."

I held the phone to my chest, closed my eyes, and took in a deep breath.

***

A couple of days went by, and I didn't hear from Connor, so I took it as my cue that we were over. I figured since I made the first move that he'd contact me again. He obviously moved on, so maybe I needed to try to do the same. Drinking had become a daily routine for me lately, downing a bottle of wine every night before bed helped me sleep.

I walked to the local store where I took my VHS tape that my mother put in the safety deposit box and had it converted to a DVD. The minute I got home, I put it in my DVD player and sat on the couch. My eyes filled with tears when she appeared on the screen. She was more beautiful than I remembered her. Her long blonde hair was like mine, and we shared the same eyes. No wonder why my dad drank so much; I was the spitting image of my mother, and he was reminded of her every time he looked at me.

"Happy 18th Birthday, angel! I'm sorry I can't be there with you physically, but I am with you spiritually. You're all grown up now, and you'll be heading off to college soon. Make sure you go somewhere you can stay on campus because I want you to have the full college experience like I did. I wish I could have watched you grow up, but God had other plans for me. Once college is finished, you'll get a fantastic job, meet a wonderful man, get married, and have children of your own. Please follow my advice and do it exactly in the order. I know being raised without a mom was tough on you, Ellery, but I know you're a strong woman, and you can handle anything that's thrown your way. You deserve only the best, my sweet girl, and don't you ever forget it. I'll be with you and guide you through the rest of your life. Remember, there's nothing more beautiful and peaceful than the sunset setting over the blue ocean waters. Live your life in peace, baby girl, and remember that I will always love you."

I sobbed as I watched her say goodbye. If there was a time I ever needed Connor, it was right now. I picked up my phone and dialed his number; I just needed to hear his voice. He didn't answer, and this time, I didn't leave a message.

I called Mason and asked him if he and Landon wanted to go to a club. I desperately needed to get out of this damn apartment and forget about my life for a night. Mason loved the idea, but said it would only be the two of us because Landon wasn't feeling well. I put on my short black skirt, a black and white color block halter top which showed off my cleavage, and my high black boots. I curled my hair and put on more makeup than I usually wear. I wanted to look and feel sexy, even if it was for just one night.

Mason whistled as I opened the door. "Look at you, sexy kitten."

I smiled and twirled around. "You like?"

"Like? I love, and you may just totally turn gay men straight."

I smacked him on the arm, grabbed my purse, and left for the club. We were in the cab and my phone started to ring; it was Connor. I didn't answer; I wasn't going to think about him tonight.

We walked into the club, and I pulled Mason straight to the bar. "Line up four tequila shots with lime!" I shouted to the bartender. He lined up four shot glasses, each with a lime in front of them and some salt. I licked the salt, downed the shot, and sucked the lime. "Hell yeah!" I yelled.

"Your turn!" I yelled at Mason. We both did two shots each and then hit the dance floor. It was packed and there was a lot of bumping and grinding going on. I danced like I never had before. Tonight was about me and having some fun; for the first time in a long time. After dancing for a while, we headed back to the bar. "Line em up! This time, eight tequila shots," I said. Mason was all for it as we slammed them down together. I slammed six, and he could only do two. The room was starting to spin, but I was feeling good. The floor was thumping beneath our feet as I dragged Mason back to the dance floor. I was enjoying the music as we were moving back and forth against each other when I felt someone grinding up against my body. I turned around to this sexy looking man who was trying to talk to me.

"Hey, I'm Chris, and you are one beautiful woman."

I smiled as I danced with him, swaying my hips from side to side as he grabbed my waist. He turned me around so my ass was up against his erection. I wasn't paying attention; I was too drunk to care. I was watching Mason a few feet away from me, dancing with some random girl when I felt his hands take a tighter grab on my hips. I moved my hands up and down his arms, taking in his muscular form as I moved my body up and down his. I turned around and came to a complete stand still when it was no longer Chris at my side, it was Connor. His eyes were enraged as he looked at me.

"Let's go now!" he ordered. My heart started racing and I started to sweat. What the hell was he doing here and why?

"What the fuck are you doing here, Connor?"

"Why don't you tell me that Ellery?!" His voice was angry.

"I'm having fun."

"You look like a total slut on this dance floor, and thank god I was here or who knows what that asshole would have done to you."

I jerked my arm out of his grip and headed towards the bar. I held two fingers up to the bartender as he put two shots of tequila in front of me. Connor weaved in and out of the crowd, coming after me. I downed one shot and picked up the next glass as Connor grabbed it from my hand. "You're drunk, and we're leaving; let's go." He threw some money on the bar and grabbed my hand, pulling me out of the bar with Mason following behind.

"Let go of me, Connor Black!" I screamed as I tried to get out from his grip. I was resisting so much that he picked me up and carried me to the cab, kicking and screaming all the way.

"Ellery, knock it off or so help me."

"So help you what, Connor?!" I yelled as he put me in the cab and climbed in next to me. I looked at him as he stared straight ahead.

"You have no right!" I said.

His angry eyes turned to me. "I have no right? What the hell do you think you were doing in there? Were you trying to get yourself raped? Look at you, and the way you're dressed, you're just asking for it."

I started hitting his chest. "Fuck you, Connor!"

Mason grabbed my arms as Connor grabbed hold of my wrists, trying to calm me down. The cab pulled up to the apartment building. Connor and Mason got out as I sat there with my arms folded.

"Get out of the cab, now!" he yelled. I glared at him and then flipped him off.

"Real mature, Ellery," he said as he leaned into the cab and dragged me out of it. He threw me over his shoulder, carried me straight to the bedroom, and threw me on the bed. I watched him pace back and forth across the room, running his hands through his perfectly tousled hair.

"I can't believe you, Ellery. I came here tonight to surprise you, and I find you dry humping some guy in a club, drunk off your ass. What the hell were you thinking?"

I sat up on the bed. "I was having fun instead of being cooped up in this apartment, crying over you every damn day!"

He stopped and looked at me. "Do you think this has been easy for me?"

I put my hand over my mouth and ran to the bathroom. I leaned over the toilet as the alcohol made its way up my throat. Connor walked up behind me and held my hair back with one hand while he rubbed my back with the other. He got me a warm cloth and wiped my mouth as he helped me up off the floor.

"Let's get you in your pajamas and into bed. You have your injections tomorrow." He took my nightshirt out of my drawer, and I grabbed it out of his hands.

"Let me help you," he calmly said.

"I don't need your help; I can do it myself." I undressed as he watched me. I slipped on my nightshirt and climbed into bed. He left the room, and I heard the TV turn on. He slept on the couch.

***

The next morning, I stumbled out of bed and walked towards the kitchen. Connor was standing there, leaning up against the counter and waiting for the coffee to brew, looking as sexy as ever.

"Good morning; you look like shit."

I frowned as my head was pounding. "Yeah, well, we all can't look as perfect as you."

He grinned as he handed me a cup of coffee. "Do I get a hug?" he asked as he held his arms out.

I walked past him. "Sluts don't give hugs."

He rolled his eyes and sat at the table while I went into the bedroom to get dressed.

***

We arrived at the hospital in silence. I walked a few feet ahead of him and heard him say, "I don't understand why you're so mad."

"You called me a slut, Connor."

"I said you looked like a slut, Elle."

I shook my head, "Same thing, you idiot."

We reached the office and the nurse took us promptly to the room. I changed into the thin gown and sat on the bed, waiting for Dr. Murphy.

"Are you even going to look at me?" he asked.

"I'm so mad at you, Connor Black, I could scream."

He walked over to me and tried to take my hand, but I pulled away. "If you think I'm going to apologize, then you're in for a surprise because I'm not. What you did last night was unacceptable and immature."

I looked straight into his eyes. "At least I didn't take the guy home and fuck him like you do with random strangers!"

He turned away. "Why did I even bother coming here?"

"I don't know, Connor; why the hell did you?"

Dr. Murphy walked in and looked at us. She could feel the

tension in the room. "Hello, Ellery, Mr. Black." She smiled.

We said hello as she flipped through my chart. She walked over and put her hand on my knee. "Are you ready for this?"

I looked at her with sadness in my eyes. "Let's just get it over with."

I laid myself down on my side, and Connor sat on the edge of the bed, facing me. I pointed to the chair. "You; go sit over there." He sighed and shook his head as he sat in the chair.

"Ok, Ellery, here's the first injection."

The prick of my skin was the easy part. My body started to burn from the inside. I clenched the sheet of the bed with my fists as my knuckles turned white. I wouldn't look at Connor even though I wanted him to hold me. I was stubborn, and I wanted to do this on my own. As soon as the second injection pierced my skin, I let out a cry of pain as my body felt like a raging fire that couldn't be extinguished. Fuck it, I needed him. I held out my hand and looked at him, and he was by my side in an instant. I clutched his shirt as hard as I could as he wrapped his arms around me and kissed my forehead.

"You are the most stubborn person that I've ever met."

I cried into his chest as Dr. Murphy injected me with the last injection. She patted my arm and walked out the door.

***

I walked into the apartment and laid myself on the couch.

"Are you going to be comfortable there?"

I didn't say anything; I was still mad at him, but I wasn't sure at this point why. He knelt down in front of me, his piercing green eyes looking into mine.

"Would it be ok if I gave you a kiss? I've really missed those lips."

In all honesty, who could resist him, but I'll be damned if I didn't try. I clamped my mouth shut, and he laughed. He ran his finger softly over my mouth and up my cheek. He leaned into me and softly brushed his lips against my mouth. It didn't take long before I gave in and my lips joined his. I parted my lips so that his tongue had access to my whole mouth. The kiss was light and soft. He broke our kiss and looked at me. He didn't say anything at first; he just stared at me.

"I've never loved anyone like I love you, Ellery, and no matter what we've been through, or are going to go through, nothing will ever change the way I feel."

Tears started to swell in my eyes as I cupped his face in my hands. "I love you too. And I'm sorry, again."

"I think we're going to spend our lives apologizing to each other." He laughed.

I sat up, letting him sit next to me. He pulled me onto him so my head was resting in his lap. He gently stroked my hair as I fell asleep.

Chapter 42

We spent the next couple of days in bed catching up on sex. "Christmas is next week, and I'm taking you to get a tree."

I looked at him and pouted. "You mean we have to leave this bed?"

Connor smiled. "We do, but I promise we won't leave it for too long." He took my hand and led me into the shower.

We spent the day picking out the perfect Christmas tree. Connor made arrangements to have it delivered while we bought the lights and ornaments. We decorated the tree as we sipped wine and ate Chinese food. We made love by the tree with the lights brightly cascaded down around us as we laid on the floor wrapped in a blanket.

"My mom wants you to come over for Christmas," he said as he ran his finger up and down my arm.

"I would love that; I miss your family."

"I talked to Peyton, and if it's ok with you, we're going to spend Christmas Eve with her and Henry and then Christmas day at my mom and dad's, unless you have other plans?"

"That sounds perfect to me, and I wouldn't want to be anywhere else."

***

It was the day before Christmas Eve, and we were heading back to New York first thing the next morning. I got out of bed and started a pot of coffee. Connor emerged from the bedroom with his hand behind his back.

"What are you hiding, Mr. Black?"

He smiled and kissed me on the lips. "A present for you." He handed me the beautiful white box with a pink satin bow. I opened it and pulled out a beautiful white, spaghetti strap sundress.

"Oh ,Connor, it's beautiful!" I smiled as I held it up to me.

"You're going to wear that tonight for dinner."

I cocked my head to the side. "You're taking me to dinner?"

"Don't I always? But tonight will be our last dinner in California for a while, so I wanted to make it special."

I put the dress down and wrapped my arms around his neck. "Thank you, I love it." It didn't take long before he picked me up and carried back to the bedroom for our routine morning love making.

***

We walked out the door and there was a limo waiting for us.

"A limo? How classy, Mr. Black."

He smiled and opened the door. I slid in and gasped when I looked at the driver. "Denny, what are you doing here?"

He turned and looked at me with a smile. "It's good to see you, Ellery."

Connor slid in next to me and shut the door. "Why is Denny driving us in California?" Connor just smiled.

"I need to blindfold you."

I looked at him and smiled. "Don't you think that's a little too kinky with Denny here?"

He lightly laughed and shook his head. "Trust me; we'll be using this in the bedroom, but for now, where I'm taking you is a surprise, and I don't want you to know till we get there." He took out a black cloth and put it over my eyes.

"Are you ok?"

"Except for being incredibly turned on, yes."

The limo stopped, and Connor took my hand and helped me out. He stopped and told me to take off my shoes. My heart was racing a mile a minute with excitement. As soon as my feet touched the sand, I stopped and listened as the waves crashed to the shore. Connor reached over and took off the blindfold.

"I'm guessing you know where we are."

I stood there; my feet softened by the sand as I look out and saw a white canopy sitting in the middle of the beach.

"Is it just us here tonight?" I asked.

Connor smiled as he kissed me softly on the cheek. "Yes baby; I rented out the entire beach just for us."

He took my hand and led me down the beach to the white canopy. Inside the canopy sat a round table draped in white linen, white roses, and two chairs covered in white fabric. I was speechless at the beauty of it all. The best part was that the sun was going to set soon, and we'd be here to watch it.

"Connor, how and when did you do all this?"

"Do you like it?"

"I love it; you're so amazing."

"Dinner will be here soon, so I thought we could take a walk along the water."

He took my hand as we walked along the edge of the shoreline; the water hitting our feet. He stopped and pointed to the sky. "Look the there; sun is starting to set." I felt an overwhelming sense of peace and comfort at that moment. Connor took my hands and held them as he faced me, taking in a deep breath.

"Ellery, from the first moment I saw you, I knew instantly that I needed you in my life, and I set out to make sure that happened. You kept calling me a stalker, and you were right; I did stalk you, but for good reason."

I smiled as he continued. "You're different from anyone that I've ever met. You're strong, kind, good-hearted, forgiving, and loving. You're also incredibly stubborn, a smart ass, and very independent, and that's everything I love about you. You've certainly given me a run for my money since I've met you. You've challenged me and brought out a man I thought I never could be. You've shown me things that I never would've seen if you weren't in my life. You've filled the void in my heart and soul that I never knew existed until you weren't by my side." Tears started to fall down my face.

"I was simply a man with no meaning until I met you, and I'm proud of whom I've become because of you. We've been through a lot together, and we will continue to go through a lot, but we'll conquer whatever life throws our way, together. I want to thank you for being my best friend, and my lover."

Suddenly, he got down on one knee and pulled a small velvet box from his pocket. The tears wouldn't stop flowing down my face. "I want to be more than just your lover; I want to be your happily ever after, your best friend, your husband, and I want you for my wife. Will you marry me, Ellery Lane?" He opened the box and took out the most beautiful ring that I've ever seen.

I looked at him, crying as I nodded my head. "Yes, Connor; I will marry you."

He put the ring on my finger and stood up, hugging me and twirling me around. We kissed passionately and then looked up at the sunset.

"I wanted to propose here because I figured you'd want your mom to be here with us."

I was touched in so many ways by this man. We stood and watched the sunset over the ocean waters wrapped around each other and never wanting to let go.

He led me back to the table as we ate dinner and talked. "I saw the tape your mom made for you; the night we got back from the club, and I slept on the couch. I turned the TV on, and it was playing. That had to be so hard for you watch."

"It was at first, but then it was comforting at the same time. It was amazing to see her, and I regret not getting the contents of that safety deposit box sooner."

I kept looking at my ring that gracefully sat on my finger. It was a four-carat, platinum princess cut diamond with smaller diamonds going down the band.

"A beautiful ring for a beautiful woman." He smiled.

He stood up and took my hand and led me to a large white tent that was filled with fluffy pillows and blankets.

A huge grin crossed my face. "Sex on the beach?"

He nodded his head. "Yes, sex on the beach."

He walked over to me and slid the spaghetti straps off my shoulders, allowing my entire dress to fall at my feet. I stood there in only my white lace panties as his tongue traveled across my neck and up my jaw line before meeting my mouth with his.

"I want to make love to you all night; first here, and then at home in every room. When you walk tomorrow, you'll be reminded of our passionate night; one I never want you to forget."

I braced myself for the amazing hot sex that was about to take place. I craved him like chocolate. He laid me down on the soft pillows and watched me as he took off his shirt and removed his pants and boxers. Every time I look at him, it amazes me how blessed this man was in the "goods" department. He bent down and laid himself on his side, propped up on his elbow as he softly stroked my breasts, paying special attention to each hardened nipple as he twisted them in his fingers. I ran my hand through his hair and brought his head closer for a kiss. Our lips grew hot as our tongues were reunited with each other. With finesse, he moved his hand up and down my torso and into my lace panties, feeling my wetness and my ache for him.

"Christ, Ellery, you're so wet," he moaned. His lips broke from mine as he kissed each breast, making his way down to my belly button and kissing me softly inside my inner thighs. He gently inserted his finger in me and feeling the wetness before inserting another. I gasped at the pleasure and arched my back for him to go deeper. His tongue ran circles around my swollen area forcing me to release my pleasure to him. He quickly placed his mouth where his fingers had been, sucking lightly and licking every sensitive area. My heart was beating rapidly as his erotic moves were scorching my skin. He brought his mouth up to mine

298

and gave me a taste of what he loves so much. I reached down and took him in my hand, stroking the length of him with long soft strokes. Groans came from the back of this throat as his mouth was lightly licking behind my ear.

"Connor, I need you inside me now. Please, I need to feel you." He moaned, and before I knew it, I was flipped on my stomach as he entered me slowly from behind.

"Is this how you want me?" he asked.

"Yes," I whispered.

He sat up and moved fluently in and out of me. He reached his hands around me and grabbed my breasts, squeezing them and pinching at each nipple before moving his hand down and rubbing my aching spot.

"Don't come just yet, baby, I need you to come with me."

"Harder, Connor; fuck me harder, right now!" I demanded.

I was never usually that vocal, but something inside me snapped, and I wanted him hard and fast. He took in a sharp breath as he moved faster in and out of me. He was bringing me to orgasm quickly as I screamed his name, and we both felt each other's release. "Fuck," he said as he pushed himself deeper into me releasing all his pleasure into my body. He proceeded to kiss up and down my back before collapsing on me. I could feel his heart rapidly beating as he was trying to catch his breath. I wrapped my arms around his neck and stroked his hair.

"I love you," I whispered.

"I love you too, baby."

We spent a couple more hours in the tent, drinking wine, and talking. Then as promised, we made love in every room back at my apartment.

Chapter 43

Before we left for New York, we stopped by Mason and Landon's apartment so that I could give them their gifts and show off my gorgeous ring. They made us some Mimosas and an elegant breakfast before we headed to Connor's plane. Denny was there sitting in a seat when we arrived. I ran to him and gave him a hug.

"You knew, didn't you?"

He smiled and kissed me on the cheek. "Of course, I knew, and congratulations."

***

We arrived in New York and back to Connor's penthouse.

The Christmas holiday was beautiful and well spent with family and friends. Connor and I spent New Year's Eve hosting a party at the Waldorf Hotel with about 200 people. We rented a room for the night and rang in the New Year by making passionate love. He wrapped his arms around me as I laid my head on his chest.

"What's wrong, babe?" he asked.

I looked up at him. "What makes you think something's wrong?"

He smiled and ran his finger across my lips. "I can tell when something's bothering you." I sighed and laid my head back down.

"Talk to me, Ellery; tell me what's on your mind."

I ran my hand lightly across his chest. "What if this trial doesn't help me?"

"It will help you."

I sat up and turned towards the edge of the bed, letting my feet hit the floor.

"You can't be so sure of that, Connor."

He sat up and clasped his hands on my shoulders. "I can be sure because I have faith. It's a new year, and a new beginning for us, for our future, and nothing's going to take that away. You will get better, and we'll be married and have the rest of our lives in front of us."

I wasn't so sure, and I was scared. "There's something I want to talk to you about." The seriousness of his tone made me feel uneasy. I turned to face him as he pushed my hair behind my ear.

"I've made an appointment with my doctor to have my vasectomy reversed."

My eyes grew wide. "What? Connor, no, you can't."

He looked at me with a surprised look. "Listen to me; I want this because I want a family with you, and if we can have our own child, that would be amazing. I'm not saying it'll work, but there's a 50/50 chance, and I think we should try it."

I sighed. "But my genes suck, and you know it."

He laughed and planted a kiss on my forehead. "Your genes are beautiful." I smiled as he took me in his arms.

"I guess I'm just scared."

"Don't worry baby. Everything is going to work out; you just wait and see."

***

We stayed in New York for a couple more weeks so that Connor could tie up some business deals, then we headed back to California for my last round of injections.

"Well, this is it, Ellery. Are you ready?" Dr. Murphy asked.

"As ready as I'll ever be." I smiled.

Connor took a hold of my hands and planted them firmly against his shirt. I smiled as my hands began clutching the fabric with each burning injection.

"One month from today, you'll be back here for blood work," Dr. Murphy instructed.

Connor took my hand and helped me from the bed. He pulled me into an embrace and whispered in my ear, "Now we wait."

Epilogue

I stood at the edge of the shoreline, looking out into the depths of the water. Today was my mom's birthday, and there was no place I felt closer to her than here. I wished so bad she and my dad could have been here to see Connor and me, and how happy we are. If there was a time in my life that I needed my mom most, it was now.

I stood and watched the waves as they crashed into the shore, remembering the day he brought me to this place 10 months ago.

Connor took my hand as he led me, blindfolded; to somewhere he called a surprise. I was still in my wedding dress because he wouldn't let me change out of it; he said he wanted the honor of undressing his new bride.

"Are you ready, darling?"

"Yes; I was ready forever ago."

He laughed as he removed my blindfold. I gasped as I stood in front of what felt like one of my paintings. Standing before us was the Cape Cod style house I painted in my picture.

"Connor, what is this?" I could hardly speak. I looked around and we weren't in New York anymore; this looked like the Hampton's.

He took my hand and led me to the porch. "This house is your wedding present."

My heart started racing with excitement. This house was exactly like the one I painted. I was breathless, speechless as my mind tried to figure out what was going on. He picked me up and carried me through the door.

"Do you like it?" he asked.

"Like it? I love it, but I don't understand."

He smiled and gently kissed my lips. "This is our second home. We'll spend our weekends and summers here."

He put me down and took my hand as he led me to the back of the house. Tears started to roll down my face as I stepped out onto the deck and took in the beauty of what stood before me. He had everything built just like I painted. I admired the short stone wall that went around the property. There was an archway that sat over small steps, leading to the beach. My favorite flowers lined the walkway. But the one thing; the very one thing that made the property so perfect, was the lighthouse that sat off to the side of the house. Connor stood behind me and let me take it all in. I turned to him as he softly wiped away a couple of tears that sat upon my cheek.

"You don't have to say a word, Ellery, I know how much you love it; I can tell by the look on your face. This was built for you because I love you. I want to give you every dream you've ever dreamed, every happy moment you never had, every bit of love you've ever lost, and most importantly, a family. This home, our home, is my future with you, and we're going to spend the rest of our lives making beautiful memories here."

I gulped because I didn't know what to say. I was an emotional wreck at the generous and loving nature of this man. It felt as if I was living in a dream; that reality was some other realm that I traveled from and refused to go back to. I looked into his seductive eyes and held his face in my hands.

"I could never understand my purpose in this world. I've had nothing but pain and loss my whole life. But now I know why God saved me the first time. It was so I could find you. Then he saved me the second time so I could love you forever. This house is perfect; you're perfect, and no one will ever take that away from us. Our love is infinite, and I'm going to spend the rest of my life showing you."

I pressed my lips against his, and we fell into a deep passionate kiss. He picked me up in his strong arms and carried me towards the house.

"Let's get you out of this dress, Mrs. Black." He smiled.

***

Connor walked up behind me and wrapped his arms around my expanding waist, resting his hands on my stomach and laying his chin on my shoulder.

"How are my two girls doing?"

I put my hands on his as he rubbed my tummy tenderly.

"Your daughter has been very active today, and she kept me up all night."

He nuzzled his face into my neck and softly kissed me.

"She's like her beautiful mother, and she's going to be a fighter. I can't wait to see her and hold her in my arms," he whispered.

I smiled as I interlaced our fingers. "I can't either. She's the reason God saved me a third time. She's our little miracle."

The End...

A Big Thank You

I hope you enjoyed reading Forever Black and taking the emotional journey with Connor and Ellery. I want to thank everyone who purchased this book and read it. This is my first long awaited novel, and I couldn't wait to share Connor and Ellery's story with you.

I would love for you to join me on my social links:

Facebook Page:
www.facebook.com/Sandi.Lynn.Author

Twitter:
https://twitter.com/SandilynnWriter

Goodreads:
http://www.goodreads.com/author/show/6089757.Sandi_Lynn

Blog:

www.authorsandilynn.com

The next installment of the Forever Black Trilogy is *Forever You*, which is a Forever Black novel **retold** from Connor's Point Of View with new and additional scenes not in Forever Black.